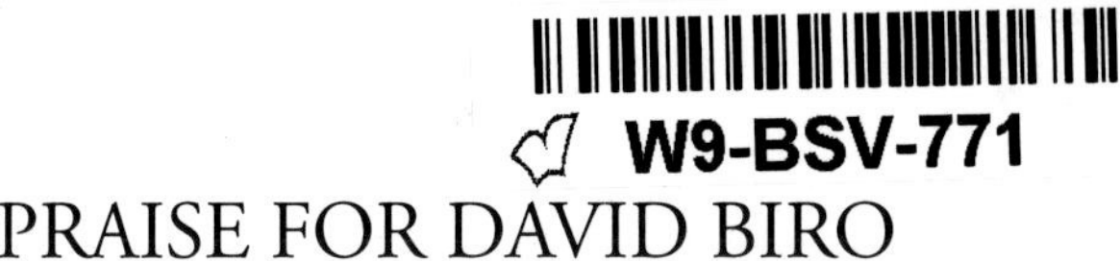

PRAISE FOR DAVID BIRO

THIS MAGNIFICENT DAPPLED SEA

"Plenty of heart and compassion. Biro's ambitious dive into the mysteries of family origins will move readers."

—*Publishers Weekly*

"Physician and author Biro examines the secrets that people carry and how they shape and distort the ways one sees the world. A story of interconnection and the boundaries that too often keep us apart."

—*Booklist*

"*This Magnificent Dappled Sea* by David Biro is a deftly crafted novel by an author with a genuine flair for originality and the kind of narrative storytelling style that both entertains and provokes thoughtful reflection. The kind of literary work that will linger in the mind and memory long after the book itself has been finished and set back upon the shelf."

—Midwest Book Review

"David Biro has written a glorious novel about connections over time, through war and displacement to life-affirming twists of fate that change the course of the lives of Luca Taviano, an Italian boy, and Joseph Neiman, a rabbi. Grief and love are intertwined in the experience of Italian Jews, and this beautiful novel tells that story, weaving in and out of time as secrets are revealed and redemption is lost and found. Brava!"

—Adriana Trigiani, bestselling author of *The Shoemaker's Wife*

"*This Magnificent Dappled Sea* is a superb read. It has fascinating, original characters you care about and a masterful plot that will captivate you as it slowly unfolds. But it's more than just entertainment. On a deeper level, it's an important novel with a beautiful beating heart. It's the kind of book the world desperately needs right now. You'll be a better person for having read it."

—Julianne MacLean, *USA Today* bestselling author

"David Biro's novel *This Magnificent Dappled Sea* is the beautifully rendered tale of Luca Taviano, a boy in a small Italian village who is diagnosed with leukemia, and his devoted nurse, Nina Vocelli, who leads a herculean effort to find a bone marrow donor who could save Luca's life. This is a captivating, well-crafted story of family secrets, love, loss and forgiveness, and our inherent human connectedness."

—Jane Healey, bestselling author of *The Beantown Girls*

AND THE BRIDGE IS LOVE

"What marks David Biro as a fine writer is his warmth, his emotional accuracy, and his ability to let his characters catch us by surprise—and these talents are all happily at work in his moving new novel *And the Bridge Is Love*."

—Matthew Kneale, Booker Prize–shortlisted author of *English Passengers*

AND THE BRIDGE IS LOVE

ALSO BY DAVID BIRO

This Magnificent Dappled Sea

One Hundred Days: My Unexpected Journey from Doctor to Patient

The Language of Pain: Finding Words, Compassion, and Relief

AND THE BRIDGE IS LOVE

A Novel

DAVID BIRO

Published by Lake Union Publishing, Seattle

www.apub.com

ISBN-13: 9781542027229
ISBN-10: 1542027225

Cover design by Rex Bonomelli

Printed in the United States of America

To the women who inspired this: Grandma Helen, Aunt Pearl, Cousin Katherine, many of my patients over the years, and most of all, my mother.

There is a land of the living and a land of the dead
and the bridge is love, the only survival,
the only meaning.

—Thornton Wilder,
The Bridge of San Luis Rey

1991

PROLOGUE

Gertie Sundersen was making good time in the early-morning August heat, halfway through her run and more determined than ever to break her previous record in the upcoming New York City marathon. "Not bad for a sixty-year-old broad," she mumbled to herself in between breaths. She had even made the front page of the *Bay Ridge Courier*, just below the cover story about Mayor Dinkins and the rioting in Crown Heights: "Local Star Athlete Still Going Strong." A young reporter came to the apartment last week to take her picture. She stood in the living room next to her grandmother's Norwegian tapestry, which Thorvald had happily left behind when he ditched her six years ago. She wondered whether the bastard had seen the paper. Her daughter in California definitely hadn't seen it—a shame since she apparently was a runner too. Well, at least someone in the world may have read it and taken notice.

At Cropsey Avenue, Gertie exited the running path along the Narrows and took to the streets. She always included Coney Island and the boardwalk on her runs. They brought back memories of childhood and outings to the beach with her parents: Nathan's hot dogs and cotton candy; the amusement park rides and aquarium; the ocean, where her father had taught her how to swim, where he had taught her to be the best damn butterfly swimmer in Fort Hamilton High School history.

If it weren't for her bad shoulder, she'd still be competing, maybe doing biathlons and triathlons instead of marathons. "Can you see me now, Papa?" she called to the sea.

By 7:00 a.m. the path along the water was no longer empty. There were other runners, a couple walking hand in hand, a fisherman baiting his rod. The exhaust from the growing number of cars on the Belt Parkway vied with the strong smell of the sea. Up ahead, a freighter passed beneath the Verrazzano Bridge, dwarfed by the elegant steel expanse that stretched across the Narrows, all the way from Staten Island to Brooklyn. Gertie picked up the pace, determined to take the last mile at full speed, her lungs heaving, her legs pounding the pavement, the finish line in sight.

—

Maria Benedetti had been full of energy her entire life, spending it mostly in the house, cooking, cleaning, rearranging. Lately, though, she couldn't stand to be inside at night and would do anything to avoid being there, which was why she found herself roaming the streets of Bay Ridge in the early hours of the morning. Her daughter, Livy, realized how hard it was for her mother to sleep in a house full of memories, and a year after her father's death, she had arranged for the sale of her parents' attached two-story brick home in Bensonhurst and the purchase of an apartment a few blocks away from hers in Bay Ridge. It hadn't helped.

"Everything has his smell," Maria complained to her daughter, "the couch, the bureaus, even my clothes."

"We can buy you new things, Ma," Livy replied.

But Maria adamantly refused to part with these reminders of Jim. Instead, she invented all sorts of tasks and errands to busy herself, and when she couldn't sleep, she walked the neighborhood, her old one at first and then her new one. It had been almost a year since the move, and Maria still felt like a stranger in Bay Ridge. Although Bensonhurst was practically next door, the two places couldn't be more different. In Bensonhurst, everyone knew each other. Maria and her friends would sit on the porch, gossip about their neighbors, and make sure the kids on the street played nice.

In Bay Ridge, it was the opposite; practically no one talked to her, and Livy was always so busy with her nursing duties at the hospital. Plus, the neighborhood was such a minestrone of different people and their different cultures that it made Maria's head spin. A Korean deli stood next to an Irish bar that was followed by a Norwegian bakery. There were Chinese take-out restaurants everywhere she looked and a Middle Eastern market that took up an entire block. Where had all the Italian shops gone? she wanted to know. Why wasn't there a place nearby to buy fresh mozzarella or decent cannoli?

About to cross Ninety-Seventh Street, she was nearly run over by the crazy boy who sped around the neighborhood on his red Vespa at all hours of the day and night. "Hey!" she called out after recovering her balance. "Watch where you're going before you kill somebody!" but the *pazzo* didn't even turn around.

In the distance, the Brooklyn tower of the Verrazzano Bridge loomed over Fourth Avenue. It was the one thing, besides being close to Livy of course, that still brought a smile to her face. Somehow the massive bridge was so heavy and light at the same time; the cables draping from one tower to the other reminded her of the beautiful pearl necklace Jim had given her the year before he passed. At the end of Shore Road, there was a path that led to the water and a bench at the foot of the bridge. She would sit on the bench after a long walk and gaze up at the bridge and down at the water, watching the boats pass in and out of New York Harbor. It calmed her restless insides.

She headed for the path as the sun peeked above the ridge.

Corinna Hale removed the blanket from her tote bag and laid it down on the grass so she had a full view of the Narrows and the Verrazzano. Early morning was one of her favorite times of day, when the park was empty and quiet except for the chatter of birds and the slight traffic on the Belt Parkway. She could read in peace for an hour or so before she was due to work at the Senior Center. Her head still buzzed from the book she'd finished yesterday, *The World According to Garp*. What a wonderful cast of eccentrics and misfits: one-eyed boys, women without tongues, men walking upside down, transsexuals, asexuals. Now *there* was a world where she could easily fit in, she thought, glancing down at her right hand—one large thumb and two pincer-like fingers, what the doctors called a lobster claw deformity. Maybe she should send John Irving a fan letter, put in a recent picture of herself wearing her moped helmet and gloves, a flask of whiskey in her five-fingered hand.

Corinna grabbed a book from her tote and lay down on the blanket. Today she had decided to go with something a bit more serious, a book she returned to again and again, Thornton Wilder's *The Bridge of San Luis Rey*. Not that *Garp* wasn't about important matters, like love, but *Bridge* was about all of life and love, from beginning to end, as chronicled by a Franciscan friar who had witnessed the death of five random strangers when an Incan rope bridge collapsed in Peru. More so than Irving, Wilder delved into the darker side of love. Even in the most perfect union, like that of the twins Manuel and Esteban, one always loved less than the other, and in this difference lay a universe of pain. Yes, that's what Corinna had always suspected, even though she had limited experience in that department—that love was overrated, toxic even. Every time she read something like *Garp*, which seemed to contradict that message, she went back to Wilder's unhappy twins, to douse the desire that would rekindle in her bones, to reassure herself that she hadn't missed out after all.

Overhead, a gull wheeled, and as she turned to watch its flight, Corinna caught sight of a large runner barreling forward along the water. She immediately thought of Hemingway and the running of the bulls in Pamplona, so stout and squat was this woman, so indelicate and fierce. God forbid someone accidently veered into her path.

Gertie's run ended as she crossed beneath the Verrazzano. She checked her watch and grinned—a better time than she expected. She walked a few steps forward, then back, shaking out her arms and legs. She reached into her fanny pack for her water bottle, poured half its contents over her head, and cried out with pleasure as water splashed coolly against her skin. The rest she drank in a single gulp.

When Maria reached the path that led down to the shore, she noticed the red moped parked by the side of the road. Huffing, she scanned the park below for a sign of the crazy boy, determined to give him a piece of her mind. But all she saw was a runner under the bridge chugging water and someone reading on the grass. Maria picked up her pace, careful not to lose her balance as she descended the hill, placing one foot gingerly after another. It was then she spotted the helmet on the blanket. Could that be the *pazzo* reading so peacefully, she wondered, as if he had all the time in the world? *Wait, that's not a young boy,* she suddenly realized. It was a woman in her middle years, late forties or perhaps fifties. A tiny, wispy thing, with an elfin blonde bob and sharp features that made Maria think of a bird, a yellow songbird. Still, this little bird was no innocent, and Maria was going to let her know what she thought of her recklessness.

A voice called from behind her, and when Corinna turned, she saw a woman making a beeline for her blanket—a tall, thin, striking middle-aged woman with auburn hair. There was an elegance about her as she descended the sloping path in her floral dress, her long, slim legs moving sideways, one white espadrille after another. Her face radiated a strong emotion, but at that distance, Corinna couldn't decide whether it was anger or sadness. A beautiful and tragic figure, decided Corinna, straight out of Flaubert or Tolstoy.

—

Unaware of the conflict brewing a few yards away, Gertie shoved the water bottle back into her fanny pack and pulled out the plum she'd wrapped in a napkin. It was nice and ripe, just the way she liked it. Leaning over the rail, watching a small tugboat pass and listening to the water lap against the rocks below, she wolfed down the soft, sweet fruit in a single bite. A second later she felt something hard catch at the back of her throat. Had she accidentally swallowed the pit? *Uff da*. She tried to spit out the damn thing, but it was stuck. No matter how many times she gagged and banged her hand against the railing, it wouldn't budge.

—

Corinna had risen from the blanket to meet the tragic figure moving toward her when she heard the whooping sounds. She turned to find the runner grabbing her neck in distress. She dropped her book and sprang into action. As it happened, they had just practiced the Heimlich maneuver at the Senior Center a few days ago, so Corinna was prepared. She positioned herself behind the choking victim and threw her arms around her midriff. But Corinna's arms, tiny as they were, didn't reach very far around the much larger woman. There was no way she'd be able to execute the abdominal thrusts.

From a distance, Maria watched the commotion with horror, rooted to her spot on the grass, hand clasped over mouth.

"Don't just stand there," called Corinna. "Help me!"

Maria moved forward tentatively. "Me?"

"Yes, you!" yelled Corinna. "Hurry!"

Maria ran to Corinna's side. Corinna positioned Maria's long arms around Gertie's waist and began shouting orders. Maria squeezed with all her strength, but the abdominal thrusts didn't seem to be working. Gertie was turning blue. Remembering the next step in the choking protocol, Corinna called for back blows. Maria did as she was told, ratcheting up the intensity with each new blow to Gertie's upper back. Finally, on the fifth and hardest blow, the pit was dislodged, rocketing straight out of Gertie's mouth, coming to a halt midair, then sailing gracefully down to land at their feet.

"That was close," Corinna said.

"Very close," agreed Maria.

The two women sighed with relief. Noticing that Gertie was still pale, they decided to move her out of the sun into a more shaded area. Together they climbed the grassy hill, Corinna supporting Gertie's right side and Maria her left. Entering the thick line of great oaks just below Shore Road, the three women happened upon a narrow, unmarked path. Through several twists and turns, the path wound its way up the ridge to a small hidden enclosure, a place none of them had ever noticed before or knew existed. In the center of the enclosure was an old stone bench where they settled Gertie. The bench was flanked on either side by fluted stone columns, one of which had been severed near the top. What a strange, unexpected set, they thought, as if it had been placed there long ago, in a different time and different landscape.

Even more remarkable, the women soon realized, was the view. Almost simultaneously their eyes alighted on a small opening in the twisted branches of the trees, affording them a direct line of sight to the majestic Verrazzano Bridge. Together they gazed at the slate-gray metal towers soaring skyward, the steel cables delicately draped from one tower to the other, ascending and descending, the small squares and larger rectangles moving back and forth over the curved roadway.

The women were speechless, as if all three of them had just choked on a pit and were now recovering their breath. They were dazzled by the poetry of their find; by the extraordinary sequence of events that had led them there, three complete strangers; and by the fact that, only a few moments ago, two of them had saved a life and the third had narrowly escaped losing hers.

"It looks like a giant bird," mused Corinna, "with the Narrows sweeping in from the Atlantic beneath its wings."

"Or a beautiful pearl necklace," said Maria.

"Or a harp," murmured Gertie.

They laughed uneasily at first, and then more easily. They told each other who they were, where they lived, how they lived. Gertie gestured to her old high school on Shore Road—less than a mile away—and reminisced about how she used to duck out of classes and hang out with friends in the park below. Corinna recounted moving to Bay Ridge after finishing her master's degree in library science in Boston almost thirty years ago. The minute she'd laid eyes on the bridge, she told them, she knew she was finally home. Maria admitted that, even after a year, she felt like a newcomer to the neighborhood and spent most of her days in her apartment, organizing and reorganizing and cooking her late husband's favorite Italian dishes.

"You should stop by the A & S Pork Store on Fifth Avenue," Corinna suggested. "You might find some new ingredients for recipes."

"Yeah, they have mozzarella and rice balls that'll knock your socks off," said Gertie. "Plus, you could stand to put a little flesh on your bones." She gave Maria a nudge and a wink of such friendly camaraderie, there was no way Maria could feel slighted in the least.

Soon they began to share details about the people and places they loved and took care of. From her bag, Maria pulled an accordion photo book filled with pictures of her daughter, Livy. "She looks just like you," noted Corinna. "She's beautiful." Corinna then went on to give animated thumbnail sketches of her favorite residents at the Senior Center. Gertie spoke of her past swim teams and how she'd always hoped her daughter would become a swimmer too—but stopped abruptly.

"Actually, she's all grown up and lives in California now. I don't talk to her much anymore," Gertie blurted out, somewhat defiantly. "I guess you could say I only take care of myself."

There was a pause.

"Well, then you're doing a good job," Maria countered evenly. "You're so fit and strong. I can say with the best of authority that your body is made of steel."

"I couldn't even get my arms around your torso," Corinna agreed. "The next time you're choking to death, try to have a little less muscle mass."

The three women laughed, partly because Gertie looked so gratified, but mostly with the pleasure of a life well saved.

On the heels of these smaller revelations came larger ones. Gertie had gone through a bad divorce and hadn't spoken to her husband in years. Corinna had a seizure disorder that made her liable to pass out without warning. It was part of a condition she was born with, she explained, showing them her hand. Maria, after recovering from her surprise—she hadn't noticed Corinna's hand until that moment—stammered that her hair was turning gray, forcing her to go to the salon every month to color it. When Gertie shot her a look of disbelief, Maria felt compelled to divulge something more substantial: ten years ago she had been treated for breast cancer and had to have her right breast removed.

"So that one's a fake?" asked Gertie, pointing at Maria's chest.

Maria flushed. With some difficulty, she searched Gertie's face, and when she seemed satisfied that no malice was intended, she replied, "It's an insert."

These were not the kinds of things the three women ordinarily shared with other people, much less strangers. Yet, somehow, sitting on the stone bench in the hidden enclosure, with its view of the bridge through the great oaks, the words flowed as naturally as the water in the Narrows below. As the conversation wound down, Gertie suggested they meet there next week. Corinna and Maria agreed.

That next week, Corinna brought wine and incense. She read poems and passages from her favorite books. Together the women watched the ships pass under the Verrazzano. Corinna and Maria marveled at Gertie's athletic feats, how a person her age was still so determined to test the limits of her body. Gertie and Maria had never met anyone with Corinna's breadth of knowledge, from first-aid maneuvers to nautical terms and world literature. Corinna and Gertie admired Maria's beauty and devotion to her family. Yet, while each was attracted to the others' differences, what drew them together most was a yearning for companionship, a companionship that had been missing from their lives for so many years.

"Shall we meet here the same time next week?" Corinna asked.

"Yes," Maria said enthusiastically. "And the week after that."

It marked the beginning of a ritual: every Tuesday morning at eleven o'clock on the dot, the three women gathered at this special place they came to call the Temple. It marked, too, the beginning of an enduring friendship. Over the years, they cheered for Gertie at marathons and visited her old haunts in Coney Island; they helped Corinna plan events at the Senior Center and encouraged her efforts at the Brooklyn Historical Society; they celebrated the birth of Maria's grandson Vinnie, mourned the unexpected death of his father not long afterward, and accompanied Maria to Livy's house for Sunday dinners. Gradually, the

Temple and their lives became so thoroughly intertwined, they could no longer be separated.

Still, the air and water currents were known to be tricky in the narrow corridor that divided the upper and lower halves of New York Bay, and in the spring of 2011, twenty years after the three women first came together, the winds suddenly shifted.

2011

PART I

1

Gertie

A heavily bandaged ear materialized in the darkness. She could dimly make out a covered nose, then a forehead wrapped in gauze. *Uff da.* What could've happened? Another terrorist attack in the city? Or was she back in the ER for her heart again? This time, though, she didn't have that feeling of a giant hand clamping down on her shoulder, making it difficult to breathe.

All around, such wreckage. For a moment, Gertie Sundersen thought she might be dreaming, until a dull ache at the base of her neck told her otherwise. Then she saw the circle of chairs, patients flipping through magazines, the TV on the wall, and remembered: she was at the dermatologist's office to have a skin cancer removed. She must have been dozing. How in the world had she gotten roped into this? she wondered, surveying the doctor's handiwork around her. Hadn't she made her horror quota for the year with the heart attack last winter? Shaking her head, she picked up a magazine and pretended to read.

As she glanced at the pictures, Gertie was aware of movement. From the corner of her eye, beyond the horizon of the magazine edge, she watched the Ear begin to levitate and drift toward her. Yes, it was moving all right, moving in her direction. A moment later, the Ear had settled into the seat next to her.

"First time, huh?"

First time she was ever addressed by an ear, that was for sure.

"Nothing to be nervous about. This is my eighteenth." The Ear sounded genuinely proud. "And Dr. Sandler is terrific. You can barely see the scars."

Gertie forced a smile. His eighteenth! By the time the doctor finished with him, the poor fellow would have more holes than swiss cheese.

"He's the only doctor I'd trust with my Rose," the man said, gesturing across the room to none other than a heavily bandaged nose. "We're here together. Two for one," he chuckled.

This was more than Gertie could bear. The Talking Ear and Rose the Nose.

"I'm Joe Flannery," the man introduced himself. "Rose recognized you from the Senior Center. You're friends with Corinna and the good-looking redhead, right?"

She nodded as Rose waved to her from the other side of the room.

"How about joining us for something to eat at the diner across the street? We've been here for nearly three hours already."

"Thanks, but I'll pass," said Gertie, her smiling muscles tiring fast.

On the TV the afternoon news was just starting: a bad day on Wall Street, the Dow plunging almost three hundred points; political unrest spreading like wildfire across the Middle East; and, a few hours ago, another suicide bombing in a crowded Afghanistan mosque. Images of the dead and wounded filled the screen.

"On a more positive note," said the CNN anchorman, switching tack effortlessly, "a young Norwegian just made history sailing around the world. Sixteen-year-old high school student Annie Halvorsen is now the youngest woman . . ."

Gertie jolted forward, the magazine slipping from her hand and falling onto the floor. It was her again, she realized, watching Annie Halvorsen beam before a group of reporters. She had seen her face on TV several times over the last few days and hadn't been able to get it out of her mind.

". . . the youngest woman to accomplish the 23,000-nautical-mile journey, braving violent storms and giant waves on her 28-foot sailboat."

Gertie couldn't take her eyes off the young Norwegian, her sparkling blue eyes and ruddy cheeks, the confident smile flashing across the screen. Once upon a time, she had been that age too. Not quite as pretty as Annie Halvorsen but brimming with the same degree of Scandinavian conviction when it came to the water. A while back—a long while—she'd been the captain of her high school swim team and a three-time individual state champ. She'd won a scholarship to Penn State and had been slated to compete for a spot on the 1956 US Olympic team—yes, it was true, Gertie Sundersen, the pride of the Bay Ridge Norwegian community. Chances are, she would have been on that Olympic team in Melbourne if she hadn't torn her rotator cuff during the qualifiers.

It was starting to make sense now, why she couldn't stop thinking of the young Norwegian. Annie reminded her of herself—not now, that was for sure, but back then, when she had been just as green and fiery. What a devastating blow, not being able to realize a dream she'd had ever since the beginning of dreams, standing on the medal podium, the national anthem playing in the background. Still, it hadn't stopped Gertie. After recovering from the shoulder injury, she began to coach and, four years later, watched with pride—and a little envy—as one of her protégés won a silver medal in Rome.

Nor did the injury prevent Gertie from leading an active life. She took up marathon running in the 1970s and soon after joined the

Polar Bear Club in Coney Island, one of its first female members. She'd regularly led the way into the icy January Atlantic, chanting her father's favorite expression as she left her stumbling male comrades in the dust: *bak skyene er himmelen alltid blå* (behind the clouds, the sky is always blue). He would say it whenever she had a bad day in school or didn't come out on top in a race.

What the hell had happened to that fiery young girl? About to turn eighty, she could barely walk straight anymore, let alone run or even swim more than a few laps. A bag of creaking bones and wheezy lungs with a flimsy ticker of a heart.

Gertie stared at Annie on the TV: sparkling eyes, flushed cheeks, her youthful I-can-do-anything expression. Could Gertie remember that feeling—the feeling of having practiced long and hard and then accomplishing a sought-after goal? Of seeing the world open up in front of her?

Gertie tried to remember, but it was hard and not just because of her flagging body. It was also the damn dullness of her life: the old green couch in the living room she'd received as a wedding present a hundred years ago, hardly green anymore and frayed bare in spots; the cursed Norwegian White Bear King staring at her from her grandmother's tapestry on the wall; bingo at the Senior Center on Thursdays, movie night on Fridays, and boring lectures that put her to sleep on Sunday afternoons. Even meeting Maria and Corinna at the Temple on Tuesdays was starting to get old after all these years. There was nothing new, nothing exciting to look forward to.

She tried to remember how it felt: the racing of her pulse and hammering in her chest, the fierce desire to beat her previous time, the thrill of touching the wall first. Sure, there were moments when the pressure got so bad she would throw up before a race, but she felt alive back then, the blood pumping, the nerves buzzing.

"So what comes next?" one of the reporters asked Annie Halvorsen.

What a stupid question! thought Gertie. The answer was obvious from the girl's confident smile flashing across the screen: anything and everything!

"I'm going to do it again," said Annie. "Only slower this time, so I can see more of the world."

Oh, if only Gertie were at the port in Stavanger right now. It wasn't far from her parents' hometown of Egersund on the southwest coast of Norway. If only she could shake the young sailor's hand, maybe even embrace her, so that she might get a taste of her exuberance.

"I'll start in Europe and work my way east. I want to see it all."

"That's right, Annie," cheered Gertie, who was now up and on her feet. "See it all."

When she realized the entire waiting room was staring at her, she shook her head and waved them off. *Go back to your stupid magazines and skin cancers and waiting. Not me. I'm getting out before it's too late.*

"Are you all right?" asked a nurse, suddenly appearing at her side. "We've been calling you. The doctor is ready." Without giving her a chance to respond, the nurse had latched on to Gertie's hand and was marching her out of the waiting room.

No, I'm not all right, Gertie wanted to say, but for some crazy reason, she couldn't get the words out. It galled her, being herded around like this. She'd always thought of herself as a tough son of a bitch who gave it to people straight and wanted it straight in return—a character trait most likely responsible for her failed marriage, her failed relationship with her daughter, and her tiny circle of friends. But these last few years, one medical scare after another had clearly dulled the edges. She was going soft. *Uff da.*

Dr. Sandler, clad in green scrubs, was inspecting his tray of metal instruments when she entered the surgical suite. Gertie's eyes caught the glistening edge of the scalpel. Eighteen times that thing had sliced through Joe Flannery's poor face. Well not hers, not even once.

"I'm sorry, doc," she said, pulling her hand away from the nurse, "but I can't do this today."

Dr. Sandler's eyes narrowed as he tried to determine what was going on in his patient's head. "There's really nothing to be nervous about, Mrs. Sundersen," he finally said. "As I told you before—"

"I'm not nervous," said Gertie. "I just don't have time right now."

"Mrs. Sundersen, you do understand you have a skin cancer that needs to be treated?"

Gertie nodded. "I do, but if I remember correctly, you told me it was the good kind of skin cancer."

"That's true"—the doctor smiled uneasily—"but it's also very close to your eye."

Gertie knew very well where the damn thing was. She was the one who brought it to his attention. "So what happens if I leave it alone?"

The doctor tilted his head to the side. He was clearly not used to this degree of questioning from a patient. After taking a deep breath, he explained that over time the cancer would continue to grow and become more difficult to remove.

Gertie chewed on her bottom lip while she digested Sandler's response. She pictured the sore getting bigger, moving closer to the eye, the one she could barely see out of because of the cataract. "I see," she said finally. "But it's not going to kill me, right?"

"No, I don't—"

"Then that settles it," she said decisively. "I'm going to have to take a rain check, doc. I got things to do and can't be running around like the walking wounded in your waiting room."

Gertie was out the door before the doctor had time to object. She passed through the waiting room of bandaged body parts—ears, noses, foreheads. "Sorry, fellas," Gertie muttered under her breath, "but I'm not sticking around for this party." There was a bounce to her step that she hadn't experienced for some time.

She's got things to do, she'd told the doctor. What things exactly, she wasn't sure of at the moment. But how good it felt to say that! She wanted to find Maria and Corinna and tell them about Annie Halvorsen. It was a sign, Gertie now realized. *Wake up,* Annie was telling her—telling her and Maria and Corinna and anyone else who might be listening. *Wake up, before it's too late.*

2

Maria

In the warm weather, she left her bedroom windows open, and lying in the dark, she would listen for the sounds of the sea, the water slapping against the rocks, the shifting breezes, the horns of ships. Maria Benedetti lived two blocks from Shore Road and wasn't often rewarded with those coveted sounds. Still, she listened, and imagined her two best friends doing the same in the quiet of the night. Gertie and Corinna lived in apartments on the ridge overlooking the Narrows, so close that you could taste the salt water in the air. In the old days, as Corinna once showed them with a series of sepia photos from the Historical Society, the land on the southeastern edge of Brooklyn was flatter, and instead of multistory apartment buildings on the ridge above the Belt Parkway, there was a wide stretch of low-lying sandy beach, backed by a row of impressive mansions. Maria liked to imagine walking down to the beach and dipping her bare feet into the water.

She was in bed now, her skin tingling from the touch of the sea, when the phone rang. She didn't recognize the voice on the line.

"It's Elsa," the woman repeated. "Gertie's daughter from Los Angeles. I hope I'm not calling too late."

"No," said Maria. "Not at all." She had been trying to reach Gertie's daughter for weeks, hoping she could convince her to come to New York for the party she was planning to celebrate her friend's eightieth birthday.

"Sorry I didn't get back to you sooner," said Elsa. "Gertie and I have a complicated relationship."

That's putting it mildly, thought Maria. Gertie and Elsa hadn't spoken in almost five years. *Five years!* Maria hoped things would have changed after Thorvald died, that Elsa would have reached out to her mother or that Gertie would have reached out to her daughter. Yet, somehow, the reaching just ended up in more of the same old fighting and recriminations.

"I understand," said Maria. Actually, she didn't understand, not even remotely. She couldn't understand why Elsa called her mother by her first name nor why she had always sided with her father. How in the world could Elsa blame Gertie for abandoning them when it was Thorvald who had left with another woman the year his daughter went to college?

"I've been thinking a lot lately," said Elsa. "It's time the fighting stopped. I've decided to come to New York. I want to be there for the party."

"That's wonderful," exclaimed Maria, excitement building inside her. "I was hoping to do something special for the occasion," she said, "only there aren't many people in Gertie's life. Just three really: Corinna and me of course, and Tom Jurgen, the nice man Gertie's been looking after since his wife died. To pad the list, I invited some residents and staff at the Senior Center, but it's not the same as having your family there."

"It doesn't surprise me," said Elsa, "Gertie not having many friends. She isn't the easiest person to get along with."

That's not fair, Maria almost blurted out, but refrained since she didn't want to say anything to jeopardize Elsa's decision. Gertie surely had a lot on her plate when her daughter was growing up, trying to live out her dreams and raise a family at the same time. And while Maria had no doubt what her own priority would have been in that situation, she also felt for Gertie; it couldn't have been easy. Most likely, she'd made mistakes. Still, anyone who knew Gertie could see she was a good person. There was no question in Maria's mind that Gertie loved her daughter, had always loved her, and was deeply hurt by their strained relationship.

"I'm sure the baby has a lot to do with my wanting to come," added Elsa.

"The baby?"

"Yes, I have a baby girl now. She was born two months ago."

Maria was caught off guard. She had heard about Elsa's fertility troubles, that Elsa had gone through several cycles of IVF, but as far as she knew, they had always been unsuccessful. "Gertie never mentioned—"

"I haven't told her yet, and please don't say anything. I'd like to tell her myself. In person. I want Kari to know who her grandmother is."

Maria was speechless, by the news and by the fact that Elsa had kept it from her mother. How selfish of her. Yet it didn't matter right now. Certainly not in comparison to the fact that Gertie would soon have a family again. Elsa wasn't just coming to New York—she was bringing her newborn baby, Gertie's granddaughter!

Maria couldn't possibly go to sleep now. Her heart racing after the unexpected phone call, she threw off the covers and bolted out of bed. She began fluffing pillows, smoothing down sheets, then rearranging pictures on the night table.

Ever since that Norwegian girl had shown up on TV, Gertie had been antsy. A wake-up call, she kept saying, to do something big and crazy before time ran out. Well, it certainly was crazy leaving the doctor's office before the skin cancer was removed. That wasn't a recipe for staying alive, leaving a ticking time bomb on your body, and certainly not the way Maria had dealt with her own cancer scare thirty years ago.

Yet Maria understood Gertie's sense of urgency. After all, she was getting older too; she'd turn seventy-five in September. Which was exactly why she had to act and do something big, just like Gertie said. Elsa's call couldn't have come at a better time. What could be bigger for Gertie than reuniting with her family?

After tidying the bedroom, Maria moved to the living room. She paced from one end of the room to the other, considering what to do next.

All these years, Gertie had been alone, telling everyone how happy she was to be independent and free, that she didn't care what her daughter thought of her. Maria never believed it. Not for one minute. But why didn't Gertie stick up for herself? Thorvald wasn't just unsupportive; he'd been downright abusive. Maybe not with his hands, but with his words, the way he demeaned his wife in front of Elsa, poisoned her against Gertie. The Absentee Mother, Gertie said he used to call her when she left for an event. *Mannaggia, the gall of that man!* The only explanation Maria could think of was that Gertie was too proud for her own good. She must have felt humiliated by the full-scale desertion of her family, first her husband, then her daughter—so hurt and humiliated that she just sealed it up inside of her, then sealed herself off.

After a brief rest on the recliner, Maria left the living room and entered the kitchen. The refrigerator was a mess. The gorgonzola in the butter basket was turning and gave off a bad smell.

Well, if Gertie wasn't willing to fight for herself, Maria would fight for her. This nonsense had gone on long enough. *You're right, Gertie, it's time to wake up. And when you open your eyes, I promise, you'll find life again. Elsa will be standing in front of you—a different Elsa than the one you last spoke to. She must sense the urgency too, now that she is a mother and has a child of her own. It's true, Gertie, a child, your granddaughter! I can't wait to see the look on your face. That will certainly settle you down after getting so worked up about some kid on TV, a kid who's not even related to you. Of course it will.*

Maria was dying to share the news. She dialed Corinna's number at the Senior Center, but no one could locate her. Her daughter, Livy, wasn't home either; she was probably working the night shift at the hospital.

As she wiped down the refrigerator shelves, reaching into every nook and cranny, she confided in the one person who was never not home when she wanted to vent.

All that talk of not needing a family, Jim, I never believed her. Even if it weren't so bad twenty years ago, surely it is now, after the heart attack and the skin cancer. Getting old isn't easy, Jim. You missed out on the golden years—now that's a good one, huh, golden years? She smiled. *But that's exactly why family can be such a blessing.*

When she finished with the refrigerator, Maria began arranging the spices in the cabinet in the order she used them, basil being front and center since almost every pasta dish she cooked was infused with the flavor of her husband's favorite herb.

I wouldn't last a minute away from Livy. Such a strong, hardworking woman, our daughter, having had to raise a kid all these years without a husband. And she still finds time to think of me. See these special shoes I'm wearing, Jim. Livy bought them for me. I know, in the old days I wouldn't have been caught dead in these ugly things. But you wouldn't believe how comfortable they are. Like walking on pillows. Now, tell me, how can a mother live without speaking to her daughter?

In one of the kitchen drawers, Maria noticed that a spoon had somehow ended up in the fork slot. She sighed, immediately returning the errant utensil to its rightful place.

And without speaking to her granddaughter! Oh, Jim, I wish you could see your grandson. How proud you'd be of Vinnie, all the amazing things he does. A whiz at the computer and the internet—though, come to think of it, you wouldn't know what the internet is. It doesn't matter, I don't either really. Now he's taking lessons in ancient Greek with a famous professor from Brooklyn College. He wants to go to Harvard after high school. Do you hear that, Jim? Your grandson, a genius! I know you'd be upset about the long hair and smoking. I caught him in the backyard the other day and told him so. But he's a good boy and gives us so much joy. Now, I ask you, how can I let Gertie not have a taste of that joy? Basta così! I'm going to make things right between her and Elsa if it's the last thing I do.

As she extended her arm so the vacuum cleaner could reach into the hollow beneath the cabinets, Maria felt a bolt of pain shoot down her left leg and detonate in her small toe.

Don't say it, Jim, I know what you're thinking, that I'm meddling again. That I should have learned my lesson the last time I tried to get those two back together and Gertie got so mad, she didn't speak to me for a week. Well, I don't care. She's going to be eighty, Jim. There isn't much time left.

Maria collapsed onto the recliner, exhausted. Past midnight now, everything was silent and still, the only sound an occasional car rumbling down the street below. On the end table next to the recliner stood a picture of her and the girls on the stone bench at the Temple. Maria smiled, recalling how Corinna positioned the camera on the severed column, set the timer, and raced back just in time for the click. So light on her feet that one, the youngest of their threesome, not yet seventy-three; she moved like a little bird. Corinna the Oddball was the nickname she'd given herself because of her quirks and physical differences, and to be honest, it had taken Maria a while before she was able to look at Corinna's hand without cringing—and even longer before she was able to control her emotions when Corinna walked out of a store without paying. But she understood her now. To her, Corinna was beautiful, with her smart blonde bob and nimble movements.

Maria reached for the picture on the end table. Gertie wasn't exactly her type at the beginning either, the way she could be so gruff and abrasive at times and how she never cared about the way she looked or dressed. Yet over the years, Gertie, too, had become beautiful in her eyes—the opposite of Corinna, with her large, powerful, confident limbs, ever the great athlete and competitor. She passed her hand over the glass frame and the figures locked arm in arm beneath it. The Three Musketeers. One of the first books Corinna had read to them at the Temple.

Remember what you once told me, Jim? That you couldn't look the other way anymore? You were talking about the bribes everybody took at the union, that someone had to say something—that you had to say something even if it cost you your job.

Well, I can't look the other way anymore either, Jim. I'm going to patch things up with Gertie and her family before it's too late—even if it costs me.

3

Corinna

The Senior Center occupied a ten-story, gray concrete building on Shore Road, overlooking the Narrows, filling a natural niche for many older members of the Bay Ridge community as their incomes dwindled and it became too difficult to care for themselves. While visitors might have felt a dispiriting and dull quality about the place in its earliest years, it had recently undergone a series of revitalizing changes, thanks in large measure to the efforts of Corinna Hale. This Sunday afternoon was a perfect example. Corinna had invited a professor from Brooklyn College to lecture on Virgil's *Aeneid.*

When the Professor finished his talk, Corinna rose from her chair to applaud. It was brilliant, much more compelling than anything they'd heard at the Center in ages. But as she scanned the first-floor TV lounge where they had brought in a lectern and set up five rows of folding chairs for the occasion, Corinna noticed that the residents and guests looked more bored than excited. Had they been listening to the same talk?

Meanwhile, Maria, sitting to her right, raised one eyebrow and pointed at her watch. "I haven't forgotten," Corinna whispered under her breath, though she still didn't understand why she had to go down to the banquet hall in person. They were only adding two more people to the party list, plus a high chair for Elsa's new baby. Couldn't they just inform them over the phone? But Maria was always so particular, and there wasn't any point in arguing.

Gertie seemed equally nonplussed by the Professor's moving description of the torrid love affair between Queen Dido and Aeneas. She, too, stood up the minute the Professor finished, only not to clap. In sweatpants, sweatshirt, and a towel draped around her neck, she bounced from one foot to the other, the spitting image of Rocky Balboa training for his next fight.

"That's funny," said Gertie when Corinna mentioned the resemblance. "But I don't box. I'm heading over to Fort Hamilton to work out with the high school swim team."

Corinna glanced at her friend sideways. "Isn't that supposed to be off limits? Didn't the cardiologist—"

"Screw the cardiologist and dermatologist and the rest of those ninnies. They keep warning me not to do anything too strenuous, but I think the opposite is true. Slowing down is what's going to kill me, not speeding up."

Corinna studied her friend. When they first met, Gertie had just turned sixty and was still running marathons. Gertie the Bull, she liked to tease her. That big, round white face, the flattened nose, broad shoulders, and muscular thighs. Gertie didn't mind the nickname. She knew her attractiveness lay in her strength and determination, not her features. And they were still there, only without the solidity. She had started to sag even before the heart attack last year. Now she was in a full-blown wilt. No, she probably shouldn't be swimming with a group of teenagers. Then again, how could Corinna tell her that when she routinely ignored the advice of her own doctors?

"So," said Gertie, "how about giving me a lift?"

"On the chopper?" asked Corinna, surprised. Gertie constantly reminded her friend that she didn't need to be motored around town; she preferred to walk on her own two feet. "Since when—"

"Haven't you been listening to anything I've said? It's time we start changing things around here. We can't keep doing the same stuff over and over. I've been thinking of getting a Vespa of my own. We could race down Shore Road. Maria too."

The idea of the three of them racing Vespas down Shore Road made Corinna laugh. It also made her wonder whether Gertie might not be going as soft in mind as she was in body. Ever since she started obsessing over that Norwegian girl on TV, she'd been acting very strange.

"Don't look at me like that," said Gertie. "You've always been a kook yourself, riding around on your red chopper, high as a kite. I'm beginning to think maybe that's what keeps you so young at heart. Still, it doesn't mean there's not something new and exciting out there you could be doing too." Gertie pulled Corinna over and whispered in her ear. "Do you see what I see?" she asked, motioning to the lectern with her chin.

The Professor, dapper in his tweed suit and paisley bow tie, held a stack of books under his arm while answering a question from someone in the audience. When he saw Gertie and Corinna looking over, he extended his free hand and waved.

"He's been staring in this direction ever since the talk started," said Gertie, a sly smile spreading over her face.

Corinna felt herself blush. Was it true?

"The two of you are like peas in a pod—how much you both love to read the classics, the work you did together on the Verrazzano Bridge for the Historical Society. Don't get me wrong, Maria and I appreciate your brainy side too, but a lot goes right over our heads. Wouldn't it be nice to have someone who really understands you?"

Yes, it would be nice, thought Corinna.

"Two peas in a pod," repeated Gertie with a wink.

"Fine, get your stuff," said Corinna, preferring not to discuss the subject any further until she had time to think it through. "I'll take you to the high school."

They passed Maria on the way out. She was helping one of the residents unlock her wheelchair and looked puzzled when she saw her friends leaving together. *Don't worry,* Corinna reassured her with a raised hand, *I won't forget the guest list.*

"We also have to find something new for Maria," Gertie said, taking the helmet Corinna handed her. "She's so focused on that family of hers that she hardly ever thinks of herself. At first, I thought maybe I could pawn Tom off on her. That man may look like a bear, but he's really just a teddy bear who needs someone to mother him—cook, clean, take him to the doctor. Did you know he passes out whenever he gets a shot? A firefighter who once ran into burning buildings and received a gazillion commendations for bravery. *Uff da.*"

Corinna smiled, well aware of Tom's issues. She was also used to her friend's bluster. Although Gertie might not admit it, she didn't always mind the attention of the annoying teddy bear.

"No question, Maria would be a heck of a lot better at the mothering job than me. The only problem is she won't ever look at another man. Not after being married to that perfect specimen of humanity, good old Jim, the gold standard of husbandry."

Corinna laughed as she pictured Maria singing the virtues of her late husband. "Put that helmet on, will you," she said, climbing on the Vespa.

"My other idea is a dance class," said Gertie, wrapping her arms around Corinna's tiny middle. "She always talks about how she and Jim used to light up the dance floor at parties. So I found this group that meets over at the Greek church on Eighty-First Street. Mostly younger people, but there's a few old-timers there too. I say we sign her up."

Corinna liked the idea a lot, especially if it gave Maria something to do besides obsess over birthday parties and family interventions.

"Hey, is this all she's got?" Gertie shouted as they navigated the sharp curves along Shore Road. "I can run faster than this chopper."

Corinna also liked the positive energy Gertie exuded. It was contagious. She pulled over in front of the high school. "Have a good swim," she told her friend. "But try not to push it."

"Sure thing, Boss."

Corinna watched Gertie jog toward the pool entrance, moving faster than she had in a long time. Maybe her friend was right: maybe they had fallen into a rut and needed to liven things up. Wasn't that why Corinna called the Professor a month ago? He was a thousand times more interesting than listening to another boring geriatrician or financial planner.

But would the Professor ever think of Corinna as more than just a colleague? She grasped the clutch in her curled-up hand. Would he ever be interested in her?

Two peas in a pod.

It was true.

But would he ever . . . ?

She could hear Gertie's voice in her ears: *Why the hell not?* whispered the Bull.

4

The Temple

Corinna was at the Temple, setting up before her friends arrived. Empty beer cans littered the grass in the enclosure and a faint smell of alcohol lingered in the air. After clearing away the garbage, she laid down a thatched mat and lit a dozen incense candles, arranging them in a circle. Today it was the myrrh scent she had picked up at the Lebanese market on Third Avenue.

She unwrapped the square of tinfoil and studied her recent purchase from Mr. Tongue Ring. It looked almost like a brownie. Corinna smiled, eagerly bringing the hash up to her nose. The smell alone sent a calming wave through her body.

Until she thought of Maria. Corinna was almost sure she'd spotted Maria's grandson lurking in a doorway a few feet from Mr. Tongue Ring's corner the other day, and she suspected Vinnie might be in cahoots with her drug dealer. If that were indeed the case, then Maria's heart might be the next in line to stop beating. Supportive as Maria and Gertie always were, this was one area where the Musketeers did not see eye to eye. The only reason they tolerated Corinna's drug habit was because they believed her doctor sanctioned it. Then again, hashish probably wasn't what the neurologist had in mind when he suggested alternative therapy. She'd better find out if Vinnie was working with Mr. Tongue Ring; she owed that to Maria.

There they were now, walking up the grassy hill, Gertie the Bull with the new bounce in her step and Maria, the redheaded Italian beauty, Helen of Troy in her new orthopedic clunkers. Corinna welcomed her friends into the Temple with a glass of wine. "It's a vino nobile di Montepulciano from Tuscany." She smiled, admiring the picture of the medieval castle on the bottle. "The Professor recommended it."

"Is that so?" said Gertie, winking in her direction.

Maria replied with a frown, "Haven't we had enough of the Professor's recommendations with that boring old Greek poem he has us reading now?"

Corinna ignored them both. "How about a toast," said Corinna, holding up her glass. "To new beginnings."

"Yes, I like the way that sounds," cheered Gertie.

Maria seemed happy with Corinna's choice of words too. Smiling, she nudged her friend to say more.

"Right," said Corinna, "and to the big bash just around the corner."

"Oh no, that's not what I had in mind," said Gertie. She told her friends that she'd been rethinking the party and had come to the conclusion that it was a lousy idea.

"How could you say that?" asked Maria. "It's your eightieth. Of course we're going to celebrate a milestone like that. Tell her, Corinna."

Gertie didn't give Corinna a chance to respond. "You're wrong, Maria. It's just a number, not an accomplishment. There's no time to waste on stuff like that anymore."

"What's gotten into you, Gertie?" asked Maria.

"It hit me the other day at the doctor's office," she answered. "All those old ninnies, sitting in the waiting room, watching themselves fall apart. I mean literally fall apart, one piece of their body after another. That's not living, in my book; it's giving up. The way I see it, we should focus on what's important now and ignore the rest. That's why I decided to keep the skin cancer," she said, running her finger lightly over the dime-shaped scab under her left eye. "I'm going to race in a swim meet for seniors at the Y in two weeks, and that won't happen if I agree to getting carved up like a turkey. Just look at Corinna's buddy at the Center, poor Mr. Flannery. Now, if you want to celebrate after I win the 200-meter butterfly, I'd say fine, let's do it. But not for a silly birthday. Better cancel the damn thing, Maria."

Maria fidgeted on the bench and looked as if she was about to say something when Gertie patted her on the shoulder.

"I know you're disappointed, Maria, but I'm right about this," Gertie said. "You'll see for yourself, once we all start to live a little again. In fact, if you really want to make me happy, take the dance class at the Greek church I suggested. Doesn't the thought of you back on the dance floor, doing the tango or the foxtrot or whatever it was you liked to do back in the day, get you excited?"

Maria's eyes filled with tears. "That's not it. You don't understand."

Corinna sensed Maria's anguish, even though she'd never been enthusiastic about her friend's scheming, especially going behind Gertie's back and talking to Elsa. If she ever pulled something like that with her, Corinna would be furious. But she'd gone along thus far, and if Elsa really had had a change of heart, maybe Maria wasn't so wrong after all.

Realizing she had best steer the conversation to another subject, Corinna looked down at her watch and feigned surprise. "Oh dear," she said. "I completely lost track of time. Quick, Maria, fetch me my binoculars."

Maria eagerly complied.

"Your favorite show is about to start, Gertie," said Corinna, flinging the binoculars around her neck. "Everyone assume their positions."

Maria wiped down the stone bench with a Kleenex from her bag, then took her spot next to the eastern column. Gertie ambled over to the opposite side, a step or so higher on the slope of the enclosure. And

Corinna, the shortest of the three by far, climbed onto the bench and stood between them on tiptoe, the only way she could see through the small opening in the branches of the giant oaks to the Verrazzano and the Narrows in the distance.

"Here she comes," Corinna informed them, peering into the binoculars. "Right on schedule. It's a freighter. Two stories, with a tower at starboard. Only half full of cargo. I see someone in the cockpit. A redhead like you, Maria, with a bushy beard. It looks like he's drinking coffee and smoking a cigarette."

"The name, Corinna," demanded Gertie, rubbing her hands together as she did before a swim meet.

"Right, I'll read it out. The first one to guess the place of origin wins the big prize. Ready?"

"Ready," Gertie and Maria said together.

Each gazed intently through the opening in the trees, toward the freighter with its rainbow-colored cargo containers, passing under the Verrazzano. Corinna couldn't take her eyes off the redheaded man in the cockpit. She followed his right index finger as it rose up and into his nose. "You're not going to believe this. The captain is picking his nose."

"The name, Corinna!" Gertie and Maria both shouted.

"Sorry. Here we go. It looks like our first vessel is the *Lugubria* from . . ."

Gertie sounded out the name slowly. "Lu-gu-bri-a. Lots of vowels. Eye-talian would be my guess."

"Then you'd be wrong, my friend."

"Yugoslavia?" ventured Maria.

"There's no such place anymore," explained Corinna. "You'll have to be more specific: Croatia, Bosnia, Serbia, et cetera. But I'll give you all of them. And the answer is no, no, and no."

Gertie guessed Germany and Maria South Africa, then they went through the rest of Europe and Africa.

"Come now, ladies. Shall I give you a hint?"

Gertie waved her off. "How about Argentina?"

"You're getting warmer."

Gertie thought long and hard, then finally called out, "Peru."

"Bingo."

"Yes!" Gertie cheered, throwing her hands in the air victoriously.

"Peru, indeed," said Corinna. "Once home to the mighty Inca Empire, one of the largest the world has ever seen. Only, its star was short lived—not quite one hundred years old when the Spanish arrived with their guns and horses."

"Also the setting of that book you read to us," Maria chimed in. "The sad one about the twins and the old rope bridge that collapsed."

"*The Bridge of San Luis Rey*." Corinna stepped off the bench and grabbed her tote. "Yes, but there'll be no sadness here today, Maria. In fact, I have a special treat from the Norwegian bakery for our big winner," she said. "Forgive me if I don't attempt to say the name."

"*Krumkake*," said Gertie, accepting the pastry. "Kroom-ka-ka," she repeated slowly, pronouncing it in the thickest Norwegian accent she could muster.

"What a melodious word!" observed Corinna.

"I hope you also brought some *tyttebær*," said Gertie with the utmost seriousness. "We always fill our *krumkake* with *tyttebær*."

Corinna and Maria turned to each other and laughed.

"And I didn't forget you, Maria." Corinna reached back into her tote. "For today's runner-up, we have a special Eye-talian cannoli," she said, pinching her fingers together and shaking her hand in the air in imitation of her friend's favorite gesture. "Though I'm afraid they're nothing like your Jim's," she conceded.

"You could say that again. He used to make them with fresh ricotta," said Maria. "He'd spend hours rolling the dough. You never tasted anything like them, isn't that right, Gertie?"

"You bet," replied Gertie without hesitation, though they all knew she had never tasted Jim's cannoli, had never even met their legendary maker, since he'd died before the women became friends.

"And a little something for me as well." Corinna broke off a piece of hashish and placed it in the hookah bowl. "You ladies don't know what you're missing."

Corinna's head drifted backward as she sucked on the hookah's hose. Maria savored her memory-filled cannoli. Gertie turned to the Narrows and the freighter in the distance with its colorful cargo containers.

"That's it," Gertie shouted, rising from the bench.

"What are you talking about?" asked Maria.

"I want to see the world, I want to see it all—that's what she said, remember?"

"Who?" asked Corinna, after releasing a cloud of smoke from her mouth.

"Annie Halvorsen, that's who," answered Gertie, her arms outstretched. "And that's exactly what we ought to do. Screw the party, Maria. Screw the books and guessing games, Corinna. I'm tired of watching the ships come and go. Let's get off our asses and take a ride on one of those ships. That's what I want to do. See the world. Maybe get a berth on the *Lugubria* and visit Peru. See the Incan ruins and whatever's left of the bridge of San Luis Rey. It doesn't matter where we go," she said, stomping her foot on the ground, "as long as we go. Somewhere far away from here, the farther the better. What do you say, girls?"

Maria glanced uneasily at Corinna and picked at her cannoli. Corinna opened her copy of the *Aeneid* and began to read. Both pretended they didn't hear the question.

5

Maria

Olivia Donofrio flinched when she entered her kitchen early Sunday morning and found her mother scrubbing dried marinara sauce off the oven grate with a Brillo pad. Though still half-asleep and disheveled, she was the spitting image of the handsome older woman standing in front of her: tall and thin with a thick mane of auburn hair and high, angular cheekbones reminiscent of Sophia Loren's.

"It's only me, Livy," said Maria. "Why don't you sit down and let me make you breakfast? You must be exhausted after your double shift at the hospital."

"I'm fine, Ma. How many times do I have to tell you, it's not your job to clean my house." Livy glanced at the dishes drying in the rack and the leftover pasta on the table, then slammed her hand on the counter. "Your grandson is a big boy now. *He* should be doing this, not you." She stuck her head out the kitchen door and yelled: "Vinnie! Wake up and get downstairs right now."

"It's okay, Livy, let him sleep."

"No, it's not." She exhaled loudly and shook her head. "By the way, Ma, how are the new shoes working out?"

"Like night and day," she answered, not quite truthfully. The pain that tore down the side of her left leg continued to come and go, but it didn't bother her in the least, as long as she could still manage her own home and help Livy with hers. As she filled the coffee maker with water, Maria pressed her left foot into the linoleum floor until her entire body tingled.

"For God's sake, Ma, sit down and let me do that." Livy led her mother to the table and guided her into a chair. "How about some eggs?"

"Don't make a fuss, Livy." Maria sat back and gazed out the window into the backyard. It didn't feel so bad giving her feet a rest and waiting for the throbbing in her toe to subside. The throbbing in her head too, ever since Gertie started talking about seeing the world.

Livy set out a pot of coffee and a plate of toast. "I have some of that cranberry jam that Gertie brought over."

"Lingonberry," Maria corrected her. "It's a Norwegian thing with a funny name. Tittabear, they call it."

Livy, already absorbed in an article on the front page of the *New York Daily News*, didn't respond.

Maria moved closer to the window for a better look at the buildup on one side of the sandbox: cigarette stubs. She hated that Vinnie smoked, even if it was only once in a while, as he claimed. A little beer was one thing, but smoking was a killer. She'd need to have another talk with Vinnie. "You shouldn't be so hard on him, Livy."

Her daughter nodded without looking up from the paper.

"Such a smart and hardworking boy."

Livy took a sip of coffee.

"Maybe it's not so bad he lets loose once in a while. If your father were alive, he would be so proud—"

"Really, Ma?" asked Livy, when she finally registered what her mother was saying. "Vinnie, who takes the car out without a driver's license? Whose best friend has purple hair and a ring hanging off his tongue? That kid better wise up before he ends up in jail."

"That's not fair, Livy, and you know it. Let me remind you of a young girl who was once Vinnie's age and did a few things we'd all like to forget."

"Maybe, but I wasn't at the top of my high school class and didn't have a chance of getting into an Ivy League school. He better not throw it all away."

"He'll be fine," Maria assured her. "The fruit doesn't fall far from the tree."

Livy sighed deeply, then returned to the *Daily News* while Maria waxed on about falling fruit and all the nice things Vinnie had done recently: donating books to Corinna's library at the Senior Center, going shopping with his grandmother, volunteering at the hospital where his mother worked.

"Family," mused Maria thoughtfully. "That's what really matters."

She listened to Livy breathe, taking in and expelling air. She smelled her smell mixed in with the coffee and jam. How lucky she was to have a daughter she was close to, who made her breakfast and bought her special shoes. A grandson who carried her groceries home from Key Food and always wrote her the sweetest cards on her birthday. People who loved her. People who needed her.

"That's what really matters," she repeated with conviction.

As she spread some lingonberry jam onto another piece of toast, Maria felt a twinge of guilt. When it came to family, she had so much and her best friends so little. Maybe that was why Gertie was upset, why she suddenly wanted to leave Bay Ridge. Maybe down deep, despite what she said, Gertie was scared of being alone.

"People need people they can count on," Maria said.

Older people especially, she thought. That was why the party was so important, so that Gertie and Elsa could start being mother and daughter again. Gertie might not be able to see it clearly now, but she would soon enough. Then she'd realize what she'd been missing all these years. Of course she would.

"Boy is Gertie going to be surprised," said Maria.

"Yeah," mumbled Livy.

"She really needs this right now, a lot more than a silly vacation."

Livy nodded without lifting her head from the newspaper.

Maria began to laugh. "What a crazy idea!" She laughed a little louder. "Can you imagine the three of us? Three old ladies in bathing suits?"

"What's that, Ma?"

"Taking a vacation. Can you imagine?"

Livy finally looked up.

"That visit to the skin doctor must have really thrown her for a loop," said Maria.

"Are you kidding?" said Livy. "What a great idea! When was the last time you took a vacation?"

"Well . . ." She pretended to think for a moment. "There was the trip your father and I took to the Canary Islands."

"Oh for God's sake, Ma, that was a million years ago."

"I remember it like yesterday. The water was so clear, you could see down to your toes. And there were so many birds with all those gorgeous colors. I told you about the pink flamingos, right?"

"You might have mentioned it"—Livy smiled—"once or twice."

"Gertie's got it in her head that we should go to the Canaries or Peru or some other far-off place."

"Good for Gertie," cheered Livy. "You could show her the pink flamingos."

"That's not funny, Livy. Not for us, at our age. You remember what happened when Gertie had the heart attack at the Center last year? They had to rush her to Lutheran. A few minutes more and she would've been dead. That's what the doctors said."

"I remember."

"You think an ambulance would have come so quickly in the Canary Islands? For all I know, they don't even have hospitals over there."

Livy gave her mother a look. "People your age travel all the time. Ask your doctor if you don't believe me. And if you're so afraid to go by yourself," said Livy with a wink, "maybe you could bring along your boyfriend."

"What in God's name are you talking about?"

"Only what Vinnie tells me. Apparently, he's been asking about you, Ma."

"He who?"

"You really don't know?" she asked incredulously. "The professor from Brooklyn College who's doing the independent study project with Vinnie."

"The professor?" repeated Maria.

"The one with the fancy bow ties. A famous Latin and Greek scholar. I'm impressed."

"Well, I'm not," said Maria, her surprise turning to irritation.

"I just meant that it would be nice to have a man along."

"That's enough, Livy."

Livy took her mother's hands in her own. "It's okay to talk to another guy. Dad's been gone for a long time, and he'd want you to be happy."

"I am happy."

"Just don't rule anything out, Ma. The two of us can't be widows forever."

She pinched her fingers together and shook her hand in the air. "I have everything I want. My family. My memories. Two great friends. My life is full."

Maria couldn't believe her daughter would even suggest such a thing, especially about that pretentious man with his boring old books and fancy wines. They had absolutely nothing in common.

"Besides, Ma, it's not like life with Dad was perfect."

"What's that supposed to mean?" snapped Maria.

"It means that you didn't see eye to eye on everything. I remember a lot of yelling in the house when—"

"Basta!" Maria cut her off. She wouldn't tolerate any disrespect to her husband's memory. Her Jim had meant the world to her. Simple, honest, and good to the bone. A garbage man who never took a bribe and worked his way up the sanitation ladder to become union secretary. A family man who put his wife and daughter above everything. No man on earth could replace him.

Just then the refrigerator door banged shut. They turned to find Vinnie shuffling to the cupboard for a glass. He was tall and skinny with a mop of brown, tangled hair that reached down to his shoulders and covered most of his face.

"Rough night, huh, Vinnie?" asked Livy. "You look like crap."

"Livy!"

"What, you're going to tell me you don't agree?" she asked, gesturing to her son, who was having difficulty standing steady and keeping his eyes open.

Vinnie filled his glass with milk and began drinking listlessly.

"Did you even say hello to your grandmother?" asked Livy. "Your grandmother who spent all morning cleaning up your mess?"

"It's okay, Livy."

"No, it's not. What does he think this is, a hotel?"

"Jesus, Ma, give it a rest," pleaded Vinnie, his voice dragging like the rest of his body. "Hey, Granny."

"Morning, Vinnie."

Livy dumped her coffee in the sink. "You know what, Ma, maybe I'll go away with Gertie and Corinna. I could use a vacation before I lose my mind in this nuthouse."

"Vinnie," said Maria after her daughter had gone back upstairs, glad to have an opportunity to talk to her grandson alone. It was the reason she had come to Livy's house so early in the morning. She'd finally figured out a way to help Corinna too. It came to her late last night as she tossed in bed, unable to sleep. "I have a favor to ask you."

"Sure, Granny, what's up?"

She reminded him of the family tree he'd made for her last Christmas, with all their relatives going back to Calabria and Sicily. "I know you did a lot of research on the computer to put it together."

Vinnie looked like he was ready to doze off.

"I was hoping you could make one just like it for Corinna."

"Hmm?"

"Corinna, my friend from the Senior Center. You know, the one you just gave all your old books to."

"The midget with the red Vespa?"

"Please don't say such things, Vinnie. It's hurtful. Besides, she's not a midget. Just a little smaller than most and with a few birth defects . . . *mannaggia*, now you have me talking that way too. Shame on both of us!"

"Sorry, Granny," said Vinnie.

"Corinna's a special person. She used to come to your baseball games. We cheered for you on the sidelines. And she's smart as a whip. I bet she reads more books than your famous professor. Gertie and I have learned so much from her. As a matter of fact, she has us reading Homer now, though I can't say I'm crazy about it."

He nodded.

"I feel awful for her, Vinnie. She has no one besides me and Gertie. No family whatsoever, at least that's what she says. But I don't believe her. I have a feeling something must have happened, something she may be ashamed of. Well, I'd like to find out more and see if I can help make things right."

"Maybe she doesn't want you to find out."

Vinnie was right about that. Whenever Maria had asked Corinna about her past, she'd tense up and tell her to mind her own business. But Vinnie's Christmas project had shown her that you could learn about people in less direct ways. And despite the risk—the one time she probed a little too far, Corinna didn't show up at the Temple for two weeks—Maria believed it was worth it. Just as she had convinced Elsa to give it another go with her mother, she might be able to do the same with someone in Corinna's family, whoever might still be around. How could that not be a good thing?

Maria turned to Vinnie as he was leaving the kitchen. "I'm not sure if this helps, but I think Corinna's father might have been a minister."

Vinnie looked up. "A minister?"

It did sound strange, thought Maria, considering how unconventional and anti-everything-religious Corinna was. But every aspect of the silence and mystery surrounding Corinna's past was strange to her, strange and deeply upsetting.

"Her last name is Hale. Corinna Hale. H-a-l-e."

"Corinna Hale," Vinnie repeated, then laughed. "Whack job."

"What's that, Vinnie?"

"Nothing, Granny. Just give me a little time and I'll see what I can dig up."

"Come here, Vinnie, and give your grandmother a kiss."

Vinnie shuffled over and planted a half-hearted kiss on his grandmother's cheek. Maria was so excited she barely smelled the lingering smoke and beer on his breath.

6

Corinna

She was almost halfway there when she realized she'd forgotten her purse. This was so unlike her. Yet the whole thing was so unlike her. Why should she go to such lengths to impress him? High school Latin had been a hundred years ago and not her strongest subject. Did she really have to read Virgil in the original?

Yes, she thought, shifting the Vespa into a higher gear and passing the cyclist in front of her. It first dawned on her last Sunday at the Center when Gertie pulled her aside. The Professor had indeed been looking at Corinna because she was the only one in the room who understood what he was saying, especially the part about how even the best translations pale in comparison to the original Latin. Gertie was right—they were like two peas in a pod.

Her conversation with Joe Flannery this morning only strengthened her resolve. She'd been at her desk in the library. "What are you reading there, Boss?" he asked.

She probably should have lied.

"Never heard of it," he said. "Thriller? Romance?"

Corinna smiled, turning over her English version of the *Aeneid*, and headed to the shelves to find the book he'd ordered, the latest in a murder mystery series by some hack writer. Pure, unadulterated rubbish.

"Now, this here is a book," he'd said, taking it from her. "Maybe not one of the classics you like, but it sure gets the blood running. You ought to try it."

There was nothing terrible about Joe Flannery. In fact, he was her right-hand man at the Center. Despite the endless merry-go-round of skin cancers, the latest casualty being his heavily bandaged left ear, he was in excellent health and always offering to help out, at the library, on field trips, even in replenishing her liquor stash—as it turned out, they had similar taste: single malt whiskey, preferably Jameson. No, she liked Flannery and his Irish jolliness and generosity; she liked the man a lot. Only, he was so un-epic. So un-Virgilian.

Not like *him*.

Corinna parked the Vespa outside Marlowe and Co. Booksellers in Park Slope. She loved the way the old wooden floorboards creaked under her feet when she entered the store and listened closely for the heartbeats of the books, stacks of living, breathing books, row upon row. She wasn't, however, happy to see the owner at the register; she had hoped to find his infinitely more accommodating wife instead.

She raised her hand to get his attention, but he ignored her.

"Cretin," she muttered to herself, still not sure why he held a grudge against one of his best customers. It had to be pride. How many times had she caught his mistakes, confusing the Brontë sisters on one occasion and denying that Wilder had won a Pulitzer for *The Bridge of San Luis Rey* on another. A bookseller for thirty years, with his stinky pipes and hanging glasses, you'd think he'd know. Or maybe he never forgave her for the time she left without paying. It might have been *times* plural, come to think of it, but who was counting? Besides, his wife never seemed to care, and the Center always paid in the end. What was the big deal?

The owner pretended to be busy examining invoices, then warmly greeted a customer who arrived after her. Periodically, he glanced over or, more accurately, glanced down, exaggerating the neck-craning efforts one would use to track a scampering infant or a darting insect. The other customer, a middle-aged man dressed in a tailored suit, noticed and unconsciously began to mimic the owner's antics.

Corinna was used to it by now, the story of her life, and it no longer bothered her. The truth was, she had come to regard her singularities more as strengths than as handicaps, especially when she ran down the list of residents at the Center—drooling, wobbling, huffing and puffing, complaining about one ailment after another—all of whom were not that much older than she was. Look at poor Gertie, and even Maria. Well, not Corinna Hale, she was holding up quite well, thank you very much.

From her eclectic readings in the academic and popular scientific press, she embraced the notion that her Lilliputian dimensions—four feet eleven and under ninety pounds—were the key to her success. She had half the cells, half the metabolism and waste products, half the buildup of genetic mutations. No wonder that, at seventy-two years old, she was zipping down Fifth Avenue on a moped and about to read Virgil in the original Latin.

But patience had never been part of the package, especially when there was no reason for it. She would not be put off another second. When the cretin finished with the man in the suit and was about to help yet another customer who had appeared from God knows where, she stepped forward. "Sorry," she insisted, "but I've been waiting."

She told the owner what she wanted, once and then a second time before he reluctantly acknowledged her.

He rolled his eyes and headed back to the stacks, returning with a handful of copies of the ancient Roman classic, which he dumped on the counter in front of her, then turned quickly to his next customer, a young college girl.

She picked the oldest one from the pile. It had no jacket cover and the cloth was worn and smooth, its green color faded. She opened the book and inspected the paper, brittle and dog eared at the edges. She held it close to her nose and breathed in the musty vanilla smell. How she loved that smell!

"I'll take it," she said, smiling as she walked out of the store. "You can put it on my tab."

She was already speeding away on her Vespa when the owner appeared on the street chasing after her.

The wind in her face felt good as she zipped down Fourth Avenue, Virgil in the front basket. She would start as soon as she returned home, work her way through all twelve books, line by line. When the going got tough, she'd take down notes and ask the Professor about it afterward. They'd discuss and debate famous passages as she gained proficiency in the language. *It's true, Professor, how much better Virgil is in the original Latin!*

"Hey, watch where you're going," she shouted at a livery cab driver who almost ran her off the road.

She hadn't felt this way for as long as she could remember, at least not in the real world. The world of books was another story. There, she found a vast selection of passionate lovers: Romeo, Mr. Darcy, Count Vronsky. They were always more than enough for her, since real people were always such disappointments. Men especially, beginning with her father, the kindly pastor, respected by the entire Boston suburb of Parkside for his compassion and intellect. Somehow it didn't matter that she was smart too, that she valued the books in his library as much as he did. Instead of praise, which he bestowed so generously on just about everyone else, he seemed to have only pity for her: "My poor little Corinna!" he would say, looking down at her with sad eyes, whether she'd done something good or bad. A man of God who couldn't see beyond the flesh to the soul inside, one that was worthy and deserving of so much more.

Corinna pulled back on the throttle, almost flooding the engine, and honked her horn at no one in particular.

It wasn't until she'd come to the Senior Center (after an unhappy stint as a college librarian) that she found a real home, a place where she felt comfortable and wanted. Even in her early thirties, she fit in with the old people and cranks, never embarrassed by people whom everyone else was embarrassed by. Instinctively, she knew how to handle them, when to push and when not to. She constantly drummed up new ideas and activities to spark their interests: art and music classes, lectures on a variety of subjects, outings to the Brooklyn Botanic Garden and the aquarium in Coney Island. The administrators quickly realized how lucky they were and gave her more and more responsibility. Eventually, Corinna came to oversee almost every aspect of life at the Center. There, she was the boss, and people like Joe Flannery and his wife, Rose, listened. They respected her. They cared about her.

Corinna whizzed down Fourth Avenue, the lights green as far as she could see, slowing only for a police car parked on the corner of Fifty-Ninth Street.

Then, later on and even better, came Maria and Gertie, the only real friends she'd ever had. Who would have thought the three women would become so close after that crazy day by the Verrazzano. They were all so different: Gertie the Bull; Santa Maria, Helen of Troy; and Corinna the Oddball. Maybe it was their differences that brought them together. And maybe each secretly wished they could be a little more like the others. They cared all right, like sisters in a way.

She first realized that about six months after they met, the morning Gertie and Maria rushed to her defense at Dunkin' Donuts. A customer hurled an insult at Corinna for sneaking in front of him to grab a napkin. "Who you calling a freak?" Gertie glared at the man, the size of Tom Jurgen but forty years younger, her umbrella within inches of his fuming face. "Let's go, Corinna," said Maria, taking her hand, "the coffee is better at Bagel Boy anyway." It had nothing to do with pity.

Somehow Maria and Gertie understood how she felt—since the world treated her badly, she was entitled to treat the world badly in return.

Her two friends cared, and she cared right back.

But that was one kind of caring. *This* was different.

She stopped for a red light on Sixty-Eighth Street, next to a yellow school bus full of children.

This was *very* different.

Two young girls waved at Corinna from the bus. Another stared. A boy stuck out his tongue and laughed. She waved to the girls.

How nice he was when she first called last month to invite him to lecture at the Center. "Of course, I remember you," said the Professor. "From the book we worked on together at the Historical Society, *The Bay Ridge Chronicle*. You wrote the chapter on the Verrazzano Bridge."

She most certainly did. It was the first time she had ever been published, and she was thrilled to see her words in print.

"I was so taken by the detail about the reciprocal gifts of stones," he went on. "Three stones chiseled from the Verrazzano Castle in Tuscany and cemented into the bridge in New York, while similar-sized stones removed from the bridge went to fill in the holes on the castle walls. What a wonderful gesture!"

Corinna agreed.

"I wasn't aware of the ceremony held at the castle every year to commemorate the bridge's opening in 1964. In fact, I wrote a letter to Count Luigi Cappellini, who now owns the property, and we've been corresponding ever since. The next time he's in New York, he promised to get together. You should come, and bring your friend Maria too."

Corinna was surprised, not only that he remembered her, but that he remembered and admired her work and asked her to join him the next time the count was in town.

"I would love to give a talk at the Center," he said. "I would be honored."

He said it again when she introduced him a few weeks later. Imagine that, a professor of classics at Brooklyn College honored to be speaking to a group of senior citizens.

She decided to take the long way back and looped onto the Belt Parkway. She wanted to ride along the Narrows and feel the wind in her hair. She wanted to see the great bridge from a distance and up close.

Then, last Sunday, he'd showered her with praise for the library she'd built at the Center. The residents should be grateful that someone with discriminating taste like Corinna Hale was overseeing their literary interests, he'd said.

No one had ever praised her like that before.

She was blushing now, five days later, as the cool sea breeze blew against her cheeks.

"My only criticism," he said, smiling directly at her—just as Gertie had said—"is that the classics section could be enlarged."

Not to worry, Professor, she was taking care of that.

The delicate lines and curves of the Verrazzano sparkled in the distance. Not a cloud in the lovely blue sky.

Why shouldn't she have what everybody else in the world had? What Gertie once had, even though it had gone terribly wrong? Or what Maria once had, even though it didn't last nearly as long as she would have hoped?

Corinna approached the bridge, the concrete mooring on the Brooklyn side rising in front of her. She could hear the sound of the wavelets lapping around it. The massive steel beams drove upward to support the underbelly of the great steel bird, stretching its wings toward Brooklyn and Staten Island. She turned off the highway and sped down Shore Road, excited to break open her copy of Virgil.

Arma virumque cano.

I sing of arms and the man.

7

The Temple

Gertie had been hectoring her friends ever since she arrived at the Temple. The big swim meet at the Y was next Thursday. She'd like to leave Brooklyn soon afterward, the sooner the better. They could celebrate her birthday in Peru or wherever else they decided to go, she offered, thinking it might help with Maria, who couldn't get Gertie's birthday out of her mind.

Maria, meanwhile, tried every excuse in the book to convince Gertie that international travel was a terrible idea. She went through a list of recent disasters happening around the world: food poisoning on cruise ships, volcanic ash clouds over Europe, earthquakes and tsunamis in the Far East, and, of course, the ever-looming threat of al-Qaeda terrorists. She produced an article from the *Daily News* about the skyrocketing costs of travel, especially during the prime seasons of spring and summer. But Gertie wouldn't listen. A mule couldn't be more stubborn, she thought. The only thing left to do was stall—stall, stall, stall until the party.

Corinna had promised to help Maria, despite how much she'd always talked of traveling abroad, especially on one of those elegant cruise ships they loved to watch from their perch at the Temple. Maria was grateful, and didn't question why Corinna suddenly seemed so dead set on staying close to home.

"*Attenzione*, ladies. I spy an impressive vessel out yonder," announced Corinna, leaping onto the stone bench and peering into her binoculars. "An old schooner from the South Street Seaport."

"How beautiful the water looks today," remarked Maria. "Don't you love when the breeze makes those little waves? What do you call them, Corinna?"

"Wavelets," she answered.

"And the sparkles the sunlight makes when it hits the water," continued Maria. "It's like all the little waves, the wavelets I mean, are bouncing and talking at once. Like fireflies. Millions of them. Look, Gertie."

Gertie strained to see the old sailboat, surrounded by all that sparkling blue water, now passing under the Verrazzano and inching toward the horizon. "I wonder where it's heading."

"Me too," said Maria.

Gertie reached down to massage a cramp in her right calf. Maria knew she'd been getting them ever since she started swimming again. It was the good kind of pain, though, she'd said when Maria questioned her about it, the kind that made her feel alive again. "For Pete's sake, girls," Gertie suddenly cried out, "let's get the hell out of Bay Ridge."

Maria took a deep breath, trying not to get exasperated. Clearly, their stalling tactics weren't working very well. But Maria was prepared. She had devised a last-ditch plan in case her other arguments failed. She motioned to Corinna, only Corinna was puffing away on her hookah and no longer following the conversation.

"Fine, you win, Gertie," said Maria. "Let's go away then."

"Really?"

Maria nodded. "And I've got just the place."

"You have?"

"The Taj Mahal," announced Maria with a big smile. "Livy talks about it all the time. One of the seven wonders of the world. Those were her exact words."

Gertie looked shocked. "Not exactly my first choice," she conceded, "but why the hell not? Let's go to India then."

"No, not India," said Maria, swatting away the suggestion. "I meant Atlantic City. Donald Trump's hotel. We can sign up for the bus at the Center. I heard Rose Flannery won over a hundred dollars at the slot machines last weekend."

"You're joking?"

"I most certainly am not. The Taj is supposed to be one of the top hotels in the world. We could splurge and get a suite, one with a view of the ocean, especially if we go midweek."

Gertie shook her head. "That's not what I had in mind, Maria. I want to go somewhere"—she pointed to the sailboat in the distance—"somewhere far away from here."

"Atlantic City is far away. The last stop in New Jersey. Over four hours by bus."

"Don't you understand, Maria?" Gertie squeezed her friend's hand. "We meet here at the Temple every week to watch the boats come and go. That's part of what's special about it. We wonder where they're heading, who the people on board are, what they want."

Maria agreed. "It's fun to wonder."

"Yeah, but it's not real," said Gertie. "Don't you see? We should be the ones on the boat."

"I'm sorry, but—"

Gertie squeezed Maria's hand harder and then gave it a shake as if that might help. "We watch the boats because we don't like who we are. The same reason we love listening to Corinna's books. They take us away. Isn't that right, Corinna?" she yelled, trying to get her attention.

Corinna's eyes were closed. She sat on her mat, one hand on the hookah, the other on her precious copy of the *Aeneid*, swaying back and forth like an ancient priestess.

"Corinna, you understand what I'm saying, don't you?"

Corinna stopped swaying for a moment and opened her eyes ever so slightly. "Yes," she whispered, "take me away, take me away."

"See that, Maria. She's sick of imagining too. It's time to go."

Maria didn't know how to respond. She thought she'd come up with the perfect solution, a compromise of sorts, where the three of them could go and view the sea and ships from another place. But Gertie wasn't interested in compromising and now Corinna appeared to be siding with her.

"How many times have you told me about that trip of yours to the Canary Islands? The water so clear you could see down to your toes."

"That was a long time ago," Maria answered. "I can't do that now."

"Why not?"

Because of the big surprise I've been planning, that's why, she wanted to answer, she wanted to scream out loud. "Well . . ." She fumbled for something to say. "I'd probably get sick on a ship, all that rocking back and forth."

"We could take a plane."

Maria sighed, realizing it was pointless; Gertie would never give in. "I'm happy here," she told her. "Livy needs me. Vinnie too. He seems to be going through a rough patch."

Gertie emitted a snort of disbelief. "That's what you think. They need you like a hole in the head."

Maria winced at the hurtful words, until she convinced herself they weren't true, that Gertie was just angry. "People need you too, Gertie," she continued. "Me and Corinna, for instance, and Tom." And soon, Maria hoped, if all went according to plan, Gertie's own daughter and granddaughter. She hoped that with all her heart.

"Just try and picture it, Maria, the palm trees and the paella."

Maria thought for a second, then answered: "We could get paella down the block at Sancho's. It was voted best Spanish restaurant in Bay Ridge."

Gertie threw her arms in the air and leaned over toward Corinna. She tapped her hard on the shoulder. "Open your eyes, Corinna. Snap out of it. We're going on one of those ships you love so much. You hear me? We're going to the Canary Islands. No, scratch that, we're going to Italy. Yes, that's exactly what we'll do. Follow in the footsteps of Aeneas and the Trojans. We can eat some real Eye-talian cannolis for a change, Maria, not the fake ones from the Norwegian bakery." She picked up the bottle of wine and filled their glasses. "Better pack your bags, girls. I'm not taking no for an answer."

8

Gertie

It was happening again. After a hard run along the water, Gertie reached into her fanny pack and took out a plum. As she wolfed down the sweet, soft fruit, the pit got caught in her throat. She couldn't breathe . . .

Corinna was lying on the grass nearby when she heard the whooping sounds. She dropped her book and sprang into action. Only she couldn't wrap her tiny arms around the much larger Gertie . . .

Maria spotted the commotion as she walked down the footpath. She rushed over to help, doing her best to follow Corinna's directions, but the abdominal thrusts weren't working. Gertie was turning blue. Corinna called for back blows. Maria ratcheted up the intensity, until finally the pit . . .

But no, this time the pit was *not* expelled. It was still stuck at the back of Gertie's throat and she couldn't breathe . . .

Maria and Corinna headed up the grassy slope by themselves. They would discover the secret enclosure without her, the stone bench and fluted columns, the dazzling view through the opening in the giant oaks. They would see all this without her . . .

Wait, she called to them. She was screaming now: *Don't leave me here alone!* But no sounds emerged from her mouth. She gasped for air, everything getting darker and darker . . . going black.

With a jolt, Gertie awoke, clutching the mattress with both hands. *Uff da.* It was dark inside the apartment, except for a few strips of moonlight that had slipped through the blinds. She could dimly make out the telephone on the night table. Should she call Maria? She would understand since she'd had a few night terrors of her own. Only Maria never called Gertie on those occasions; she called her daughter.

Gertie had a daughter too. What time was it now on the West Coast? she wondered. Maybe Elsa hadn't gone to bed yet. But how could she call someone she didn't speak to? *Who's this?* She imagined Elsa answering the phone, not recognizing her mother's voice. Or even worse: *Why should I be there for you, Gertie, when you weren't there for me?* The Absentee Mother—that was what she'd called her the last time they spoke. The name came from Thorvald, who loved to bash her over the head with it whenever she left home: "There she goes again, the Absentee Mother. Swimming and coaching always more important than family. Thank God for your grandmother, Elsa. I don't know what we'd do if Mor Sundersen wasn't here to help out around the house."

It wasn't fair. He knew she wouldn't give up her swimming career. And from what she could remember, he was even supportive at the beginning, almost as excited as she was about the next step on the way to the biggest prize of all, the Olympic Games in Melbourne. Then suddenly he wasn't, and that was before she screwed up her shoulder. He wasn't interested in anything—not the swimming and definitely not her. She could never pinpoint exactly when the change took place, or why he changed. Who the hell really knew why anyone changed!

Regardless, it wasn't true what he said. She wasn't a bad mother, was she? Hadn't she made up for the absences when she returned home—taking Elsa to the park, buying her ice cream, reading to her at night? Yes, she might have missed one or two birthday parties and some softball games, but she knew *Goodnight Moon* by heart and loved to recite it to Elsa before bed. Didn't that count for anything?

Maybe it didn't. Maybe Elsa needed more—more things, more time, more love. Maybe she *was* a bad mother.

No. She gripped the mattress harder. She wouldn't call anyone. She'd just stare at the strips of light on the walls, watch them inch across the ceiling, slowly, ever so slowly, and wait out the night.

In the morning, Gertie filled a bowl with fancy Greek yogurt and, as she regularly did, tried to picture herself in the yogurt company's popular advertisement: scaling rugged Greek mountains with a group of wrinkled but nimble old shepherds. This morning she was having trouble, after the nightmare and now the swelling around her eye. She must have brushed against the skin cancer in her sleep. When she awoke, it was bleeding and the area around it all bruised. She stabbed at the tasteless white paste in the bowl in front of her. How would she be able to practice this afternoon? The swim meet was just over a week away. One more mouthful of the yogurt was about all she could stomach. Maybe she'd never make it up those Greek mountains anyway.

Gertie was also depressed by the article in the *Daily News* that Maria had cut out for her. It never occurred to her how much a trip to Europe might cost. Flights alone were now running over a grand. Where the hell was she going to come up with that kind of money, considering the miserable state of her finances? All she really had was her monthly social security check. Her savings account had been nearly wiped clean when her fridge pooped out last year and she had to splurge for a new one. And she'd just spent all her bingo winnings on Maria's dance lessons. Maybe she could try to pawn some of her jewelry? Or organize a garage sale? Only, nothing she had was worth very much.

Maybe her dour cardiologist was wrong and she didn't have to take all of her heart medications—the blood pressure pill alone cost over two hundred bucks a month. Maybe she could return whatever pills she had left and get a refund. And why keep splurging on the fancy Greek yogurt? How much was it helping anyway? On the other hand, she probably shouldn't give up everything at the same time, considering the fragile state of her body. Never mind, she'd find a way to come up with the money—whatever it took.

Her first priority was to get Maria on board, even if she had to resort to trickery. She'd ask Maria to accompany her on an errand this afternoon. On the way, they'd just happen to pass the travel agency. She hoped that some of their glitzy posters and enticing brochures would help change her mind.

When Maria didn't answer her phone, she called Livy's house. Vinnie picked up: "Who?" he asked her.

"Maria," repeated Gertie. "Is she there?"

"Who?"

"Your grandmother, Vinnie," she shouted into the receiver. *What is wrong with kids these days!*

"Sorry, no. Haven't seen her. My bet is," he added after a pause, "she's at Key Food."

Gertie's bet too. Maria spent half her life shopping. The reigning queen of Key Food, they liked to tease her. "I'll head over there now, but if you hear from her first, tell her to meet me on the corner of Ninety-Third and Third Avenue at noon. That's near Kon Tiki Travel, but whatever you do, don't tell her I said so. Got it?"

"Sure thing."

Suddenly realizing it was a weekday, Gertie wondered why Vinnie was at home. "Don't you have school, Vinnie?"

"Yeah, but I'm doing some work on the computer. A background search on your friend from the Senior Center."

"Corinna? Why in the world . . . ?"

"Granny asked me to see what I could dig up on her family."

Uff da, Maria, why do you always have to butt into everyone's business? One of these days you're going to get into big trouble.

"I found something interesting," said Vinnie, sounding pleased with himself. "I'm pretty sure she has a rare genetic disease, an enzyme-deficiency disease. That's why she's a midg—" He stopped mid-sentence to correct himself. "I mean, that's why she's so small and has that funny hand. It's also associated with sterility and other hormonal abnormalities."

Gertie had always suspected a genetic disorder might be the case. So did Maria, although they rarely discussed it. Probably because it was such a big part of how everyone else saw Corinna, they didn't want to make it an issue for them. "And the seizures, is that part of it too?" she asked.

"Yeah." Vinnie chuckled.

"What's so funny, Vinnie?"

"Nothing."

Gertie's calf was knotting up again.

"Another thing," said Vinnie. "She's not from Brooklyn."

That didn't surprise her. You could always tell a transplant from a local, and Corinna never quite fit in. She was far too educated and cultured, in Gertie's opinion. Plus, there was always something mysterious about her, and this was part of what made her attractive to Gertie and Maria. Corinna made a point of never mentioning her past. She'd been at the Senior Center forever, she insisted, and there was no before. Gertie, unlike Maria, wasn't one to pry. Yet she couldn't deny she was a little curious now. Such a strange bird, that Corinna, there must be some story to account for it all. "So where's she from, Vinnie?"

"I'm pretty sure she was born in—"

A clicking noise interrupted Vinnie before he finished. "Where, Vinnie? I couldn't hear you."

"Sorry, that's the other line. I gotta go."

Gertie held the buzzing phone at arm's length and frowned. She had known Vinnie since he was a baby, and for most of that time, she would agree with Maria that her grandson was special, a handsome, smart, athletic young man. And equally impressive was his affection toward his grandmother, the way he would hug her, walk her to church, help with the groceries. But lately, he'd been looking more and more like a hooligan, with his long hair and weird behavior. There was something not quite right with that kid. How could Maria not notice?

It took a while for Gertie to maneuver into her shoes. Her feet swelled up in the mornings, another screwed up part of her aging body. What a shame, since she'd always considered her feet one of her best features—long and slender without any of the skin conditions that plagued so many swimmers. She grabbed her jacket from the coat closet, slammed the door, and hurried out.

Her heart was racing. The pounding in her chest wouldn't let up, as if it were trying to tell her something.

9

Corinna

She had been at it for two days now, glued to her desk in the Senior Center library, moving back and forth between the Loeb edition of the *Aeneid*, a Latin dictionary, and a Latin grammar book. It hadn't been easy, and she had hoped the Professor would have returned her call by now. Only a few more pages and she'd be finished with book four.

The phone sat on the right side of her desk. It was one of those old-fashioned rotary-dial phones. Maybe that was the problem—the wiring had gone bad. She picked up the handset and inspected the connections on each end. They appeared fine. She walked over to the wall, removed the phone jack, and reinserted it. Nothing wrong there either. She pushed down the buttons on the cradle, then let go. The dial tone buzzed loud and clear. Everything seemed in good order, which was what she suspected and why she never replaced the phone with one of the fancy new digital gadgets that wouldn't last a year.

She returned to Virgil's epic poem, the part where Queen Dido promised to help the homeless Trojan warrior Aeneas because she, like him, was no stranger to bad luck and was eager to comfort those in pain . . .

That's nice, thought Corinna. She herself was no stranger to bad luck and pain.

The stillness in the room unnerved her. When was the last time the phone rang? Maybe the problem lay with incoming calls. She phoned the front desk and asked George to call back. "Everything okay, Ms. Hale?" he asked when she picked up a minute later. He reminded her about the group scheduled for physical therapy; they were waiting in the lobby. She had completely forgotten. He also told her that Gertie Sundersen had called and left a message to meet her and Maria at Kon Tiki Travel at noon.

She didn't understand the grammar in the passage before her and put it on her list of questions for the Professor, which now ran over twenty pages. She glanced at the phone. Why hadn't he called back? There were so many things to discuss.

The goddess Venus wanted to ensure Dido's feelings for Aeneas never faded, so she asked Cupid to light a love-fire in her bones . . .

Corinna herself began to feel hot. It started in the chest but quickly spread upward, to her neck and face. She decided to try the Professor again and dialed the number. She waited until his answering machine came on, then hung up.

Cupid worked his magic on Dido, awakening her sleeping desires and unused heart . . .

Corinna's body was burning up.

desueta corde . . .

She looked up the words in the dictionary: a heart that was unused, unaccustomed, out of practice.

The heat rose to her head, concentrating and intensifying. She felt dizzy . . . that hot and dizzy feeling that came before an attack . . . dizzier and dizzier . . . until everything went dark.

"Corinna! Corinna!"

She heard someone yelling her name. Opening her eyes, she found Joe Flannery staring down at her.

"Are you okay?"

She couldn't answer right away.

"Should I call an ambulance?"

She was baffled by the urgency in his voice, until she realized that she was on the floor and grabbing the left side of her chest with her hand, not a gesture to be taken lightly in the Senior Center. "No, I'm fine," she said, the words finally materializing. She withdrew her hand and laughed uneasily. "I'm fine."

"Thank God," said Flannery. "I wasn't sure whether you were having one of your spells or if this was the real thing. I was scared I might have to perform CPR, and to be honest, even though the training session was only a few weeks ago, I can't remember a thing."

"No need for that, Mr. Flannery," she assured him, noticing the panic in his voice. Somehow Flannery was always around when she passed out. He was there at the Botanic Garden a few weeks ago too, the water bottle in his hand the first thing she recalled when she came to. "No need," she repeated, "but thank you."

Flannery reminded her that the group for physical therapy was waiting downstairs. He would have taken them himself, but he had to go to the dermatologist. "Another skin cancer, the sixth in the last two months, if you can believe it."

"Oh my." Corinna feigned surprise, even though everyone at the Center was aware of Flannery's ongoing skin problems. In fact, there was a running bet in some circles as to which part of his body would be the next to go.

"I see Dr. Sandler on Fourth Avenue. If you ask me, he's the kind of person you should be inviting here to talk, not the Greek professor who puts everyone to sleep." Flannery gave her the big thumbs down sign. "I mean, skin cancer is more of a priority for us than those silly old love poems, don't you think?"

"I'm not so sure," she replied. "But I'll take it under consideration."

"Good."

"As long as you give those silly old love poems a chance too. You may be surprised at how much you like them."

As they walked toward the door, the phone rang. Corinna jumped to answer it.

"Hello," she said, grabbing her list of questions and the Loeb edition of the *Aeneid.*

But it wasn't him, the voice too deep and coarse. Her head dropped.

It was Tom Jurgen, looking for Gertie. *When wasn't he looking for Gertie?* Tom explained that Gertie was neither at home nor with Maria, and he was starting to worry. Corinna told him that she hadn't seen her.

"Will you please tell her I called? It's important."

"Sure," she said, hanging up the phone.

"Everything all right?" asked Joe Flannery at the elevator bank.

"Everything is fine," she lied.

"Sounds like you were expecting someone else."

"No," she said.

10

Gertie

Kon Tiki Travel stood a few blocks from Key Food, sandwiched between Frank's Photo and Betty's Beauty Salon. It was a closet of a store, with three small desks staggered down the center, each of which had a phone and a computer. Posters advertising exotic and not-so-exotic destinations covered the walls. There was a circular display filled with brochures at the entrance. A man in a short-sleeved Hawaiian shirt and straw hat sat at the middle desk talking to a customer on the phone.

"Afternoon, ladies," said the man, covering the receiver with his hand. "Have a seat and I'll be with you in a second."

Maria didn't move. The only reason she hadn't turned around and walked out was probably because she felt bad for Gertie, whose eye was puffy and bruised after the bad dream she had had last night.

"So," said the man, after finishing his call, "you gals thinking of getting away?"

"She is," replied Maria.

He invited them to sit. "And why not you, Mrs. . . . ?"

"Benedetti," Gertie answered for her. "She's plenty interested, just a little shy."

"Well, let me tell you, Mrs. Benedetti, you couldn't have picked a better time. There are some plum deals out there if you know where to look." Although the travel agent was talking to Maria, he kept looking back at Gertie.

"What's the matter, mister?" snapped Gertie. "Never seen a girl all black and blue before?"

The agent was suddenly tongue tied.

"The truth is"—she leaned forward and whispered across the desk—"I like it rough. The rougher the better. Ga-beeesh?"

"Gertie!" squawked Maria, turning the color of her hair, then a few shades redder. "She has a skin cancer," she explained to the agent while blotting her face with a Kleenex and then glaring at her friend. "One that she better take care of *pronto*."

"I'm sorry," said the man, clearly flustered.

"Don't be," said Gertie. "Just stick to your job."

"Absolutely," he replied, gradually recovering his composure. "As I was saying, I can recommend some wonderful places, sunny and warm and easy to get to. Boca Raton, for example, or West Palm Beach. They're running a special at the Seahorse Resort in—"

"Do we look like we want to go to Florida," interrupted Gertie, "with the rest of those ninnies? I'd rather set myself on fire."

"You're absolutely right, what was I thinking? You gals want something more sophisticated, I can see that now. How about Bermuda? Or England? The *Queen Mary* leaves from Red Hook, passes right under the Verrazzano. Biggest passenger ship on the high seas and very elegant. I could get you a plum deal."

"How about you stop with the plums already—I'm allergic. I almost died choking on one a few years back," said Gertie. "But I'm sure Corinna would go wild for a berth on the *Queen*, don't you think, Maria?"

"Corinna?"

"The third member of our party," Gertie answered the travel agent. "She should be here any minute. Corinna has a thing for boats."

Maria thrust her hands in the air. "This is ridiculous. I'm not going anywhere. Why can't you—"

"I completely forgot," said Gertie. "No *Queen Mary* for Maria. She gets seasick. Besides, we want something a lot more challenging than snoozing on deck chairs all day. Maria may not be so good on the water, but you should see her on a mountain. She's done Everest twice."

"Is that so?" he said, glancing at Maria, who was almost as red as before. "Well, I'm impressed, Mrs. Benedetti. But wouldn't you want to go somewhere more relaxing at this point in your life?"

"I don't want to go anywhere at this point in my life."

"How about Machu Picchu?" proposed Gertie. "Or a safari to Africa?"

"What's wrong with you, Gertie?" asked an exasperated Maria.

The agent, who clearly thought they would be signing papers by now, was also starting to wonder. "You're not serious, ma'am, are you?"

"You bet I am. Maybe not chasing after lions, but I sure as hell don't want to be sitting by the pool with a bunch of zombies."

"I understand," said the agent, sitting back in his chair and pondering. "I understand," he repeated, tapping his pencil on the desk. "Of course!" he announced suddenly. "Italy. The Grand Tour: Venice, Florence, and Rome."

"Now you're talking." Gertie clapped her hands. "My friend here is a real Eye-taliano herself who makes the best *pasta fagioli* in Brooklyn and would kill for a good cannoli. But she's never set foot in the homeland, isn't that right, Maria? Italy might be the perfect place for us."

"Wonderful. Then let me recommend some excellent packages. All very strenuous, in terms of the sightseeing, but nothing you gals can't handle, I'm sure. Here, let's have a look."

As he pulled out a brochure, they heard a clattering behind them, then someone clearing his throat. They turned to find the Professor. He was spinning the brochure rack around, trying to get their attention.

"Excuse me, but I couldn't help overhearing," said the Professor. He wore a brown corduroy suit with a blue paisley bow tie and spoke with exaggerated formality. "You may not be aware, ladies, but I, too, am contemplating a trip to Italy." As he smiled, his hazel eyes lit up.

Maria eyed Gertie accusingly. "Don't tell me he's in on this too?"

The Professor stepped forward. Tall and wiry, his movements were somewhat awkward but spry. "Vincent told me where I might find you."

Gertie shook her head. She told that boy not to say anything about the travel agency. Now she was convinced: something was definitely wrong with Maria's grandson.

"Please don't settle for one of those dreadful tours, ladies," urged the Professor, undeterred. "Let me offer my services instead. You might remember I lived in Rome for several years and spent a good deal of time traveling around the country. I will be your guide. Your *cicerone*, as they say in Italy."

"Chicherony." Gertie playfully nudged Maria.

"I'll take you on a personal tour of the Colosseum and the Forum. We can visit Nero's Golden House and Augustus's palace. I've studied those places and know them inside out. Trust me, it will be far superior to any tour—"

"That's awfully kind of you"—the agent waved him off—"but the ladies are looking for a professional, and I have just the—"

"Right you are, sir, and now they've found one." The Professor adjusted his bow tie and continued his pitch. "I'm not only familiar with the ancient city but also well acquainted with present-day Rome. After visiting the ruins, we'll take a cappuccino at Sant'Eustachio and dine at Al Moro. Only the best for my discerning friends."

Gertie couldn't help but smile, watching the Professor's angular limbs set and reset. All he needed was a top hat and cane to take his show to Broadway. She wondered whether Corinna put him up to this, her idea of applying pressure. But that wasn't what Gertie had in mind when she asked for Corinna's help; the trip was supposed to be for the Three Musketeers alone. Then again, at this point, she'd be willing to do anything to persuade Maria. "Maybe the Professor has a point, Maria. We've never been to Rome. And it might be nice to travel with someone who speaks the language and knows his way around."

Maria grabbed her bag from the floor and rose to her feet. She'd had enough. More than enough. "Fine, then it's all set, Gertie. You can go with the Professor to Italy. I need to get back to my groceries."

"Yes, you do," agreed Gertie, who thanked the agent and asked him to put together a few options, promising she'd be in touch shortly.

As they were leaving, the Professor offered Maria his hand. "Ah, Maria, wait till you see the view from the Janiculum Hill. Bernini's *Apollo and Daphne* at the Villa Borghese. And the food, the glorious food—*carciofi alla romana* and *bucatini all'amatriciana*. You'll never want to leave."

What a smooth talker, marveled Gertie, watching the Professor's hands dance and eyes sparkle. If she didn't know better, she might think he was trying to seduce Maria too—first Corinna and now Maria. Oh yes, he must have been quite the player back in the day, with his dainty bow ties. So unlike Tom with his baggy clothing, gruff mannerisms, and tendency to nod off whether they were listening to a lecture or watching a fast-paced action thriller.

Then again, maybe they weren't so different after all, these men, even at their ages. She remembered the night Tom came over to her apartment a year or so ago. They had been playing gin rummy, and in the middle of a game, he threw down his cards: "I'm feeling something here, Gertie," he blurted out, reaching across the table with his massive fireman's hands. "How about you?"

She was caught off guard, completely and utterly off guard. Although she had known Tom for years—they'd all grown up in Bay Ridge and attended the same high school, Gertie, Tom, and Gertie's cousin Hannah, Tom's wife—he rarely ever had a word for her, and when he did, it was typically to joke about her masculine qualities.

"We're not too old," pressed Tom. "Are we, Gertie?" Well, yes, she might have said, having lost that kind of desire so long ago she could barely remember what it was like. Yet she felt bad for the man, so lost at sea after Hannah died. There was something awful about his neediness, and she didn't want to make it worse. So Gertie went along with him. She let their knees jostle under the table; she let him squeeze her hand when she laid down a card. But later, when they were watching TV and he tried to pull her toward him and touch her, she had to put a stop to it. "What the hell are you doing, Tom?"

What a perverted lot, these men! Who knows, maybe that's what had turned Thorvald against her all those years ago. Not because she wasn't around for their daughter—the Absentee Mother—but because she wasn't around for *him*—the Absentee Wife. It made him mad, all right, the nights she was too tired or not in the mood or simply wanted some space. She shook her head. Now it was making her mad too—that that might have been the reason for his change of heart.

"Why don't you save your energy," Gertie told the Professor, afraid that his efforts would only sabotage her travel plans. "Maria's still on the fence. I think it might be better if you let me work on her."

Maria glared at her friend.

"In the meantime, would you mind doing us a favor? Maria left her groceries at Key Food."

"Why, of course," replied the Professor, delighted to be of service. "I'd be happy to transport them for you."

"Oh no," objected Maria. "My grandson—"

"Please, Maria," insisted the Professor. "Vincent has more important things to do with his time. You must be aware that Vincent and I—"

"Yes, yes, I know all about the independent study project."

"Excellent. Then let's leave Vincent to attend to his Greek grammar while I oversee the groceries." He smiled, half bowed, and rushed off before Maria could say another word.

"Wow, that man is something else," observed Gertie. "I wonder how Corinna puts up with all his shenanigans. Now that I think of it, Corinna was supposed to meet us here. She must not have gotten my message."

As they made their way down Third Avenue, Maria walked a step ahead of Gertie, her lips sealed, eyes to the ground.

Gertie knew the drill. "You're giving me the silent treatment?"

No answer.

"*Uff da*, Maria, why do you always have to be so damn stubborn?"

"I could ask you the same thing," Maria fired back.

11

Corinna

Stunning—the way the night lights illuminated those mighty wings and spine, a giant, delicate creature presiding over the dark waters below and gunmetal-gray sky above, bringing together the jutting land masses of Brooklyn on one side and Staten Island on the other. The cars passed back and forth, back and forth, as if measuring time. A small tug on the Narrows plied its way eastward. Otherwise, everything was quiet and still, a full moon hovering in the distance like a ghost.

This might be the best time of all and the best place, even better than the Temple—here, on top of the Senior Center, her private roof deck that no one but the maintenance people knew about. She came late at night, up the ladder and through the old, dented door that never shut completely, when everyone was asleep or gone for the day. Her private balcony overlooking the Narrows. Many times she thought of bringing her friends, to show them what it was like at this height, to share the stunning view, but now she was glad she hadn't. This was hers. "Mine, do you hear?" she shouted at the moon.

She turned on her music box. The sounds of Johann Sebastian Bach calmed her instantly. She took another nip from her flask, now almost half-empty. A chill radiated down her chest, then a surge of warmth.

She gazed upon the sparkling steel bird, one minute imposing and vast, the next within reach like a child's toy that she might take in her hands. She closed her eyes and listened to the sounds of the violin, sweeping to and fro like the water below. She moved to its beat, quiet and peaceful, until a sudden chord threw her off balance and broke the spell.

"Why?" she shouted at the Professor who wasn't there. "I would have gladly shared all this with you, the view and the music. I would have read Byron to you: 'Ten thousand fleets sweep over thee in vain . . . Upon the watery plain.'

"Can't you see I have a passion for it? A passion that I waste on them, especially on Maria?

"'A shadow . . . like a drop of rain . . . sinks into thy depths with bubbling groan . . . Roll on, thou deep and dark blue sea.'

"Such lovely music beside these glorious lines and curves, the sky and sea, moon and stars, Johann Sebastian and a Tuscan red, here on my private rooftop! You would have liked it, I know.

"Perhaps Maria would have liked it too, but not the same, just as she didn't appreciate Virgil or Horace. Believe me, I tried. She could scarcely remember any of the names or places in the poems. But I remember them all: Argos and Tyre, Carthage and Latium, Myrmidons and Danaans. We are the kindred spirits, Professor, can't you see?

"I bought an old Loeb edition of the *Aeneid* at Marlowe and Co. The cover is worn and smooth, the pages yellow and musty. I bet you love that smell as much as I do."

She had had the book with her earlier today when she spotted the Professor making his way down Ninety-Fourth Street with a cart full of groceries. A young kid with another cart trailed behind. She pulled the Vespa over to the curb in front of him. The book was right there in her basket when she called out his name.

"Just in time to give an old man a tow," he replied with a smile. "I have quite a load here." He took the handkerchief out of his breast pocket to wipe the perspiration from his brow. "Nothing like a little exercise to get the blood flowing."

She reached into her basket for the book and turned its spine in his direction. She asked if he was having a party.

"A party? No," he said, "these are Maria's groceries. I offered to help."

"Oh?"

"I was at the travel agency," he explained, "inquiring about flights to Rome."

"Rome," she said, "the city that Aeneas founded."

"The very one."

"Rome with its seven hills and ancient walls. The yellow Tiber. 'I set no limits on space and time,' decreed Jove in the *Aeneid*. 'I will give them an empire without end.'"

"I had no idea you were such a classicist, Corinna."

"Just an enthusiastic student, Professor." She blushed. "I'm reading Virgil with Maria and Gertie now." She held the book up for him to see, so he could not possibly *not* see. "But I'm afraid they aren't very interested."

"Then you must help them, Corinna."

"I'm trying."

"And help me too. I offered to be your guide."

"My guide?"

"Yes, why waste time with those second-rate tours when you can have someone like me, who lived and studied at the American Academy in Rome?"

Huh?

"I know that city like the back of my hand."

She tried to make sense of what he was saying.

"I could show you all the important sites."

What?

"You understand, Corinna, I see that now. You and I see eye to eye."

Yes, she wanted to say, *it's true. Like two peas in a pod.*

"So I ask you to help me, to make your friends understand too."

"Help you?"

"With Maria," he replied. "She seems very resistant. Yet I know how much she would appreciate . . . she's a wonderful woman . . . well, the truth of the matter is . . . I like her very much."

"Maria?"

"Yes, from the first time I laid eyes on her."

Her head was spinning. "Maria?"

"Will you help me?"

She jumped on her Vespa, turned away, and raced the engine to drown out his words.

"No," she shouted at the moon. "No, no, no!"

She gazed over the rooftop to the glorious bridge. She reached forward and hoisted it on her back. She flapped its steel wings in the air, feeling its enormous size and power. She flapped harder and harder until her arms slipped and fell away. "You are blind," she shouted. "You are all blind!"

The wine burned going down her throat.

"Come, Maria," she said to her friend who wasn't there. "I've changed my mind. I'll show you now. Come and see my stunning rooftop view. Here, have some wine. Come closer. Stand on the stool, so you can see better. Do you see, Maria?"

Corinna filled with hate. The hate blotted out everything else, all the goodness that surrounded her friend—Santa Maria, Helen of Troy—who cooked for her when she was sick, helped her install the new filing system at the library, took her place at the Center when she had to be somewhere else. Maria, who picked her up at the police station after she got caught shoplifting at the Lebanese market, who was incredibly calm, didn't utter a word of reproach, never even told Gertie about the incident. It didn't matter now, none of it, not one shred of that overbearing goodness.

Her body was on fire with hate. "Come closer, Maria. Have a look at this stunning view."

And then, when her friend stood beside her, entranced by the sight, Corinna pushed, pushed with all her might and watched as Maria flipped over the ledge and fell through the air, story after story, ten in all, until she hit the pavement with a loud thud, and lay motionless on the ground.

"There," Corinna sighed, then finished off the wine. Who was she kidding, thinking that someone might like her? *And you, Gertie, how could you be so cruel, planting that seed, that filthy, rotten seed in my head?*

"Liar!" she shouted at the moon. Corinna would never be able to attract a man. She wasn't the slightest bit attractive. She wasn't even normal. A freak, just like her brother had said.

It made her stomach judder and heave until she expelled every drop of ugliness through her mouth. She belonged on a deserted beach along with Queen Dido, encircled by the growing flames, licking and burning, consuming every well-preserved cell in her youthful body.

12

Maria

It was drizzling as she walked up Shore Road toward the footpath. Maria disliked the dampness, the way it seeped under the skin and bogged her down, not just her feet but also her knees and hips, her back and neck. It packed a chill too, even in this mild spring weather, and she didn't want to catch a cold.

But it wasn't just the rain that bogged her down. They had argued and Livy had become angry. It started with Vinnie, as it always seemed to these days. He'd come home late again, after hanging out with those troublemakers down the block. As always, Maria defended her grandson, even though she harbored doubts of her own.

"You make excuses for everyone, Ma," said Livy. "You used to do it all the time for Dad. When he got pissed the meatballs were too soft or his shirt wasn't ironed just right. The whole house would shake."

It's true, her Jim had a temper, like lots of Italian men. He often lost his cool and said mean things. She would never forget the night he threw his dinner plate against the wall, smashing it to pieces, sending rigatoni and sausage flying through the air. He'd roared that the meat wasn't just soft, but raw. "*Che cazzo fai*," he'd cursed. "Are you trying to poison me?" She was afraid of what he might do next, the way he glared at her and his neck veins bulged.

"You don't understand, Livy. Your father was under a lot of stress."

"Oh, I understand all right. My father was a hothead we had to tiptoe around, terrified he might explode any minute."

There were plenty of reasons for Jim's behavior that Livy wasn't aware of: the problems at the union; the infighting and backstabbing; and worst of all, the threats from the Mafia if he didn't follow their orders. It wasn't easy for an honest man like her husband; yes, he exploded once in a while, but he never once hit her and always apologized in the end. He'd make it up to her by bringing home a little something the next day, a bouquet of flowers or a cheesecake from Paneantico and, one time, a lovely pearl necklace. "He was a good man, Livy, and you know it."

"Jesus, Ma, you need to get a life. Stop living in the past, especially when you hardly remember it. And stop telling me how to raise my kid. I can do that just fine on my own."

Maria wasn't so sure. Poor Livy. She had so much on her plate, raising a teenage boy without a man in the house all these years, while working full time at the hospital. No wonder she became upset at the drop of a hat. If only she'd let Maria help out more, the way she did when Vinnie was younger.

Gertie, too, was adding to the bogginess. When that woman got an idea in her head, nothing would change her mind. She was starting to think that maybe they should forget the party altogether. Elsa should just fly to New York with the baby as soon as possible, before her mother picked up and left. Yes, that's what she would do—she'd call Elsa right after the Temple and tell her to get on the next plane.

The tree line thinned at the eastern end of Shore Road. As Maria crossed the street, part of the bridge came into view, the Brooklyn tower rising upward into the sky. But everything in front and behind had been erased by the dense cloud cover. What a strange sight, she thought, as if a terrible accident had wiped out entire sections of the great steel structure. It reminded her of the bridge that collapsed in Peru, from the sad story Corinna had read to them a while back, *The Bridge of San Luis Rey*. One of the twins had died in the accident, the one who loved more than the other. Corinna had said she always believed love was that way—unequal and unfair. Maria wished her friend weren't so cynical and hoped that, with Vinnie's help, she might be able to change Corinna's mind.

Someone called out her name. She wheeled around to find Tom Jurgen trudging up Shore Road. The old firefighter with his tree-trunk legs and giant hands was soaked, his hair matted against his forehead.

"Gertie never said anything," he said, clearly agitated. "She never said—"

"Never said what, Tom?" asked Maria. "Why are you so upset?"

"I saw him, that's why. He told me everything."

"He?"

"The Greek teacher who gives those talks at the Center."

"The Professor?" asked Maria.

"He told me about the trip. That you're all going to Rome. That he was going to be your chicherony or something."

So that was what had been troubling him. "Relax, Tom, no one's going anywhere."

"Then why . . . ?"

"Because he's crazy, that's why. The two of them, one crazier than the other."

"The two of them?"

"Gertie saw some young girl on TV," explained Maria, "who sailed around the world. Now she's got it in her head that she wants to do the same."

"With him?"

"With him or anyone else who'll go." Maria realized the minute she finished speaking that it was the wrong thing to say.

Tom stuttered and shook: "But . . . but . . . but . . ."

"Try to calm down, Tom. I promise, no one is going anywhere. Remember, we have a big surprise in store for Gertie that's bound to change everything."

Tom didn't look convinced. He took a step to the left, then the right.

"Go home, Tom, before you get sick. Everything will be fine."

As Maria made her way down the footpath, she decided that enough was enough. The Professor had become a menace that needed to be stopped before he ruined all their lives—before he filled Gertie's head with more nonsense about Rome; before Corinna bored them to death with another Greek classic; and before Tom had a nervous breakdown. *Basta cosi!* As soon as she returned home from the Temple, she'd call Elsa in Los Angeles and then track down the Professor and set him straight.

13

The Temple

Corinna was at the Temple when Maria arrived. She pretended not to notice her while she arranged the incense candles.

"I need your help, Corinna."

Corinna turned around and laughed. "Hah!"

"Gertie is dead set on going to Italy."

Corinna snickered. "I heard about your travel plans."

"I would hardly call—"

"Not from you."

Maria sighed. "No, of course not, because you know I think it's a terrible idea. I thought you did too. Why would you encourage Gertie—"

"I heard about it from the Professor."

"The Professor?"

"I was surprised, too, considering all the unflattering things you said about him. You do remember what you said, Maria?"

"Yes, and I was wrong. That man is even worse than I imagined. He's a menace who's wrecking our lives."

"Oh really," Corinna said. "But that doesn't stop you from flirting with him."

"What?"

"From leading him on."

"What are you talking about, Corinna?"

Just then Gertie entered the enclosure with her knee-high rubber boots and slicker. The bruising around her left eye had faded. A bandage hid the skin cancer. "Settle down, girls. I could hear you all the way from Shore Road."

Corinna turned away to light the incense candles. She inhaled deeply after finishing. Gertie and Maria waited for her to list the ingredients, but she went straight to the wine instead. She poured herself a glass and, without a word, drank it.

"What, no toast today, Corinna?" asked Gertie.

"Right," she said coolly, pouring herself another glass. "It's a frascati from the Castelli Romani region. How fitting—we can toast your upcoming trip." Corinna waved her glass and faked a smile.

Gertie looked at Maria.

"She's mad," explained Maria. "Don't ask me why."

"Me, mad," said Corinna. "Hah!"

"Apparently, she spoke to the Professor."

"Your *cicerone*, I hear." Corinna's eyes were flashing. "Hah!"

"That's just what I wanted to talk to you girls about. I have something important to say and I want you to listen."

Gertie took her seat on the stone bench and regarded her friends sternly.

"This is it for me," she said. "The last time I come to the Temple unless the two of you agree to go away with me."

"You're not serious?" asked Maria.

"This isn't easy for me," conceded Gertie. "We've been coming here for twenty years. Ever since that crazy day you two saved my life. Our special place. Our thing. What do the Eye-talians say, Maria? *Cosa Nostra*, right?" She nudged her friend. *"Cosa Nostra."*

Maria laughed nervously. She glanced over at Corinna, who was picking at the cork and about to pour herself another glass of wine.

"A special place for someone who doesn't go to church or believe in much of anything anymore. Just look at that magnificent bridge," Gertie continued, gesturing to the opening in the trees. "Gateway to the world, all right. Boats from every port on earth pass beneath it, entering from the Atlantic or heading back out. Now, Maria, don't get teary eyed on me. This has been a gift, sharing this with the both of you. It's kept me going all these years."

"Me too," agreed Maria.

"The problem," said Gertie, "is that everything has changed."

"You're right about that," said Corinna. "Everything *has* changed."

"I'm not sure why or when exactly. Maybe it was the heart attack. Or the stupid skin cancer. The nightmares. I can't say."

"You're not scared, are you?" asked Corinna dryly.

"That may be part of it, sure," admitted Gertie, "but not the whole story. I hear this voice inside my chest, thumping against my ribs, warning me: time is running out."

"That's crazy," said Maria.

"My bet," said Corinna, rolling her eyes, "is that you'll outlive us all."

"Maybe. But it doesn't change how I feel. And how I feel is changing the way everything looks. Like our bridge," explained Gertie, gazing at the Verrazzano through the branches of the great oaks. "Its vastness used to make me feel big, but now it makes me feel small. And the horizon doesn't take me out anymore—it shuts me in. I feel like I'm in prison. If I don't get out of here soon, I'm going to explode. It's my last chance to feel like Annie Halvorsen—to feel the way I used to feel. Time is running out."

"Your mother lived to ninety-five," protested Maria. "And the cardiologist said—"

"*Uff da*," said Gertie, waving her off. "I've made up my mind. Made my reservations and put down a deposit. I'm going to Italy with or without you."

"As far as I'm concerned," said Corinna, "you can both go wherever you want and take that idiot professor with you." She scoffed at Gertie. "Two peas in a pod. Hah!"

"What are you talking about?" asked Gertie. "I don't get it. You of all people should understand."

"Understand?" shouted Corinna. "What do either of you understand about me? It doesn't matter. Go ahead with your plans. I'm fine right where I am."

"You're fine watching life pass you by?" asked Gertie. "People and cars and boats? Reading about Aeneas and Odysseus sailing from one end of the Mediterranean to the other? You don't want to see those places for yourself?"

"No, I don't. And certainly not with the two of you."

"Maybe then it's you who's the scaredy-cat around here, Corinna."

"Please!"

"Oh, I think you're scared all right. Scared of leaving the Center and all the people you feel safe around. Scared of anything new and different. You're a hypocrite, Corinna. The truth is, we all are. We're a bunch of pathetic hypocrites."

"Screw you, Gertie," Corinna fired back, rising from the bench. She circled the enclosure, pretending to tidy up, adjusting the tarp, straightening out the mat, checking the incense. "You know what, Maria? You're right," she said after her third lap around. "Gertie is dead set on this. Nothing I can say will change her mind." She took out her hookah and packed the burner with hash. "Stubborn as a mule, isn't that how you put it the other day?"

Maria ignored her. "I understand how you feel, Gertie, and I promise, when the time is right, we'll go away. Just not now."

Gertie threw up her hands. "You want to wait until I'm dead and buried?"

"Nah," said Corinna, taking a hit on her hookah. "Just until the party and Maria's big surprise."

"Corinna!" Maria's face turned red.

"A surprise." Gertie clapped. "Let me guess: You bought me a gift certificate to the diner? Or maybe you went all out and hired a male stripper?"

"Hah! That's a good one, Gertie. It's a shame we didn't think of it. Look, Maria, you might as well tell her the truth, now that we're all laying our cards on the table."

Gertie turned to Maria. "What is she talking about?"

"Don't be shy, Maria," prodded Corinna. "Tell her."

"Please, Corinna—"

"Sorry, but I don't think we can wait on this," said Corinna. "Gertie's in a rush. She might be gone tomorrow, sailing around the world with young Annie Halvorsen. If you don't tell her, I will."

"Maria?" Gertie questioned her friend.

Maria had no choice but to answer. "Elsa," she murmured, almost inaudibly, "is coming to New York."

"What?"

"Elsa is coming to the party."

Gertie stood up and swallowed hard. "What's that supposed to mean?"

"'What's that supposed to mean,' she asks," repeated Corinna, fondling her hookah as if it were a dear pet. "Are you kidding? She's been at it for quite some time now, our little eager beaver, isn't that right, Maria?"

Maria looked sick as she watched Gertie pace back and forth across the enclosure.

Gertie stopped suddenly. "You begged Elsa to do this, am I right?" She shook her head. "How could you?"

"No," said Maria, "it wasn't like that. She wanted to come."

"Bullshit. I know you, Maria. And I know my daughter." Gertie spat into the bushes.

Maria could only mumble and stutter.

"Damn you, Maria, how many times have I told you! This is none of your business."

"But—"

"But nothing. It's between me and my kid and has nothing to do with you. Lord knows, I've given her chances, plenty of them. But she's made up her mind and nothing is going to change it. Sure as hell not you."

"Elsa is bringing her baby, Gertie."

"Baby?"

"She wanted to surprise you."

"Baby?" repeated Gertie, as if she didn't understand what the word meant. She repeated it over and over again, and for a moment, the shock seemed to dampen her anger. "Baby?"

"It's true. After all those years of trying."

"And she never called to tell me?"

"How cute," said Corinna, still fondling her hookah. "A little baby as peace offering."

"Peace offering, my ass!" roared Gertie, rage taking over once again. "Screw that. I've gotten along just fine without her and her baby, and I'm not about to fold now because my heart is skipping a few beats."

"A baby girl, Gertie," Maria pleaded. "Your granddaughter."

"Grandma Gertie," Corinna called out. "It has a nice ring to it."

Gertie seethed. "How could you, Maria? To me, of all people."

"But I did it *for* you."

"Now that's where you're wrong. You did it for yourself. That family bullshit is your thing. Stop forcing your values down my throat. I haven't had a family for as long as I can remember, and it doesn't bother me in the least. Can't you get it through that skull of yours?"

"I just wanted—"

"It's not about what you want. It's about what I want." Gertie was screaming now. "You've gone too far. You've crossed the line!"

"Crossed the line," giggled Corinna, drawing an imaginary line on the mat with the hose of her hookah.

"With me and with you too," she said, pointing to Corinna. "Hey, wake up. It's not just me. She's meddling in your life too. You hear me, Corinna? Your life too!"

"Damn right, she is," said Corinna, laughing.

"I mean it, Corinna. You better watch out. She's got Harvard on the case. Darling little Vinnie."

"Mr. Smarty-pants?"

Gertie shook her head. "That's fine if you want to joke about it, but don't say I didn't warn you. Harvard is searching the internet right now as we speak, and before you know it, he'll have your family showing up for a big reunion too."

Corinna finally looked up. "My family?" She chewed on the words, trying to make sense of them.

"I'm done here," announced Gertie. "And I take back what I said before. I don't need either of you. I'm going away on my own."

"Gertie," Maria called after her. "Gertie!"

But Gertie wasn't listening. She had already left the Temple and didn't turn back.

Maria was beside herself. She grew dizzy, replaying their conversation over and over in her head, trying to figure out what went wrong. How did this happen when all she wanted was to help her friend? But no matter how much she tried, she couldn't make sense of it. Losing her balance, she fell to the mat.

Meanwhile, Corinna had risen to her feet and was now standing over her.

"You!" she said to Maria, with a wild look on her face. "Santa Maria, hah! What was I thinking? You're just as selfish as everyone else."

Maria foundered, unprepared for another attack.

"*I* decide what I want you to know about me," shouted Corinna. "Not you, Maria. And not that delinquent grandson of yours either."

"What?"

"Come on, Maria, you have eyes. You see who he hangs out with. That other delinquent with the purple hair and a ring hanging from his tongue—who just so happens to be my drug dealer. If I had to bet, Vinnie is part of the operation."

"No, it's not poss—"

"Better stop him, Maria. Stop him right now. Or I'll turn the little shit in myself. He'll be going to Sing Sing instead of Harvard!"

Corinna raced around the enclosure, gathering her belongings and throwing them in the tote. Then she stormed out too.

Maria was alone now in the Temple. Without Corinna's tarp for protection, the rain beat down on her mercilessly. She felt like a ship taking in water, growing heavier and heavier, starting to sink.

PART II

14

Vinnie

Vinnie was having a hard time concentrating. A few hours ago, he'd smoked a joint and still felt the effects. As a matter of fact, he almost got busted by the track coach, who saw him and his friends coming out of the sports shed. That's all he needed, especially after what happened to Zach. Two-week suspension plus the threat of notifying colleges. Man, that's fucked up.

"Odysseus, we are told, is *polytropos*, a man of many turns and twists," explained the Professor, his hazel eyes sparkling as he discussed the scene in Homer's text. They were sitting across from each other at a card table set up in the living room for the tutorial. "Clearly, the Greek hero is several moves ahead of Polyphemus in this mental chess game. When the cyclops cries out for help and his friends ask who blinded him, he replies 'outis'—'nobody'—precisely what Odysseus just told him. Which is precisely why nobody comes to his rescue." The Professor erupted into laughter.

Vinnie tried his best to smile. He'd never had such a brilliant and enthusiastic teacher. *Never.* Most of the time, Vinnie got swept right up. But that was some potent weed. Right now, he'd rather be lying in bed and chilling to the Red Hot Chili Peppers.

"Clever man, Odysseus," said the Professor. "Like you, Vincent." He winked at him.

Why'd he just do that? wondered Vinnie. Did the Professor suspect something? Or was the weed just making him paranoid?

"Are you all right, Vincent? You look a little under the weather."

He lied. "I think I'm coming down with a cold."

What the hell was he doing? Vinnie asked himself, registering the disappointment on the Professor's face. This was his ticket out of Bay Ridge, his ticket to the major leagues, to fucking Harvard, and he went and got high before the session. The Professor had promised to help Vinnie, convinced him he was a perfect fit for his alma mater and that he could count on the support of his daughter, who taught classics there. A perfect fit? Vinnie could kick himself in the ass for his stupidity.

"How about some tea, Vincent? It will make you feel better."

Tea?

The Professor was already loping toward the kitchen before he could say no, he didn't like tea, and he was pretty sure it wouldn't help at the moment.

Vinnie tilted his head back and closed his eyes. His friends teased him about hanging out with the old man, wondering what he could possibly talk to him about for two hours at a stretch. The truth was he liked talking to the Professor and reading the old Greek epic, and not just because of the Harvard angle. It was about the *only* academic thing that got him excited these days, a hell of a lot more than calculus or social science. Translating Homer's text felt like breaking an ancient code. You pieced together the foreign words until a picture emerged, one that catapulted you back in time—almost three thousand years in this case. And the coolest part was that none of it seemed so old or foreign. Vinnie knew these people. He had the same fears and desires as Odysseus and the cyclops. It was as if the vast universe of space and time had suddenly collapsed, and he was neither here nor there, but somewhere above, looking down.

"Why don't you try to tackle the next passage, Vincent," the Professor urged him from the kitchen.

Yes, that was why he liked these books so much. They took him away, the farther the better. He was so damn sick of Bay Ridge. School was a bore; his mother was constantly on his case; even his friends were getting on his nerves. He'd been in the same place with the same people way too long. He needed to get the hell out of Brooklyn.

Funny, Granny said her friend felt the same way, the old Norwegian lady who used to run marathons. Like she was in prison and had to escape. That was why she wanted to go to Europe and kept badgering Granny to go with her. Funny, how two people so different—she was over sixty years older than he was—could want the same thing. Must be another instance of the space-time collapse. Or maybe just the weed playing tricks on him.

"Here we are," said the Professor, placing a pot of tea onto the card table. He poured his student a cup.

Vinnie felt obliged to taste the greenish liquid that looked like piss.

"You might want to add a lemon wedge," said the Professor.

Vinnie thanked him, but he'd had more than enough tea already. What a character the Professor was. So formal on the one hand, with his teas and bow ties and erudite chatter, and a real mess on the other. His handwriting was illegible. His books and papers and empty cups were strewn all over the apartment. He was constantly searching for things he misplaced. A lot like himself, come to think of it. Another old-timer a lot like himself! *Wow, this was getting super weird.*

Vinnie wondered if he might be losing his grip. His life, he realized, was chaotic—reading ancient Greek one minute and dealing drugs the next. He didn't always love zigzagging between the two, but he did love the extra cash. It gave him the freedom he otherwise wouldn't have, to go to concerts, buy a pricey pair of vintage sneakers, and take his girlfriend out to dinner once in a while. Granted, the new stuff scared him a little—pot was one thing, pills another, even if the margins were better. Man oh man, what would the Professor say if he found out?

After finishing his tea, the Professor opened his book, eager to pick up where they had left off. Vinnie, however, still struggled to keep his eyes open. "Should we call it a day, Vincent?"

"Yeah," he answered. "I'm sorry."

"Quite all right." The Professor patted him on the back. "We'll meet again when you feel better."

The Professor was cool. He knew when to back off. Not like his mother, who never took her foot off the gas pedal: "Better not let us down, Mr. Genius!"

For a moment, Vinnie considered opening up to him, confessing his boredom and bad habits, maybe even sharing his worst fear, that he wasn't as smart as the Professor thought he was and that he'd fall flat on his face at a place like Harvard. Something told him the Professor might understand. No way, he couldn't chance it. There was too much at stake.

Just as he was leaving the apartment, the Professor called out: "By the way, Vincent, I met your grandmother at the travel agency the other day. Unfortunately, it didn't go very well. I'm afraid I may not have made the best impression. I'd like to give it another try," he said, his fingers moving so quickly it looked like he was signing.

Damn. Vinnie hoped he wouldn't bring that up again. He was surprised when the Professor first mentioned his grandmother, stuff about her and her friends, how nice and helpful they were to the residents at the Senior Center. But then it started getting weird, him going on about Granny's magnificent red hair. Granny was almost seventy-five and the Professor had to be even older. What was he thinking? Then the Professor told him what a great dancer she was. *Granny?* She could barely walk up a flight of stairs without wheezing. Besides, the two of them couldn't be more different, and Granny made it pretty clear she wanted nothing to do with him.

"The problem is I don't have her phone number or address. The other day I helped her with her groceries, but she had me drop them off at your house."

Screw it! He had already disappointed the Professor once today. Besides, how could he refuse to help a person who was doing so much for him? *Manus manum lavat, right, Professor?* Why not let the old man have another go at her, even if it was a losing battle? And if by some miracle the Professor changed Granny's mind, so much the better. She could use having someone else in her life, just like his mother always said. It might even mean he'd be relieved of his grocery-carting duties. A win-win all around!

He gave the Professor Granny's address and number, then said, "That reminds me, Professor. My grandmother asked me to see what I could dig up on her friend Corinna. It's actually turning out to be a little more complicated than I imagined. I could use your help."

"Of course, Vincent."

"Have you ever heard of the Kindertransport?"

15

Gertie

Walking up the footpath, Gertie muttered every Norwegian curse word she could think of: "*Fua, deg, raua* . . ." The rain came down harder now, and the ground was a thick, muddy soup. She kicked and splashed with her rubber boots, spraying water and bits of dirt in every direction. It almost felt good, this railing from top to bottom. All she needed was something in the middle, to throttle with her hands. A piece of mud hit her in her bad eye. She felt it drip down the side of her face.

Uff da, Maria. How could you? You know me better than anyone; you saw me try, Lord knows how many times, to talk sense into that child. I abandoned her and her father, she told me. Who would believe such nonsense? Somehow he must have brainwashed her but good, because nothing I ever said about him carried any weight—not his drinking, his selfishness, or that passive-aggressive crap. "Your mother has more important things to do," the bastard liked to say in front of Elsa.

"Well, it was true," Elsa responded, whenever Gertie brought it up.

"No, it was not," insisted Gertie. "Just because I wasn't always there didn't mean I didn't love you."

"Bullshit," said Elsa.

But I made peace with it, Maria. I learned to live my life and not let it upset me. You know that. You also know I would never get down on my hands and knees and grovel like a dog. Yet I'm sure that's just what you did. Poor old Gertie, going fast, one thing after the other, her heart, her eyes, her skin. Get over here quick, Elsa, before there's nothing left of the old bag.

How could you grovel like that? It makes me sick just thinking about it.

By the time she reached Shore Road, Gertie was winded and her right calf had started to cramp. The park next to the Verrazzano's Brooklyn anchorage was empty, and she considered resting on one of the benches for a while. Only she feared Maria and Corinna would be up any minute. As she passed the giant cannon and pyramid of black metal balls, she wished she could feed in a few and fire them off, one after another—boom, boom, boom.

As soon as she returned home, she would call Elsa and tell her it was all a big mistake. Maria didn't know Gertie was planning a trip and wouldn't be there for the party, so she'd better cancel her plans. Elsa would be thrilled, no doubt. Gertie could see the smile spreading across her face three thousand miles away. She'd apologize for the confusion and for Maria's badgering. She might even ask for a picture of the baby, though the truth was she didn't want to see the baby, a baby Elsa never even told her about. *Uff da*. Besides, how could Gertie have a granddaughter when she didn't really have a daughter? It made no sense.

Elsa would be thrilled all right.

How could you, Maria?

And you too, Corinna, for going along with it and not saying anything.

She'd stop at the travel agency on her way home. There was no use waiting anymore, no one left to convince at this point; she was on her own. Fine with her. She was used to it by now. She remembered Coach Sully whispering in her ear just before the state championships her last year of high school. She was up against Lily Waters, who had beaten her twice earlier that season in her best event, the 200-meter butterfly: "Don't look at me," Sully had said. "Don't look at your parents in the stands either. You're the only one in the water. No one is going to push you across the finish line. So swim your heart out, Gertie."

How could she have known then that her fiery, young coach with prematurely thinning hair wasn't just giving her a pep talk but a life lesson?

She beat Lily Waters by eight-tenths of a second that day, the length of a fingertip. Sully's military-style training sessions had paid off. She wished she could thank him. Coach Jackson at Penn State, too, who worked with her on weekends and holidays to prepare for the Olympic trials. And the girls she mentored after her career ended, like Carly Johnson, who won the silver at Rome. They taught her that she could be happy, almost as happy, watching on the sidelines.

It was her father's idea, the swimming. As far back as she could remember, he would take her to Coney Island on the weekends. They'd go just after the winter thaw, when the water was off its bitter lows and the beach was empty, her father pretending they were at the inlet in Egersund where his father had taught him to swim. At first, he would toss her into the ocean and watch her thrash about to keep afloat. When she mastered buoyancy and grew accustomed to the freezing temperatures, the real lessons began. "Not with your arms and legs by themselves," he explained. "Swim with your whole body, one motion, like a fish." When he saw how quickly she picked it up, how fast she was able to move, how flushed her cheeks became when she popped out of the water, he nicknamed her *rokesild*, red herring. "But you eat *rokesild*, Papa," she said to him. "Yes, and I will eat you too," he answered, taking her in his arms and smothering her with kisses. For a moment, she felt his warm face against her cold, wet skin, and she was back on the beach in Coney Island once again.

As she walked down Fourth Avenue, remembering those days and imagining the days ahead, Gertie's anger began to subside. She had put out the fires and launched her plans: the party would be cancelled; Elsa and her baby would remain in Los Angeles; and her trip was almost on the calendar. No, *almost* wasn't good enough. She had to convert the reservations into firm dates and book them ASAP. She no longer worried about the cost—she'd wipe her bank account clean, cash in her retirement fund, withhold the rent and everything else if she had to. She was going away, and that was that. It was her last chance.

The giddiness didn't last very long. On the next block, Gertie started to feel light-headed. Her body, taut and clenched just a moment ago as she remembered pulling past Lily Waters on the final lap, had now gone slack and floppy like the muddy soup on the footpath. She had to lean against the wall of an apartment building for reinforcement. The mailman stopped and asked if she needed help. No, she answered, she was fine, now that she had eight stories of brick propping her up.

Only she wasn't fine. Had he been more observant, the mailman would have noticed that the water running down Gertie's cheeks came from her eyes, not the sky. Annie Halvorsen might have crossed the ocean alone, but that wasn't what Gertie Sundersen had in mind for herself, not now anyhow. Maria and Corinna were supposed to be at her side, as they had been for the last twenty years. Instead of meeting at the Temple at eleven o'clock on a Tuesday morning, they would be walking up the gangway of the *Queen Mary*. Instead of watching the ships pass under the Verrazzano, heading out to sea, they'd be passengers standing on the foredeck, embarking on a journey of their own. The three of them. One for all, all for one.

True, she'd always been good at being alone, but that was before. At this point in her life, she wasn't so sure. Did she feel scared, like Corinna had said, that she couldn't do it anymore, given her dilapidated condition? Or was it more a matter of habit, that she was so used to having the girls around, she couldn't imagine being without them? Regardless, she didn't have a choice right now. *Buck up,* she told herself. *No one but you is going to push you across the finish line.*

"I'm fine," she assured the mailman for the third time, trying her best to smile. "Just fine."

Crossing Ninety-Seventh Street, she caught sight of a familiar form lumbering toward her.

"You're early today," said Tom when he reached her side.

"What?"

"You usually stay down by the water longer, that place you call the Temple. It's not even noon yet."

Gertie frowned. She'd never gotten used to that man tracking her around Bay Ridge like a bloodhound. Ordinarily, she told him so in no uncertain terms. Only today, she didn't mind the sight of the old firefighter with his giant hands. She didn't tell him this, however. Instead, she chided him about the umbrella. "I don't get it, Tom, what's the point of carrying that thing around if you never plan on using it?"

"For you," he answered, opening the umbrella and placing it over Gertie's head.

The gesture silenced her, made her feel light-headed all over again. This time, though, she recovered more quickly and shook her head at him. "You are something else, Tom. Come on then, if you want," she said. "But you better keep up, because I got things to do."

"Things?"

She told him about the trip she was planning at the end of the month.

"Trip?"

"That's right, Tom. I'm going away for a while."

Tom was confused. "But I thought . . ."

"I'm going to see a bit of the world out there. You know there's a world outside of Bay Ridge, don't you?"

"But Maria said . . ."

"No buts, Tom. It's something I have to do."

There was a flickering beneath the fold of Tom's right eye, as if a tiny insect were crawling under the skin.

"You feeling okay, Tom?"

He didn't answer.

A similar flickering began at the edge of his upper lip.

That was when Gertie decided she better pop the question before the poor man had a conniption.

"Any chance you want to come along, Tom?"

"Come along?" The flickering stopped. "Me?"

"Yes, you, you big galoot."

Tom was speechless.

"I'm going with or without you, Tom. Fact is, I'm on my way to the travel agency right now. So you'd better make up your mind quick."

She tightened her grip on his arm.

Shards of sunlight poked through the clouds. She put her hand out and saw that the rain had stopped. "We don't need this anymore," Gertie said, lowering the umbrella. "Looks like the day might turn out nice after all. *Bak skyene er himmelen alltid blå.*" She thought of her father.

Tom was mumbling. "But . . . there are so many things . . . and next week is . . ."

"Behind the clouds, the sky is always blue," she translated. "Stop vacillating, Tom."

He looked up at her, his lips moving but not producing any sound. "Okay, Gertie," he said finally. "I guess I can go. Sure."

Her father's eyes were blue, like the sky. Gertie remembered his voice, deep and loud, as if it were yesterday, as if it were he and not Tom walking beside her, agreeing to accompany her to Europe. Not that her father talked much on their walks by the water: Coney Island, Breezy Point, the Narrows. But when he did, it was always about the old country, the fjords and mountains and sea; and the older he grew, the more stories he told.

That was what getting old was all about, she'd begun to realize: a growing heap of stories and memories piling up all around you, a Mount Everest of memories. The very opposite of being young, when the ground ahead lay level and bare, a vast open space that stretched on forever and ever, waiting to be explored.

The image grabbed Gertie by the shoulder and squeezed, sucking the air out of her and forcing her to lean on Tom for support.

"Gertie?"

Was there any open ground left, she wondered, beyond the ash heap of memories?

16

Maria

She struggled up the footpath, a wet, boggy mess. Each step sent a flash of pain down the side of her left leg and into her small toe. It was the one thing she could count on at the moment, the one thing that wouldn't desert her. In a way, it soothed her, these flashes of pain, and she was grateful for each successive one.

Grateful, too, for her neighbor who happened to be standing at the front door of her building when she arrived and couldn't seem to find her keys.

"Looks like you vent svimming," observed Ida Levitsky as she opened the door for her. "Vit all your clothes on."

Maria wiped the water off the tip of her nose with the back of her hand. Drowning was more like it, she thought.

"There's someone vaiting for you," said Ida, tilting her head in the direction of the sitting area. With her thick Eastern European accent and interrogating eyes, Ida fancied herself a cross between a second super and a Stasi agent. Nothing occurred in the building without her knowledge.

Maria turned to find the Professor springing up from the couch. For a second, she wondered whether she might still be under water. What in God's name was *he* doing here?

"I am deeply sorry for barging in like this, Maria, but I must have a word." The gangly Professor bounced nervously from one foot to the other. "Naturally, it would have been more appropriate . . . to call before . . ."

How did he even know where she lived?

"I can see you're upset, Maria. I don't usually . . . it's just that . . . after the other day . . . I thought . . ."

"Please, you have no idea how upset—"

"Oh, I do, Maria," he interrupted. "And you have every right, considering my behavior at the travel agency. Which is precisely why I felt obligated to apologize in person. I never meant to pressure you about Italy, that's the last thing . . ."

Why did he keep rattling on and on? All Maria wanted was to get back to her apartment and lie down.

". . . the last thing. I merely wanted to let you know that I am available, as a companion and tour guide. You must understand how excited I am at the prospect of returning to Italy, an extraordinary country so full of beauty, from Taormina to Como, the Pantheon to the *Pietà*. And the prospect of sharing that beauty with someone I . . ." The Professor suddenly paused and stared at her with his earnest hazel eyes.

No, she prayed, *please don't let him finish that thought.*

". . . with someone," he resumed, lowering his voice so that Ida Levitsky, who was listening intently from her front-door post, couldn't hear, "I like very much."

"*Mannaggia mia*," she shrieked. "What are you talking about? I'm upset because I had a fight with my best friends, not because you were pressuring me about Italy. I don't give a damn about Italy!"

As the words flew out of her mouth and she saw the stunned reaction on the Professor's face, Maria turned bright red and began to sway.

The Professor rushed over to steady her, but it was too late: together they tumbled to the floor.

"Oy," gasped Ida Levitsky. "I vill call an ambulance, yes?"

It took a while before Maria answered that it wouldn't be necessary. It was the second time in a matter of hours that she'd landed on her rump. Thank God nobody else was around to see them sprawled on the lobby floor. She noticed the Professor wore two different-colored socks, one tan, one black.

"Let me help you up, Maria," the Professor said, holding out his hand.

The man was clearly out of his mind, a *pazzo*, but then again, she wasn't very far behind. The beginning of a laugh escaped from her mouth.

"I see that, Maria." The Professor smiled back.

Maria was completely baffled. Soaking wet and cold, her head thrumming, she hadn't felt this upset for as long as she could remember. And here was this man acting like a little boy, talking nonsense about how excited he was to share the beauty of Italy with her, dapper as ever in spite of the weather and his mismatched socks, not a single hair out of place, not a drop of water on the white handkerchief neatly folded in the pocket of his tweed blazer, less than a foot away from her—Maria Benedetti—wet and disheveled and smelly, even as the man's overpowering cologne washed over her.

She used to care about the way she dressed. And once upon a time, she also used to be attractive, just like her daughter, Livy, who still turned heads with her beautiful auburn hair, high rounded cheekbones, and slim figure. Now she was just a washed-up old lady wearing orthopedic shoes and sackcloth in place of a proper outfit. What could the Professor possibly see in her, want from her, this respected man so well versed in things she couldn't care less about? It was ridiculous, absolutely ridiculous.

"You're shivering, Maria," observed the Professor. "Let me make you some tea."

What was he saying now?

"Some tea," he repeated. "To warm you up."

Did she hear him right? Where did he think he was going to make tea? Down here in the lobby? He couldn't possibly think she would invite him up to her apartment.

A clucking noise interrupted her thoughts. Ida Levitsky, who had been closely monitoring the conversation, advanced toward them and clucked like a disapproving hen. "Is everything okay, Maria?"

"Yes, Ida," Maria reassured her as she rose from the floor and stepped toward the elevator.

The Professor blocked her way. "Please, Maria, I can't leave without redeeming myself."

"Look, Professor, we both said some things we probably regret, especially me, but right now—"

"Not another word about Italy, I promise. We could talk about your friends, the fight you just had. I'll do my best to make you feel better." He held out his arm and pressed the elevator button. "I insist."

"Vat do you think you're doing, young man?" asked Ida, deeply offended by the Professor's aggressive tactics.

Maria sighed in dismay. "It's fine, Ida."

She was much too tired and upset to argue with her neighbor or with the Professor, her head too muddled, her body too wet and cold. All she wanted was to lie down and gather her thoughts. So she gave in to the crazy man and followed him into the elevator. Besides, she wouldn't mind talking to someone right now, and even though the Professor might not be the ideal person—he was a big part of the problem, in fact—there wasn't anyone else at the moment. She realized that as the elevator door closed on Ida Levitsky's horror-stricken face.

"Don't worry about me, Maria," the Professor assured her as she opened the door to the apartment. "I'll find my way. You just take care of yourself."

She was definitely out of her mind. It dawned on her as she watched a stranger wander through her kitchen, opening cabinets and shuffling through drawers. The whole thing was ridiculous, but she didn't have the strength to object. So she headed for the bedroom and shut the door. Her clothes and shoes were soaked, and it was a relief to take them off. If only she could dip into a nice warm bath and close her eyes for a while, but she wasn't that far gone to do it with him in the apartment. Still, just toweling off and putting on some dry clothes felt good—until she remembered what happened at the Temple, and her heart began to race. What had she done?

"Is everything all right, Maria?" the Professor called out.

How could everything be all right? she wanted to yell back.

"The tea will be ready in a jiff."

The cheerfulness in his voice irritated her. What was he so happy about? Did he know something she didn't? Actually, he knew a lot more than she did. The man was a genius according to Vinnie and Corinna. So maybe he could help her make sense of this mess. She took a deep breath and entered the living room. "Do you have any family, Professor?" she asked, taking a seat on the couch.

"Please call me Richard," he answered from the kitchen, just as the kettle began to whistle.

No, better to keep it formal, thought Maria, and worried that he might sit down next to her, she moved to the recliner.

"Yes and no," answered the Professor as he brought out a tray with a pot of tea, cups and saucers, little spoons, lemon slices, and folded napkins, all very neat and proper.

The attention to detail surprised Maria. Just the way she would do it, everything in its rightful place, the way she arranged her kitchen cabinets, her closets, her entire life for that matter. The little spoons, she suddenly recalled, were a gift from her mother-in-law. Where did the Professor find them? She hadn't used those spoons in years.

"My wife passed away a long time ago," said the Professor, "when the children were in high school."

"I'm sorry."

"Now they're grown and settled in different parts of the country," he continued. "I don't see them very often. Sarah takes after her father, only a good deal more intelligent. She's a classics professor at Harvard. And Daniel is out in California. He's a park ranger at Yosemite, an outdoorsy type, who loves to hike and climb like his mother once did."

"That's nice," said Maria, taking a sip from her cup. The tea tasted good, just the right temperature and sweetness. Strange, she didn't remember being asked if she took sugar. How did he know? "Family means everything to me, Professor."

"I understand," he said. "I have a grandson named Jacob, Daniel's son. We talk on the phone, and if I'm lucky, I see him once a year."

"What a shame, especially at our age. Being able to help out my daughter and watch Vinnie grow up, celebrating all the special occasions—that's what I live for now."

The Professor nodded sympathetically.

If only Gertie understood that too, thought Maria. *Then she'd realize that she needed her family a lot more than traveling around Italy.* "That's why I did it."

"Did what, Maria?"

Maria shifted uncomfortably in the chair. She hesitated at first, then gradually told him about her secret calls to Gertie's estranged daughter in Los Angeles and the surprise reunion she was planning.

"I'm impressed, Maria," said the Professor. "Maybe you could talk to Daniel and persuade him to visit with my grandson more often."

"You might be impressed, but Gertie wasn't. When she found out, she went berserk. You should have seen her, the look on her face. I never saw her get so mad."

"Hmm."

"She told me I crossed the line." Maria started to cry as she remembered Gertie storming out of the Temple.

"Don't get upset, Maria. It's probably not as bad as—"

"Oh, it is, it is."

"I see."

Maria frowned. "You see?"

"Well—"

"The same with Corinna," said Maria. "And her situation is even worse than Gertie's. The poor thing has no one but us. So I asked Vinnie to look on the computer for someone, anyone, from her family that I could get in touch with."

"Yes, he told me. In fact—"

"Corinna was even angrier than Gertie. She said things about me, hurtful things. About Vinnie too. Then she walked away. My friends walked away from me." Maria covered her face with her hands.

The Professor gently patted her on the shoulder. "You had a fight with your friends. It happens. But they are your friends for good reason. They will be back."

Maria looked up at him. "You don't know that."

"I'm sure of it."

Maria didn't share his confidence.

"But I want to be honest with you," said the Professor. "I can also understand why they became upset."

She figured as much, with all his hmm-ing and I-see-ing.

"Family is a tricky business, much like politics. You're very fortunate to have such a strong relationship with your daughter and grandson. It's not like that for everyone. I myself am envious, and perhaps

Gertie and Corinna are too. Or they simply have different relationships with their families, and what makes you happy, leaves them cold. You have to respect their feelings."

"So you're saying I did cross the line?"

The Professor tilted his head and turned out his hands. "Well—"

"Oh God, what have I done!"

"Let's just say you've come very close, Maria, which is bound to stir up the pot. That's not always a bad thing."

"How can you say that?"

The Professor leaned forward and placed his hands on Maria's shoulders. "It is true you've acted against the wishes of your friends, but I am certain everything will sort itself out in the end. In the best-case scenario, Gertie and Corinna will be happily reunited with their families thanks to your efforts. But even if that doesn't happen and Gertie and Corinna prefer to remain alone, they won't be mad forever. You will apologize for what you did, and they will do the same."

"Maybe I should apologize now. Call them up and tell them how sorry—"

The Professor put up his hands. "I would wait a bit and let the dust settle. Everything will turn out fine. You'll see."

Maria hoped he was right. She felt sick to her stomach and couldn't imagine going on like this for much longer.

"By the way, were you surprised about what Vincent discovered?"

"Discovered?"

"About Corinna."

Maria froze.

"Yes, Vincent was kind enough to confide in me, and as it turns out, Corinna and I have similar backgrounds."

Vinnie had already talked to the Professor? Please let that not be so. Corinna would kill her.

"Corinna was adopted," explained the Professor.

She stared at him blankly. "What?"

"She's not a Hale, Maria. Her surname is Hoffman. I'm almost certain she was born in Germany or possibly Austria."

Maria wondered if she'd heard him correctly.

"I realize this must sound strange, but I can assure you, it's true."

The Professor set down his cup and slowly went through the sequence of events that had led Vincent to this unexpected finding, his hands moving animatedly. "Your grandson is extremely skilled at mining the internet for information. Honestly, I'm surprised at how much he was able to learn in such a short time. He discovered that Corinna has a rare genetic disease, a disease that only five people in the country have. He managed to get the names of those people from an old National Institutes of Health registry. There was a Corinna Hoffman on the list, birth date May 26, 1938, who had immigrated to the United States from London in 1941 and had resided in Parkside, Massachusetts, just outside Boston. Hoffman, not Hale. Are you following me, Maria?"

No, she thought, *not really.*

"Next he found an announcement in a local newspaper, dated June 2002, that Jonathan Hale, the rector of Parkside's Trinity Church, had passed away. Didn't you tell Vincent that you suspected Corinna's father was a member of the clergy?"

She nodded.

"The announcement went on to say that the rector was survived by his son, Henry, and his daughter, Corinna."

"She has a brother?"

"A younger brother who still lives in Parkside. Vincent was able to contact him by phone the other day. Henry told him that Corinna had been adopted from an English agency. She was a refugee from Europe during the war."

Maria tried to process the strange news—Parkside, Europe, England, refugee—but it made her dizzy. Then again, did it matter? The important thing was that Corinna had a family. A brother. "Does Henry know Corinna lives in Bay Ridge?" asked Maria, suddenly excited about the prospect of reconnecting the siblings. "Has he tried to get in touch with her?"

"I'm afraid not," answered the Professor grimly. "According to Henry, the adoption was a big mistake that his family came to regret. Corinna was not right in body and mind—his exact words were much more offensive—and he wanted nothing to do with her."

Maria didn't understand. "What kind of a person would say such a thing?"

"Not a very nice person. Henry Hale is a bigot. An anti-Semite. He told Vincent that Corinna was a dirty Jew, a Christ killer who should have stayed in Europe and got what she deserved. It appears that Henry Hale is the one who is not right in body and mind."

Maria cringed. How awful! No wonder Corinna didn't want to talk about her family. Here she thought she was helping her friend when, instead, she was reopening old wounds.

"I must say, Maria, the story becomes more and more intriguing. I can't be sure, but my guess is that Corinna was indeed Jewish and came to England by ship. Vincent believes she was part of the Kindertransport."

"The what?"

The Professor's face lit up. "The Kindertransport was one of the few bright spots during that ugly time. Various agencies worked closely with the British government to rescue Jewish children from the Nazis, over ten thousand children in all. They were taken by trains from occupied cities to Holland and Belgium, and from there by ship to England."

Maria wondered why the Professor seemed so excited. Corinna might have been rescued from one nightmare, only to end up in another. What good could possibly come from this information?

"The point is, Maria, Corinna had a family in Europe at one time and, for all we know, may still have one there—parents, siblings, cousins."

It didn't make sense to Maria. If Corinna had another family, why hadn't she ever mentioned it?

"I'm sure she has no idea," explained the Professor. "Corinna was adopted when she was two years old, under very difficult circumstances. She probably doesn't remember anything. My bet is that the Hales never told her and may not be fully aware of her history themselves."

Could it be that Corinna didn't know? That she might actually have family other than that horrible brother Vinnie spoke to in Parkside? "Is it possible?"

The Professor beamed. "It most certainly is, Maria, and that's precisely what I intend to find out, by contacting some of the Jewish organizations that helped coordinate the transports. Meanwhile, Vincent is searching the internet for any trace of Corinna Hoffman in Germany and Austria."

The Professor's excitement was contagious. Maybe her meddling wasn't so bad after all. If Corinna had other family left, who was to say they wouldn't be kinder and more loving than her adopted family? And if Corinna hadn't known, wouldn't she be eager to know now?

"We don't have all the facts yet," cautioned the Professor, "and as difficult as this is for you to digest, it will be more so for Corinna. But I'm certain that, in the end, she will be grateful for what you initiated. This is her history after all, and I can assure you, Corinna is an enthusiastic student of history. I remember how meticulous she was in our work on *The Bay Ridge Chronicle*, digging up the most fascinating details about the Verrazzano Bridge that might have easily been missed. She'll be even more curious about her own origins."

"You're right," she said, jumping up from the recliner. "Thank you, Professor, thank you for everything." She felt like going over and hugging him, so grateful she was for what he'd just told her, but she had something more important to do first. "I have to find Corinna."

The Professor put his hand up to object.

Maria had already grabbed her purse and was heading to the door. She didn't care anymore that she was out of her mind, leaving a stranger on the couch in her living room, leaving him alone in her apartment. She didn't care one iota. All she wanted was to find Corinna and tell her what the Professor had just told her. It would instantly wash away all her anger and make her happy again. How could it not?

17

Corinna

"You're kidding, right?" Corinna asked the receptionist at the Center when he informed her that the art teacher had called in sick.

"I can try to find someone else."

Corinna checked her watch. The class should have already started. She muttered something under her breath and flung her tote bag into the closet behind the reception desk.

"No. I'll take care of it," she said.

Tuesday afternoon art class was the most popular activity at the Senior Center. Corinna had found a spirited, young graduate student at Parsons who needed some extra money and then charmed the director of a local art foundation into sending a new batch of art supplies every month. She'd always known the residents needed more than bingo and card games and movies. More, too, than outings to the Botanic Garden, Broadway shows, and museums. They needed a creative outlet, an opportunity to make their own things. She was right. Even the most withdrawn and listless residents were churning out drawings and paintings, some of which were quite impressive. In fact, they were running out of wall space to hang the work.

Today, though, she wasn't in the mood to shepherd their creative spirits. She needed to find Vinnie before he did any more digging into her family, the family she had thankfully escaped from ages ago. She couldn't trust Maria to stop him.

The class was hardly underway before she snapped.

"Damn it, Joe. Didn't I tell you not to set up your easel over there?"

Joe Flannery, who sat at the far corner of the recreation room, next to the computer station and in front of the big window looking out onto the Narrows, had just knocked over his palette for the second week in a row. Paint drizzled down the computer screen, snaked between the keys, and spilled onto the floor. Corinna rushed over with a roll of paper towels to clean up the mess, while Flannery told her how sorry he was.

"I like it over here," he mumbled when the last paint drop had been expunged and order restored. "Best view in the house."

Corinna frowned. "Maybe you should paint outside next time."

She felt bad the minute she walked away. In addition to missing chunks of skin, Flannery had a hand tremor that made him clumsy. Besides, who cared about a spill every now and then? Corinna had always encouraged her budding artists to be a little messy. Older people were generally so rigid, always trying to keep things under control. Letting loose once in a while would do them some good.

"Don't take it personally," said Rose Flannery. She was sitting with her girlfriends on the other side of the room. "He never listens to me either."

Corinna glanced down at Rose's work, wondering what she could possibly be trying to draw.

"It's the Verrazzano Bridge," explained Rose, noticing her teacher's confusion. "Did he break anything this time?"

Maybe it was Rose who should sit closer to the window, considering how little the drawing resembled the bridge. "No, nothing broke."

Juliette Ippolito, on the other hand, was a great admirer of her friend Rose's artistic skills. She told Rose she wished she could draw like her.

"You have to practice, Juliette," said Corinna. "Let me get you one of the workbooks the foundation sent over."

Actually, they could both use a workbook or, better yet, some lessons from Rose's husband. Tremors and all, Joe Flannery was by far the most talented member of the class. His portraits of residents and staff at the Center were not only technically good, they also captured an essential aspect of the person he painted—like the look of envy on Juliette Ippolito's face, whether she was admiring Rose's winnings in Atlantic City or her abstract rendering of the Verrazzano.

"Here, Juliette," said Corinna, laying the workbook down in front of her. "All you have to do is connect the dots."

After class, she would apologize to Joe. She wasn't really angry at him anyway. She was angry with Maria and her grandson. She should've found someone else to cover the class. She could hardly think straight, picturing Vinnie at his computer searching for details about her past.

"Have a look now," said Rose Flannery, proud of the latest additions to her sketch. "See the cars and trucks driving over the bridge?"

"Is that what those are?" asked Corinna. "Ah yes, now I see."

Corinna usually didn't have to make an effort at sounding cheerful around the residents, but today it was incredibly difficult with all the bad memories of her childhood welling up in her head. Maybe she was blowing things out of proportion. How much could Vinnie possibly find out anyway? Her parents were long dead, her mother for twenty years and her father for nine. She wouldn't have even heard of her father's stroke had it not been for Betty Fields, a former classmate and the only person she remembered talking to in grade school, a girl with thick bifocals, almost as thick as her own in those days, and equally unpopular. Betty worked at the public library in Parkside and had contacted her about the funeral. Thanks, but no thanks, had been her response.

"How does it look, Corinna?" asked Juliette after she connected the last dot.

"Beautiful," Corinna said weakly.

Against her better judgment, she had gone to her mother's funeral and realized immediately that it was a mistake. "I'm glad you came," her father had said when she arrived at the church. She hadn't seen him in over thirty years and he had aged, the skin billowing below his eyes and sagging around the jawline. "We've missed you." He was exactly the same, a liar and a hypocrite. She still shook when thinking of his sermons. "Who sinned," he would ask his congregation, "this man or his parents, that he was born blind? Neither one nor the other, but all mankind, so that the work of God be revealed in him."

Her father must have been in his early thirties when he'd given that sermon. He was tall and handsome and had the respect of the entire community. He smiled smugly as he looked around the church, at the Brindle boy with Down syndrome in the pew next to the Hale family, at Corinna with her crooked teeth and misshapen hand. He didn't have to spell it out: *they* were the living, breathing examples of sin seared into flesh, the glorious work of God, of all that was wrong and evil in the world. How could he think of her like that, a father appalled by his own daughter? Why didn't he ever see the positive side, her intelligence and goodness, her desire to love and be loved?

"She wanted you to have this," he'd said after her mother's funeral, without the slightest warmth. He handed her the silver-framed picture her mother had kept on her night table. The photograph was taken in their backyard by the dogwood tree. Her mother's arms were draped around her children, Corinna on one side, Henry on the other. She was five at the time, Henry three.

"I need some more red," Juliette announced.

Corinna grabbed the red paint and poured it into Juliette's cup. Before she realized, the cup had overflowed, and paint was spilling onto Juliette's lap.

"Thank you," said Juliette, who didn't seem to notice.

She'd thrown out the photograph the minute she returned home. Corinna didn't want to remember. But the next day, she felt guilty and fished it out of a garbage bin in the basement. She would keep it for the time being—the image of her mother, not her brother. She took a pair of scissors and cut him out of the photo.

"Zadie is making those sounds again," said Rose.

Zadie Sandusky was a resident with Parkinson's disease; usually rigid and expressionless, she made a loud grinding noise with her teeth when she became excited—and she was excited now, plunging her hands into every different paint color and smearing the contents on the paper in front of her.

"Just concentrate on your drawing, Rose."

Henry was the spitting image of his father, tall and fair, with arctic-blue eyes. "You shouldn't have come," he said to her that day. "You don't belong here." He was vicious and hateful. "You never did."

He used to call her "freak" and would hit her when their mother wasn't watching. One day she found him in her room with his friends, standing over her favorite doll. Henry had cut off one of its fingers and taped the toes of the left foot together. "Her doll is a freak too," he told them. She tried to grab it from Henry, but he pushed her away, then pretended to urinate on the doll while his friends laughed. He was a monster. How dare Maria pry into her past? The thought of that monster reappearing after all these years and ruining her life terrified Corinna.

"I can't concentrate," said Rose, "with all that noise."

"I can't concentrate either," said Juliette.

"Damn it, you two!" yelled Corinna. "Shut up!"

Rose and Juliette looked at each other in disbelief. Zadie had gone rigid again and stopped grinding her teeth. In fact, everyone in the room had suddenly become silent.

Corinna was mortified. She had never done anything like that and wished she could take it back. Her eyes darted nervously from one resident to another. Eventually, they settled on the stereo above the mini fridge. Yes, that was what she needed right now, what they all needed right now, some music to calm their frazzled nerves.

Her hand shook as she slipped a CD into the tray. The *Goldberg Variations*. She closed her eyes and waited for the opening aria to enter her pores, and only after the first few measures did she begin to breathe easier.

She walked over to Zadie and gently guided her hands back into the paint containers. "I want to see more of those beautiful colors. Just try not to make too much noise." She turned to Rose and Juliette. "And you two," she said with mock sternness, "back to work."

"Yes, ma'am," they answered together, glad to see their teacher smiling again.

Corinna rode up and down the tonal register with Bach, moving to his fluid rhythms, and when she glanced at the clock, she noticed the hour was almost over. The music had sped up time. It had also sped up her metabolism, lifting her spirits and allowing her to submerge the bad memories. Now that the last variation was ending, though, she worried the magic wouldn't last.

Someone was calling her name.

Joe Flannery waved from the opposite corner of the room. "I've been working on this for a while and it's almost finished," he said when she arrived at his easel. "I made it for you."

It was a portrait of Corinna astride her Vespa. She wore a red helmet that matched the red color of her bike. Her blonde hair fell straight and evenly around her head. She smiled impishly as she retracted the gears and raced the engine.

"What do you think?"

She noticed he hadn't painted any of her deformities. She didn't even look particularly small in the picture. "You really think it looks like me?" she asked.

"It looks *just* like you," he answered with a smile. "I'm going to call it *Bird in Flight*."

She was too overwhelmed to speak. "It's a good name," she finally said in a low voice. "But I think it's already taken."

He rubbed his chin. "Fine, then *Bird in Flight 2*."

"Are you trying to brownnose your teacher, Mr. Flannery?"

"Is it working?" For those who didn't know him, Flannery's smile could be hard to distinguish from a look of disgust because of the scar that pulled on his upper lip.

"Maybe," answered Corinna, returning his smile.

"Sorry about before," he said. "From now on, I'm putting my paint on the other side of the easel so that if it spills, it won't wreck the computer."

"I'm the one who should be apologizing," said Corinna. "It was an accident. Besides, how could I be mad at you, Joe, when you're always giving me such wonderful presents?" She looked at him. His face was a jigsaw puzzle of white scars and missing pieces.

Yet, for all that, Joe's face—it was beautiful.

"Hey, what's wrong?" he asked her.

"Nothing," she answered, turning slightly so he couldn't see her expression. She wondered whether the other residents saw the beauty in Joe's face too.

Flannery studied her for a time before he said anything. "Not him again, is it?"

"Him?"

"From the other day. You were waiting for his call."

The words startled her.

"You don't remember?" Flannery pretended to adjust his bow tie. "The classics professor from Brooklyn College."

Corinna blushed.

"I knew something was up when you got rid of the romance section in the library and replaced it with all that Greek crap nobody wants to read."

"I didn't get rid of it," she protested. "I just rearranged things. The romance section is by the water fountain now."

"Forget him," said Flannery. "He's not worth it anyway."

The truth was, Corinna had been so consumed with anger at Maria and fear of her brother, Henry, that she had almost forgotten about the Professor.

"Not worth it at all," said Flannery, flicking his shaky wrist as if he were swatting a fly. "A pompous son of a bitch who thinks he's better than everyone else. Not like you."

Corinna hadn't felt that way, at least not at the beginning. She had never met anyone who shared her passion for books and learning. Anyone, moreover, of his caliber, who seemed equally impressed by her intellect. It was a dream come true.

"Trust me."

Yet that was all it was in the end, a dream. The real-life person was just like every other real-life person she had known, a great disappointment.

Flannery smiled his crooked smile again. "You know I'm right."

It was all Corinna could do to hold back her tears. She was tempted to hug him, but that wasn't the sort of thing she normally did, not the sort of thing other people did to her either.

"Thanks, Joe," she said, rushing out of the room before she started to cry.

Corinna sat astride her Vespa a few minutes later. The rain had stopped and the sun was peeking through the clouds. Mr. Tongue Ring should be in his usual spot in the alley behind the high school, and hopefully, Vinnie would be nearby. She'd take the long way around, down Shore Road to the Verrazzano, then make her way onto the Belt Parkway. Picking up speed, she felt the wind in her hair, the sea on her lips. She heard Bach's music, imagined his fingers dancing across the keys of his harpsichord.

Flannery had pegged her in his portrait. Clearly, Corinna had underestimated him, probably because of his lousy taste in literature. Flannery was a talented artist. A psychoanalyst too. He intuited her feelings for the Professor. Why hadn't she noticed how perceptive he was before? Not because of his . . . no, please, let it not be because of his imperfections. She of all people.

She pulled back on the throttle, pushing the Vespa to its limit. Flannery had pegged her, all right. This was where she was happiest, flying solo—on her bike or in her library of books—a bird in flight. He was right about the Professor too. She pictured him adjusting his bow tie, his wiry limbs canted in different directions, his pompous gaze. He never liked her and never would.

Besides, she wasn't made for that kind of like. For as far back as she could remember, she was different from the other girls. In fifth and sixth grades, she watched her classmates' chests fill out and heard about their first menstrual cycles. She watched and waited, but nothing ever happened to her. Even bifocaled Betty Fields got her period. Even Betty Fields started talking to boys. The doctor said it was a hormonal deficiency that couldn't be corrected.

Of course it bothered her—being different, being essentially sexless. But eventually she came to realize that love wasn't all it was cracked up to be. She saw how it had played out for Gertie and many of the residents at the Center, who sat on the other side of the room, as far away from their husbands as possible. And while Maria believed she had been the luckiest woman on the planet, who knew how much of what she remembered was real.

Corinna exited the highway at Owl's Head Park and looped back around in the opposite direction, her favorite stretch, heading east toward the Bridge.

You're right about the pompous son of a bitch, Joe! Corinna understood her needs, and the Professor wasn't one of them. She had her Vespa and the Belt Parkway. Her rooftop deck with views of the Narrows and the Verrazzano. Her Bach and Brahms. Red wine and Irish whiskey. Hookah and hash. What more could she want?

The sunlight sparkled on the water. A tugboat towed a large freighter toward the harbor. Corinna tried to make out the name but had trouble because of the glare.

There were plenty of people who respected her, who depended on her, just as the freighter depended on the tug. People like Rose Flannery, Juliette Ippolito, and Zadie Sandusky. People like Joe Flannery. Especially Joe Flannery. She'd always felt at home at the Center. That was where she belonged.

She got off the Belt Parkway at the foot of the bridge and headed down Shore Road to the high school. She had to make sure Vinnie didn't find her brother and tell him where she lived. All that monster ever wanted was to ruin her life, and there was no reason to think anything had changed. She couldn't afford to let him jeopardize her home at the Senior Center, the only true home she'd ever had.

18

Maria

The second she spotted Corinna riding down Shore Road, Maria jumped up from the bench she'd been sitting on and rushed into the street to flag her down. She was so excited she barely felt the front wheel of Corinna's Vespa rolling over her foot.

"Jesus, Maria, I nearly—"

"There's something I have to tell you," Maria said, smiling widely.

Corinna took off her helmet. "You spoke to Vinnie?"

Maria didn't answer.

"Don't tell me you haven't—"

"Please, Corinna, this will make you happy."

"The only thing that will make me happy," said Corinna, pointing her enlarged right thumb at Maria, "is knowing that Vinnie isn't snooping around anymore. You hear me?"

"But—"

"I mean it, Maria. If you don't stop him, I will, and it won't be pretty."

"Just listen," she pleaded, wishing Corinna would let up for a second and give her a chance to explain. "You're not . . ." she said, struggling to find the right words. "You're not who you think you are."

"What are you talking about?"

"You're not . . . a Hale."

Corinna's eyes narrowed.

"You were adopted," explained Maria, gaining confidence. "Your real name is Hoffman."

"What?"

"The Hales are not your real family."

Corinna shook her head.

"It's true," said Maria. "Vinnie spoke to your brother, Henry."

Corinna recoiled, as if she'd been slapped across the face.

"Isn't this a good thing?" asked Maria, eager for her friend to digest the news and recognize the exciting possibilities that lay ahead. But Corinna had lost all the color in her face and was backing away. "Aren't you happy that Henry isn't your . . . ?"

Corinna shielded her ears with her hands.

"He's an awful person from what I heard, and I can't imagine what it must have been like to live with him. But now we know he's not your real—"

"Don't say another word, Maria. Not you and not that degenerate grandson of yours. You'd better stop him now, or so help me God, I'll call the police and have him arrested on the spot."

Maria was dumbfounded as Corinna restarted her Vespa and raced away. Why was she so mad? It didn't make any sense, but there wasn't any time to think about it. She had to get to Vinnie before Corinna did something crazy.

19

Vinnie

"Fuck!" Vinnie grabbed his friend Zach and turned him the other way.

"Whath up, Vinnie?" asked Zach. "Do you thee cops?"

"Ssh."

"Thath all I need," said Zach, whose tongue ring made him lisp, especially at stressful moments. "I'm thupposed to be home, remember?" Zach had just finished his last sale of the day, to Vinnie's grandma's friend. They could usually count on her coming by around that time, and Vinnie always stepped around the corner so she wouldn't see him. She hadn't spotted him before she left, had she? It seemed like she'd been snooping around.

"Ssh."

"They'll boot me for this. No graduation, no college. I'm finithed."

"Shut the fuck up," said Vinnie. "It's my grandmother, not the cops. I don't want her to see me. Just look the other way."

A shrill voice called out from across the street: "Vinnie!"

Too late. His army jacket must have given him away. He should have ditched it the minute he saw her.

"Vinnie!" his grandmother shouted again as she waddled toward the alley.

While her arms and legs swung wildly, Granny moved at a snail's pace, her right side dragging behind the left. Vinnie recalled what the Professor had said about his grandmother's impressive dancing skills and wanted to laugh. He wondered whether the Professor might be spiking his afternoon tea with some serious dope.

Maria was breathless by the time she reached him. "I need to talk to you," she managed to say.

"Sure, Granny. Everything okay?"

Maria regarded Zach crossly.

"Give us a minute," he told his friend.

She asked him straight out when Zach was out of earshot: "Are you selling drugs with that boy, Vinnie?"

"What?"

"Tell me the truth."

"Jeez, Granny, that's crazy. Why would you ever think—"

"I know about the cigarettes and drinking," she said. "I clean up after you in the yard. But not drugs. When I heard you were hanging out with that boy and he was selling—"

His head jerked backward. "Who told you that?"

"Please, Vinnie, be honest with me." Maria suddenly looked like she was about to cry.

He put his arm around her shoulders. "Don't get upset, Granny. No one's selling drugs here."

"Promise me, Vinnie."

"I promise."

"You've promised me things before," she reminded him. "When you swore you wouldn't take out your mother's car."

He promised he was telling the truth this time.

Maria didn't say anything for a while. She pushed the hair away from Vinnie's face so she could see his eyes. "You know how much I love you? How much your mother loves you? You've made us so proud.

You're smart enough to be whatever you want in this world. A doctor, a lawyer, an engineer. You name it."

Not this again. Vinnie had heard the spiel a thousand times and was sick of it. He had no idea what he wanted to do with his life. The only thing that mattered now was getting out of Bay Ridge and being on his own, free from all the nagging and pressure.

"I don't want anything to get in the way."

Neither did he, and that was definitely no lie.

"You don't have to worry, Granny. Let me take you home before you get sick. You're not supposed to be running around like this." He guided her out of the alley and onto the street. Arm in arm they walked silently together down Shore Road.

"I do have to worry, Vinnie." Maria stopped before they reached her apartment, when she noticed Ida Levitsky standing guard at the front door. "It doesn't matter whether she's telling the truth."

She? Who was his grandmother talking about?

"She's mad, Vinnie," explained Maria. "I thought it would make her happy, finding out about the adoption. But for some reason, it only made things worse. She's so mad right now, I'm afraid she might do something crazy."

"Corinna? She's the one who . . . ?"

"She threatened to call the police."

Vinnie was stunned. After all he'd done for that woman, the hours he'd spent researching her family history.

"I should have never involved you in the first place," said Maria. Ida Levitsky was waving to her. She waved back. "You have to stop, Vinnie. No more looking into Corinna's past. And no more talking about Corinna to anyone."

Vinnie bit down on his lower lip.

"Do you hear me?" she asked. "Please, Vinnie, be careful. I'd kill myself if anything happens to you because of my foolishness."

That thankless, fucking whack job!

Ida Levitsky had left her sentry post and was now standing next to them. "Is everything all right, Maria?"

She wiped her eyes. "Yes, Ida, thank you. You know my grandson, Vinnie?"

Ida regarded him with disapproving eyes.

Vinnie smiled weakly, then turned to his grandmother. "Don't worry, Granny, it'll be fine. My lips are sealed," he whispered in her ear. Then he planted a quick kiss on her cheek and took off down Shore Road.

Fine? Was he kidding? Fucked was more like it, totally fucked. It was clear Corinna had figured out that he and Zach were working together. Would she tell the cops? Would they arrest him, put him in jail? Jesus fucking Christ. Then again, wouldn't that get her into trouble too? After all, she was one of their biggest customers.

Fine, so she'd tell his mother instead. Or she'd go and rat him out to the principal at school and he'd be suspended. No way would Harvard ever consider him, or any other school for that matter. He'd be stuck in Bay Ridge forever.

He grabbed the railing that separated Shore Road from the park below and let out a howl.

Vinnie always thought of himself as pretty smart, not just in school but also on the street. He figured his smarts would allow him to take a few risks and not get caught. But maybe not this time. Why the fuck did he ever tell Zach to sell dope to that whack job? Because he felt bad for her, her and all her disabilities? Because he believed what she told Zach, that the dope would help her seizures? What kind of reasons were those? She was his grandmother's friend—how stupid could he be!

Through the trees, he could see the Verrazzano Bridge in the distance, the tiny specks moving back and forth along the upper and lower decks. Just the other night, he was one of those specks, driving to a party in Staten Island. Now that he had a license, he was officially allowed to take out his mother's car. What a high, sitting behind the wheel and speeding along the wide illuminated roadways. With the car windows down, he could smell and taste the sea below, while the wind whistled loudly in his ears. He never felt so free in his life. The road ahead stretched before him—a vast open space, waiting to be explored.

20

The Temple

On Friday morning, as the clock struck 11:00 a.m., the Professor listened while Vincent translated *The Odyssey*. He smiled inwardly; his favorite student had shed his cold and was much more alert today. Tom Jurgen, meanwhile, rummaged through his drawers, wondering what clothes to pack for his upcoming trip to Europe. Livy stood in front of her son's bedroom door, considering whether to disregard Vinnie's "No Entry" sign and go inside; remembering the last time she invaded his privacy and the brouhaha that ensued, she decided against it.

Outside, the sun blazed in the blue sky. A group of sailboats tacked back and forth beneath the Verrazzano Bridge. Along the water, a fisherman felt a bite and pulled back on his rod as a jogger passed by and watched. On a stretch of grass, two little boys played soccer while their mothers sipped coffee and chatted.

As she walked down the footpath, Maria heard someone crying and quickened her pace. One of the little soccer players had fallen and hurt himself. He was now in the arms of his mother, being comforted. "He's fine," the mother assured Maria when she arrived on the scene panting. "Tell the nice lady she doesn't have to worry, Johnny."

Relieved, Maria waved goodbye and started up the grassy slope toward the enclosure. Even though it wasn't their usual day, she couldn't resist stopping by the Temple. Three days had passed since the big fight. She hadn't talked to Gertie, not once. It might be the longest stretch since they'd known each other. And her rush to tell Corinna what Vinnie had discovered hadn't helped matters with Corinna in the least. Everything Maria did had the opposite effect of what she intended.

Wait until the dust settles, the Professor had advised her. She should have listened.

As Maria climbed the hill, she hoped—prayed—that the dust had in fact settled at some point during the painfully long night and that, as a new day dawned, Gertie and Corinna might have had a change of heart, awakening with the same idea. But when she peeked inside the enclosure, neither of them were there.

Maria sighed. The grass was littered with empty bottles and cans. Had Corinna been at the Temple, the place would have been spotless, a circle of incense candles purifying the air with scents of lavender and myrrh.

She plodded toward the bench, wiped the surface with a Kleenex, and took her position on the lower side, since she was the tallest of the three. Gertie usually sat on the other side, next to the decapitated column, and Corinna, the shortest, stood on the bench in between them. Maria lifted her head and peered through the opening in the trees. Today, in the sunlight, the metal beams of the bridge appeared blue, or was that just the reflection from the sky above? The cars looked tiny as they passed beneath the massive arches, the cables so light and delicate as they dipped and climbed from one height to the other. The flattened U shape reminded Maria of the pearl necklace Jim had given her. Gertie pictured the bridge as a harp, with the vertical cables as strings, and Corinna as the wings of an enormous bird that might lift off and soar through the air at any moment.

There was a sailboat on the water, gliding eastward from New York Harbor, and an old schooner from the Seaport, the same one they had seen the other day. How frail and haggard it looked next to that big tanker. Frail and haggard, just like her and her friends.

Oh, how I misjudged you, Gertie. I thought it was all bluster, your talk about being independent. I thought you were hurting inside, not being able to speak to your daughter, share things with her, confide in her. I thought you were just too proud to say so. That was why I never gave up on Elsa. I thought for sure that, when she came to her senses, you would too—that the two of you would see how silly you had been all these years and finally be happy together. Instead, I've only made things worse.

How could I have been so wrong?

Will you ever forgive me?

The large tanker inched in from the Atlantic. She waited until it got closer so she could read the letters on the side. But why bother? Gertie wasn't there to play the game, and Corinna wasn't there to dole out prizes.

Maria's hip ached, and when she shifted her position on the bench, a flash of pain ripped down the side of her leg. Her friends had deserted her, and there was nothing she could do but wait. Thank God she was able to talk to Vinnie, and thank God Corinna was wrong about him. She had left a note for Corinna at the Center afterward, assuring her that Vinnie's mouth was sealed. Hopefully, it would be enough to stop her from doing anything rash.

Gertie stood in her apartment by the window. If she craned her head far enough to the side, she could see down to the Narrows, at least a sliver of it. She was doing that at the moment, craning to get a glimpse of the bridge, maybe even the Temple, and thinking about last Tuesday's fight.

She also waited for a call from Elsa. They'd been playing phone tag the past few days, so this time she'd make sure to be home when the phone rang. Gertie's eyes burned and her lids felt like lead weights. Another lousy night. That same dream of her choking under the bridge twenty years ago: Corinna sticking a finger down her mouth, Maria pounding on her back, both of them trying desperately to expel the pit stuck in her throat.

They saved her life that day. They did so again last year when she collapsed at the Center on bingo night. Corinna started CPR after calling 911, and Maria accompanied her in the ambulance, remaining at her side almost the entire time she was in the hospital. How could Gertie have gotten so mad at them? No question, it was wrong for Maria to butt in for the millionth time. But who was she kidding, accusing Maria of being selfish? Maria didn't have a selfish bone in her body. To her, cajoling Elsa to come to Bay Ridge was like performing the Heimlich all over again. She was trying to save Gertie's life, no matter that she was dead wrong this time and only pushing the pit further down her windpipe. Nor should she have been surprised that Corinna went along with it. Who could possibly say no to Maria?

Gertie's neck hurt from craning. She couldn't see much anyway. She hoped a boat would eventually pass, one big enough for her to make out the upper part at least. She wondered what it was like down by the water now. Were there many people out? Was the water choppy or still? Was the sun making the wavelets sparkle, like fireflies jumping and talking at once, as Maria imagined? Gertie wished she could see the bridge now, especially in the glorious spring sunshine. She wished she were sitting on their bench at the Temple, peering through the opening in the trees.

Her anger had all but subsided; she'd beaten it out of herself over the last few days. Still, Gertie hadn't called either of her friends yet. She had to make a point this time, put an end to the nonsense once and for all, because if she didn't, Maria would never stop. But maybe it was time. Maria was so damn sensitive and must be beside herself.

Gertie's mouth was sandpaper dry. The fancy Greek yogurt had hardened into a layer of cement on the roof of her mouth. *Uff da*. Why couldn't they water it down a bit? No matter, she had finished the last of the yogurt and wouldn't be getting any more. Just as she'd finished the last of her medicines and had no intention of refilling the prescriptions. She had wiped her accounts clean for the big trip to Europe and hardly had any money left for extras. She was going to cross the Atlantic, the only thing that mattered now. She was going to see the world. *I'm with you, Annie Halvorsen, one last time.*

She would call Maria and Corinna after she spoke to Elsa. She'd make up with them. They were practically sisters after all. She couldn't go away being mad at her sisters. It would wreck the trip. Besides, if she couldn't get them to come in person, she wanted them there in spirit.

On the coffee table sat a red plastic envelope with the Kon Tiki Travel logo, a replica of the raft made of balsa and bamboo used by the famous Norwegian explorer Thor Heyerdahl. Inside were her expedited passport, which cost a small fortune, and her tickets and itinerary—precious as jewels to Gertie. She admired them from different angles, held them in her hands to make sure they were real. She had read the documents a hundred times during the last twenty-four hours. She would depart on the *Queen Mary* on Tuesday, May 31, from the Red Hook Terminal in Brooklyn, the day she turned eighty. Arrive Southampton, England, June 7. Three nights at the Lord Nelson Hotel near the Strand. Alitalia to Leonardo da Vinci airport, Rome, June 10. Four nights at the Hotel Teatro di Pompeo. High speed train to Florence on June 14. Three nights at the Hotel Raffaello. Then onto Venice for the final leg, three nights at the Tiziano with a view of the Grand Canal.

A masterpiece created by her smooth-talking, Hawaiian-shirted travel agent, who greeted Gertie that rainy day after the fight as if she were a long-lost friend.

She folded the itinerary neatly and placed it back in the envelope with her passport. Next, she removed the tickets.

There were two sets, one for her and one for Tom—the only possible flaw in the masterpiece. Tom wasn't supposed to be her traveling companion. He had entered the picture only because her first two choices had bailed. Tom was her ward, her responsibility, ever since she promised Hannah to look after him. When she agreed, Gertie had no idea that this big man would be such a big baby. She never backed down though, no sir, not once, mothering the baby as best as she could. But that didn't mean she had to drag him halfway across Europe with her. That wasn't part of the bargain, was it?

Yet maybe she wasn't being entirely honest with herself. She pictured him waiting outside the post office or the grocery story, waiting in the rain with his umbrella. Tom was needy all right, but he was also giving in turn. The truth was, Gertie felt safe around the old firefighter with his large hands. Plus, they had known each other a large chunk of their lives, and even if that knowing didn't mean they were always on the friendliest terms, it had to count for something.

She had better set down some ground rules though. She would have no more of that groping and pawing. If he wanted to drop his drawers, then he'd better do it with someone else. *Uff da.* "Save the honeymoon suite for another client," she'd told the travel agent. "Tom and I are just friends. We'd like our own rooms. Isn't that right, Tom?"

Gertie also wanted to make it clear that she hadn't invited Tom for his money. Not that it was a bad thing he had a little extra saved up, considering how strapped she was at the moment. But Gertie was going on this trip with or without him and would be paying her own way in full. If he wanted to treat her to a meal now and then, she could accept that, as long as there were no strings attached. Gertie was picturing the two of them sitting at an outdoor restaurant next to the Pantheon—carafe of red wine, spaghetti carbonara and veal saltimbocca, cannoli and espresso—when the phone rang.

Corinna opened the door to the roof deck. She was carrying a pail of water and a mop to clean the mess she'd made the night before, when she spotted the old schooner in the Narrows. She wished she had her binoculars. From the activity on the masts and deck, it looked like a set from the movie *Pirates of the Caribbean*. Off to its right was a massive tanker, the *Helmen* from Holland. *That would have been a good one,* she thought. *Not too hard, not too easy.* But no more games. Not for a while, maybe not ever again.

Had someone just exited the Temple? For a second, she thought it might be Maria, but before she could angle herself for a better look, the figure was gone. *Damn you, Maria, I wanted to kill you! You too, Gertie—for allowing her to go behind my back like that!*

The roof deck was a mess: an overturned chair, a crumpled mat, two empty bottles of wine, and a mound of vomit. She barely remembered anything about last night, except that she was burning on the inside and freezing on the outside, and no matter how much she moved and swayed with Johann Sebastian, she couldn't get warm. Even now, with the sun blazing, she still felt a chill.

Corinna set the chair upright, pushed the mat to the side, and mopped up the concrete floor. Her head ached and she had a bad taste in her mouth as she remembered Maria's bombshell: *Vinnie spoke to Henry. Damn you, Maria!*

Even after all these years, she was scared, deathly scared. Who knew what that monster might do if he found her?

Maria also said something before that: *You're not a Hale, Corinna. You were adopted.*

The words were only now beginning to register in the morning light.

Corinna still wasn't sure what to make of it. How could Jonathan and Esther Hale not be her parents? Her earliest memories were with them and no one else: the old rocking bassinet she slept in, once her father's, and after her, Henry's; the red sweater decorated with posies her mother knit for her one Christmas; dinners at the long oak table in the dining room. Her parents were like everyone else in Parkside, maybe somewhat stricter, not as communicative, a little cold even. But that was their way, and it applied to both their children. And if they looked at her differently, it was understandable, since she *was* different, as Henry never failed to remind her.

Your real name is Hoffman, not Hale.

She'd never heard that name before. Never.

Isn't this a good thing?

Could it be that the people she never felt at home with were not really home? Righteous Jonathan who refused to see beyond the surface of things. Meek Esther who never stood up for herself, let alone Corinna. Parents who pitied more than loved her. A brother who wanted her dead.

Corinna tried to cough up the bad taste in her mouth.

If it were true, then who was she and where on earth had she come from?

Hoffman? Who were these Hoffmans, and why would they give her up for adoption? Did she mean as little to them as she did to the Hales? *And why would that be a good thing, Maria? Why? Is there something else you haven't told me?*

Maria's words swirled around her.

Isn't this a good thing?

I don't know. Is it?

Don't you want to know?

No.

Isn't this a good thing?

No.

Don't you want to know?

She thought. She thought hard.

Yes. I want to know.

21

Gertie

"Hello?"

"It's me, Elsa."

"I know who it is," said Gertie, although for a second or so she wasn't sure. Her daughter's voice sounded strange.

"Sorry I keep missing you, but it's been crazy around here."

Crazy around here too, Gertie thought.

"Kari was sick," explained Elsa. "Really sick. She was in the hospital for a week. It was a nightmare. Thank God she's okay now."

"Kari?" Gertie said dryly.

"My baby girl. I wanted to tell you, but thought it would be better in person. We were planning to come to New York for your birthday."

"Yes, well—"

"She'll be three months old next week. I never thought it would happen, especially after what the doctors said. Incredible, huh?"

"Incredible, all right," said Gertie, trying not to sound too uninterested.

"I named her after Grandma Sundersen. Remember how cute she was in her *festbunad*, always so happy, singing to herself while she baked those delicious Norwegian pastries. *Krumkake* was my favorite."

Gertie's favorite too. And yes, she remembered her mother-in-law. "Thank God for Mor Sundersen," Thorvald would say in his passive-aggressive way; she filled in at home whenever the Absentee Mother left for a competition, making sure her granddaughter was entertained and her son was well fed. "Thank God for Mor Sundersen"—now it was Elsa telling her.

"I know what you're thinking, Gertie, but it's not like that. She was a good person. You used to call her Momma. We all loved her. Probably the only thing we ever agreed on."

"Once upon a time, you used to call me Momma too," she said under her breath.

"I hate to do this, Gertie, but we can't come to New York for the party. The doctor doesn't want Kari to travel for a while. I feel terrible."

"I'm sure you do," muttered Gertie.

"You don't believe me?"

"Look, let's not start this again. It doesn't matter anyway. The party's been cancelled."

"Cancelled?"

"Yes, so don't upset yourself about it."

"I wanted to come," said Elsa. "I swear."

Gertie gave a snort of disbelief. She didn't like playing games, but at the moment, she wasn't in the mood to fight. "Fine, I believe you."

"I was never so scared in my life, Gertie. At the beginning, we thought it was a cold. The doctor didn't even prescribe antibiotics, just Tylenol for the fever. But I knew something was wrong when Kari wouldn't take any milk. She just sat there in a daze and kept falling asleep."

That wasn't good.

"Meningitis, the doctor told us when we brought her back. The infection spread to the brain. That's why she wasn't moving."

Uff da.

"Fortunately, it wasn't the worst kind. Kids die from bacterial meningitis. Kari's was viral."

That was good.

"You should have seen the poor thing. They had her in a crib with bars all around, like a cage. IVs in her tiny arms and a tube down her nose so they could feed her. I couldn't even hold her. My baby, my poor baby."

Gertie listened as her daughter began to cry. Who wouldn't cry after what she'd been through? Still, she wasn't used to this side of Elsa. They never did anything but argue when they spoke on the phone. "Are you okay?" she asked.

"The strange part is that, when things were the scariest, I held it together and never cried. Now that Kari is better, I'm a basket case. I can hardly think straight. It would have killed me if something had happened to her. I have nightmares of Kari in that cage, wondering if I took her to the doctor too late . . . if I was feeding her the wrong food or not giving her enough vitamins . . . why it had to be her and not someone else . . . Put me in that fucking cage . . . put John there, I don't care. Anyone but her."

"I understand," Gertie said.

But did she?

It had been over forty years since she was in her daughter's shoes, and maybe she never really was in her shoes. Elsa desperately wanted a child and went through Hula-Hoops with all that fertility crap. Gertie, on the other hand, had been lukewarm about motherhood, at best. From as far back as she could remember, she had one thing on her mind, and everything else, including having kids, took a back seat. And when it happened—completely unplanned and unexpected—her doubts only grew. She was furious at her body's changes during the pregnancy, afraid it would never be the same again. When Elsa was born, Gertie felt weirdly distant, hardly wanting to hold the child or look at her for long. How could she feel that way about her own flesh and blood? Was there something wrong with her?

"Thank God she's all right," said Elsa.

Could Elsa have sensed her ambivalence, even at that early age? It always gnawed at Gertie. Was she a bad mother, like Thorvald said? An absentee mother? Thank God for Mor Sundersen. She was there when Gertie wasn't.

"Thank God," repeated Gertie.

But it wasn't like that forever. At some point, things did change. She remembered their own little medical crisis, nowhere near as serious as Kari's, the day Elsa's finger got jammed underneath the door. Elsa had just started to crawl and was behind the bedroom door when Gertie opened it. She wouldn't stop screaming. Her thumb reddened and swelled like a tomato, although fortunately nothing was broken. The next day, Elsa went right back to exploring, but Gertie was still shaken. Every time she looked at the door, or pictured it in her head, she saw the wounded little finger and a bolt of pain flashed inside her own unwounded finger.

"Gertie, are you still there?"

"I'm here," she answered. Maybe that was when she realized she wasn't so abnormal after all. Even though she often had to leave the house in Mor Sundersen's care, she missed Elsa. She missed the smell and feel of her soft pudgy skin, the way Elsa cooed in her crib and laughed when Gertie made funny faces. She would phone every night and buy her little presents. When she returned home, she'd spend as much time with Elsa as she could, just as much as the other mothers spent with their kids. Why didn't Elsa remember any of that?

"My baby is doing fine," said Elsa. "Isn't that right, Kari?"

"She's with you now?" asked Gertie.

"Sitting in my lap. She just woke up from a nap."

"I shouldn't keep you then—"

"No, it's fine. Hey, Kari, would you like to say hello to your grandmother? Oh, how cute she is! Kari says hello, Gertie."

"Tell her I say hello back."

"You know, Gertie, she has some of your features."

That isn't good.

"Your blue eyes and the dimple in your chin."

What about my big ugly nose? Poor Kari.

"Some of your expressions too."

Her expressions? Would Elsa even remember her expressions? They hadn't seen each other in ages.

"Most important," said Elsa, "she's got your grit, Gertie. A real fighter, my Kari. Isn't that right, darling?"

"A lot of good it did me," muttered Gertie.

"What's that?"

"Nothing."

"I really feel terrible about the party," said Elsa.

"Like I told you, it doesn't matter. The party's been cancelled."

"Why? What happened?"

"I'm going on a cruise instead."

"That sounds fantastic," said Elsa. "I'd choose a cruise over a party any day."

"You would?" Funny, she thought, how Elsa understood her better than her friends.

"Thing is, I really wanted to see you, Gertie. Both Kari and me."

Who did she think she was kidding? "Look, I understand this business with Kari has thrown you for a loop, but—"

"That's not fair, Gertie."

"Come on, let's not pretend. We haven't spoken for years. Why start now?"

Elsa didn't answer right away.

"Because things happen," she finally said. "It's true that Kari's meningitis scared the shit out of me. I just had a baby after almost fifteen years of trying—fifteen years, Gertie—and she was almost taken away from me. But it's not only that. Being a mother has given me a whole new perspective, helped me see things I hadn't seen before. It's also brought back memories of when I was young. Good memories."

So she did have some good memories.

"I had no idea how hard it would be, taking care of a baby. Feeding her every four hours, changing diapers, playing with her—all on practically no sleep. And the worrying, the constant worrying."

Yes, all that, thought Gertie, *and for what?*

"Or how hard being married is sometimes."

Gertie suddenly perked up. "You and John aren't getting along?"

"Sure, we get along. But you know how it is. You think John gets up in the middle of the night? You think he bathes Kari or takes her for a walk? Maybe once in a blue moon, but mostly it falls on me. I have to say, Gertie, he's pretty selfish when it comes to the baby."

She began to wonder whether this was about John or whether it was just another dig at Gertie's questionable mothering skills.

"Was Dad like that?"

Gertie laughed sourly. "What do you want me to say, Elsa, that your father was an angel? You know damn well how I felt about him."

"Yeah, I know."

In truth, thought Gertie, Thorvald wasn't a bad father. His problem was with her, not Elsa. They were married at a young age. Their parents, from nearby villages in Norway, had openly pushed to unite them. He was a handsome man with broad shoulders and strong sharp features, not very talkative, like her father in many ways. It made him attractive, at least at the beginning. But maybe Thorvald never felt the same about her; she certainly wasn't the prettiest girl on the block. Or maybe he liked her for a while and then got turned off because she didn't become the traditional wife he had hoped for, although she certainly never led him to believe she'd be anything of the kind. When the differences started mounting, neither was very good at compromising.

Both believed that they were in the right and wouldn't budge. "John doesn't hurt you, does he?" asked Gertie.

"No, of course not. It's just that we don't always see eye to eye. He wants one thing, I want another, and then we fight."

"Sounds pretty normal to me," said Gertie, which was why—and this she didn't say—the whole marriage idea was for the birds. Two completely different souls with completely different needs trying to get along. Then you throw a child into the mix. *Uff da.*

"The funny part is that you don't see it from the outside," said Elsa. "All my friends tell me how lucky we are, how lucky I am, what a great guy John is."

Always the husband, thought Gertie, shaking her head, *never the wife.* Her parents thought Thorvald was a great catch. They never saw how mean he became when things didn't go his way. He might not have been physically abusive, but he worked hard to make her—and everyone else in the house—feel like she didn't belong.

"Not that he isn't a great guy, Gertie. What I'm trying to say is that I realize now how things aren't so black and white. Maybe I was wrong to take Dad's side all the time."

"Maybe?" Gertie wanted to scream.

"But what I don't understand is why you gave up so easily. When I look at Kari, I can't see anything but her. All of me goes right out the window. I would do anything for her. Anything."

"You think it was easy for me?" said Gertie, her voice rising several notches. "Your father did a lot of bad things, but turning my daughter against me, making her think I was some cold bitch that didn't care one iota, that was despicable. And you believed him and shut me out. What the hell was I supposed to do?"

"I was just a kid then. What did I know about the world?"

True and not so true, thought Gertie. Then again, maybe Elsa wasn't wrong and Gertie had given up too easily. She was hurt and humiliated when Thorvald walked out on her. The only thing left was her pride.

Still, Elsa couldn't lay all the blame on her. She wasn't an innocent kid forever. How many years went by without Elsa ever asking for her side of the story?

"I'm sorry, Gertie. I said I didn't want to judge you, and here I go again. Nothing matters except right now. I have a baby girl, and I want her to see her grandmother."

Gertie didn't respond.

"And I want to see my momma again."

Gertie winced at the sound of the word.

"Good thing your friend is so stubborn."

"You mean Maria?"

"There were times I was pretty rude to her," admitted Elsa. "But she never gave up."

"That's Maria."

"She must be a very good friend. She was able to see past all the bullshit, and she helped me see past it."

Gertie wasn't so sure about that. You didn't get past years of bullshit after a few telephone conversations. But Elsa was right about Maria.

"As soon as you get back from your cruise, Kari and I are coming to New York," promised Elsa. "Where are you going anyway?"

"England and Italy."

"That sounds amazing. You'll have to tell us all about it when we see you."

"Sure."

"One last thing, Gertie."

"Yes?"

"Would you mind if I called you Momma?"

She pressed the phone against her ear, pressed it hard.

"I know it sounds weird after all this time, but we'll get used to it. Okay, Momma?"

"Okay."

After she hung up the phone, Gertie felt light-headed. She wondered whether she had heard her daughter correctly or simply imagined it. And if she hadn't imagined it and her daughter did indeed want to call her Momma, why had it affected her so deeply? She had convinced herself that she didn't need a family. Had she been wrong?

22

Maria

Livy's small, two-story brick house on Eighty-Ninth Street was fewer than ten blocks from Maria's apartment. Vinnie's room sat at the very top, in what used to be an attic. For years, Vinnie had pleaded for more privacy, and his mother, worn down, finally gave in and converted the cluttered storage area into a livable space. The room had low ceilings and a single, small dormer window facing the street, but Vinnie couldn't be happier. No one was allowed up there, including his grandmother, obsessed as she was with keeping her daughter's house clean and tidy.

Maria felt guilty as she climbed the last few stairs and stood before the "No Entry" sign on the door; yet she had to go in and see for herself. Flipping on the light switch, she shuddered. It was even worse than she had imagined. It reminded her of that poor town in Alabama on the news a few weeks back, completely destroyed by the twister. There were clothes everywhere, dishes with leftover food, glasses half-filled, books and papers scattered. And the smell—*mannaggia mia*—was dreadful, like the basement in her building when Manny, the super, forgot to take out the garbage. She headed to the window for some air, so that she could breathe. So that the room could breathe.

Who was this boy? she wondered, surveying the wreckage.

It wasn't long ago that she'd held him in her arms—a soft, round ball of flesh with his clean baby smell and Livy's big brown eyes—and sang to him and rocked him to sleep, her daughter's first and only child. Not long ago, too, that he started crawling and then walking, that he joined Little League and became the best pitcher on the team, that she cheered for him on the sidelines. Gertie and Corinna too. How cute he looked in his baseball uniform. The years had flown by.

Who was this boy now? she wondered again, glancing at the poster above his bed, a scruffy rock star covered in tattoos.

You could hardly see Vinnie's face behind his long brown hair. Or talk to him since he always had headphones on. "He comes and goes like a boarder," complained Livy. "I'm going to start charging him rent."

Maybe, but deep down he was still a good boy. He couldn't possibly be selling drugs. Maria would know. So would Livy. Of course they would.

The computer on Vinnie's desk emitted a low buzzing sound. Maria sat down in front of it and tapped the keyboard. A picture of the Acropolis at sunset appeared on the screen. If only she knew how to use a computer, she could have researched Corinna's past herself and left Vinnie out of it. She'd also be able to find out more about her grandson. But she was clueless about Facebook and Twitter and everything else kids talked about these days.

The desk was cluttered with books and papers and hundreds of little notes. She flipped through them and didn't notice anything suspicious, all having to do with school or friends from school or events at school. So far so good. The desk had two drawers on either side. She glanced at them uneasily. Maria knew this was wrong, but what troubled her even more was the fear of what she might find.

"Ma," shouted Livy from downstairs. "You're not in Vinnie's room, are you?"

She didn't answer.

"Ma?"

She had better say something or Livy might come up to check. She tiptoed down the attic steps. "Of course not," she told her. "I know the rules."

She knew the rules, but she didn't necessarily agree with them. Why should a kid's room be off limits to his mother? Just look at this place—a disaster area that needed to be fumigated before someone got deathly sick. She bet no one had been in there to clean for years.

Maybe Livy, too, was afraid of what she might find.

Back at Vinnie's desk, Maria held her breath as she opened the right-hand drawer. The inside was as chaotic as the rest of the room: batteries, Swiss Army knife, phone book, CDs, letters. She withdrew an envelope on top of the pile. It contained a brochure and application for Harvard. Every time she uttered the name of the school, she felt a tingle at the back of her neck. How proud she was of him, how proud they all were. A perfect score on the PSAT, the best student in his class, and soon the most likely to attend the best college in the world. Beyond their wildest expectations. Where did he get those smarts? A "scholar" was what the Professor called him, one of the smartest boys he had ever taught. *My grandson.*

Cradling the brochure in her hands, Maria felt certain Vinnie was innocent. How could he manage both at the same time, Harvard and drugs? She pictured Corinna with her hookah, slurring her words and swaying like a drunk person. Impossible.

Then why in the world would she accuse him of such things? Was Corinna so upset that she would make up something like that? Or . . .

Maria plunged her hand into the drawer in search of answers but only found more writing implements and a stack of index cards with Greek words on them. There was a photograph of Vinnie and an attractive blonde girl, the new girlfriend, she assumed. Nothing else. Thank God. She could breathe easier. It would be the same with the other drawers, she was sure now.

As relief settled in, Maria's emotion gradually turned to anger. How dare Corinna scare her like that! It was wrong, and Maria, guilty as she felt about her own backhanded behavior, intended to tell her friend.

"Ma," shouted Livy from the kitchen, "how about a cup of coffee?"

That sounded good, she thought, feeling a lot better now than she had twenty minutes ago.

Should she have a peek in the left-hand drawer first?

The second she opened it, an overpowering smell wafted up her nose, smoky with a tinge of sweet. She knew that smell. At the back of the drawer was a crumpled red bandanna. She grabbed it and found a pipe and a brownie-sized rectangle of tin foil underneath, the same sort of thing Corinna brought to the Temple. Maria's heart sank.

So it *was* true. Her grandson wasn't just drinking beer and smoking cigarettes. He was doing drugs. *How could you, Vinnie, with all your talents? How could you?*

Somewhere in the room, a phone began to ring. It seemed to come from under the bed. She bent down on her knees to look just as the ringing stopped. The phone wasn't the only thing under the bed. There was a plastic bag filled with white pills. *What now, Vinnie? Please tell me they're vitamins or aspirin.* She grabbed a pill from the bag. There was no label, only a design like a hieroglyph. Maria's pulse quickened. What would she find next, needles and heroin? *Oh, Vinnie, what have you done?*

"It's Gertie, Ma," shouted Livy from downstairs. "Pick up the phone."

The phone? How could she pick up the phone when she could barely move, let alone speak? She'd like to remain under the bed and never come out, so she wouldn't have to deal with this nightmare. She had no idea how she'd manage.

"Ma, pick up," shouted Livy again.

Maria had no choice but to answer the phone.

"I owe you an apology," said Gertie.

Her friend sounded far away.

"It's horrible," Maria said in a barely audible voice.

"You're right, Maria, and I'm sorry."

She stared at the white pill in her hand. "Horrible."

"I know, that's why I'm calling. To say how sorry I am."

"You could go to jail for this."

"Jail?" said Gertie.

"Yes, jail," she answered.

"Maria, are you all right? You're not making any sense."

"No, I'm not all right," she said, starting to cry.

"What are you crying for?" asked Gertie. "I'm admitting it was my fault, that I shouldn't have gotten so mad at you. But a crime that I could go to jail for? I don't think so. I just didn't want you meddling, but maybe I was wrong. Elsa called today, Maria. We spoke for almost an hour."

"Horrible." Maria said it louder this time.

"*Uff da*, Maria. You're the one who wanted us to speak, not me. And now I'm telling you that maybe you were right. Not that I'm ready to welcome Elsa back with open arms. No way, not after all this time. But it was different, this last phone call. We actually had a conversation. A real conversation. I'm still having trouble believing it."

Maria wasn't listening. She couldn't take her eyes off the pill. "It's all true."

"You really think so, Maria? That people can change—"

"He's a drug addict."

"What?"

"I'm holding the proof in my hand."

"Proof?"

"I'm in his room now. Under the bed."

"Under the bed? Whose bed? What the hell are you talking about, Maria?"

"Aren't you listening to a word I'm saying? It's all true, just like Corinna said. I found hash in his desk and pills under the bed. He's a drug addict, my grandson. A drug addict, Gertie, do you hear what I'm saying?" Her voice was cracking.

"Yes, now I understand."

"What am I supposed to do?"

Gertie exhaled deeply. "First thing, Maria, you need to calm down. There might be an explanation. Finding a few pills in his room doesn't mean Vinnie's a drug addict."

"It doesn't?"

"For all you know, they're not even his. And even if they are, Vinnie is a junior in high school with lots of free time on his hands. I bet all the kids at his age do crazy things. I'm not saying it's right, but it's hardly criminal."

"He's also selling drugs, Gertie, him and his friend from school. Where do you think Corinna gets her hash?"

"What? You're not serious?"

"I'm serious, all right."

"Wow, that's surprising even for Corinna, not to say anything about it. But we have to get the facts straight before jumping to conclusions. You should talk to Livy. Maybe she knows something. If you want, I could come over to be there when you tell her."

Maria felt dizzy, rising from the floor, and had to sit on Vinnie's bed to steady herself. She didn't know whether to scream or cry. "I can't tell Livy," she said, "not right now at least."

"You found drugs in her son's room. How can you keep that from her? She'd never forgive you."

Gertie might be right. Livy was still mad at Maria for waiting so long to tell her about Vinnie's joyrides with her car.

"Your call, Maria, but whatever you decide, I'm ready to help."

Maybe there was an explanation, she told herself after hanging up the phone. Vinnie was still a kid, just like Livy was once a kid who did some stupid things. She remembered the day she got a call from the bike shop down the block. Livy had walked out with a scooter. She was ten at the time, and when Maria arrived, she was standing on the corner staring down at her sneakers. She wouldn't look up, even after Maria settled with the owner and they were on their way home. She was terrified her father would find out and throw a fit. But Maria knew she didn't have to say anything, neither to her daughter nor her husband. Livy had learned her lesson, just like she did the time she got caught cheating at school. She turned out just fine in the end. So would Vinnie, right?

She stopped in the bathroom before going downstairs, threw some water on her face, and fixed her hair. She didn't want Livy to see her upset.

Her daughter was sitting at the kitchen table, reading the *Daily News* and sipping coffee.

"There's plenty left, Ma," said Livy without looking up. "I just made it."

"So," Maria asked casually, "where's Vinnie today?"

"Greek lesson, I think."

"Did he say when he'll be back?"

"You're kidding, right? That boy doesn't tell me anything unless he wants something." Livy shook her head. "I don't get it," she said, turning back to the newspaper. "I thought the Greeks were supposed to be smart. So why is their country going down the tubes, on the verge of bankruptcy, credit rating in the toilet? Maybe Vinnie ought to be studying some other language, like Chinese. That's where the future is."

The future, thought Maria, suddenly overwhelmed with doubt again. Vinnie had such a bright one, but who knew what would happen now. Livy might have had a few close calls when she was a kid, but those were minor infractions in the scheme of things. Drugs were in a different league altogether.

"Ma, take a load off. You're making me nervous standing there."

Maria told her she couldn't. She had errands to run.

"By the way, what's up with the trip?" asked Livy. "I wanted to ask Gertie, but she was so anxious to talk to you, I couldn't get a word in edgewise. I thought I'd send you as a birthday present. You're turning seventy-five in the fall and deserve something special."

Maria had no desire to go away.

"I know you don't like spending your money—"

"I said no, Livy."

"It would be good for you, Ma."

"I can't." She started to cry.

"Jesus, Ma, why are you crying?"

Maria grew more and more confused. She didn't want to say anything to Livy but now wondered if she really had a choice. Inside the pocket in her dress was the bag of pills she'd found under Vinnie's bed. Slowly, she withdrew the bag and laid it on the kitchen table. "I found them in his room."

Livy stared at the pills. "What the hell are those?"

Maria wasn't sure.

"Wait a minute," said Livy, flinging the bag off the table as if it were beside the point. "You were in his room?"

She didn't answer.

"You saw the sign, didn't you?"

"Yes, but—"

"'No Entry.' Pretty self-explanatory, don't you think?" said Livy, pinching her fingers together and shaking her hand in the air. "Goddamn it, Ma, why the hell are you always going into places you're not allowed?"

"I only meant . . . to help." Maria was having a hard time speaking.

Livy slammed the newspaper down on the table and rose to her feet. She was furious, anger pouring from her body, her arms shaking violently. "Help? That's what you think you're doing around here?"

Yes, she wanted to say.

"I don't need your help, Ma. Actually, you're killing me with all your help. This is my house. *My house*. Not yours. You hear me?"

"Please, Livy," begged Maria, holding out her hand, which now shook even more than her daughter's.

"Turn around and leave, Ma. Just go home."

23

Corinna

"I'm impressed, Corinna."

The sound of his voice made her jump.

"A grand tour of the classics, beginning with Hesiod and Homer, then moving through the great tragedians and on to the golden age of Roman poetry: Virgil, Horace, Catullus, Propertius."

Slowly she looked up to find the Professor standing in front of the stacks near the library entrance. Dressed in scholarly tweeds and a bow tie, he was inspecting the new Latin and Greek section.

"Even a few specialist editions like Ennius and Livius Andronicus. All in all, an excellent, rather comprehensive collection," he said, walking toward her desk.

Corinna's pulse quickened. She couldn't help it, even though she had tried to convince herself that her feelings for this man had been foolish, ridiculous, laughable. She'd tried hard.

"You may be the only one who's impressed," she said.

"I'm used to it," he shrugged. "A classicist in the age of Twitter—it's not easy."

Yet the gods showed no mercy, a mischievous Cupid lighting a fire in her bones all over again. And she was powerless to resist, a naive Queen Dido filling up with hope.

"Not for me either," she said. "For what it's worth."

"I know that, Corinna, which is why we are simpatico. We see eye to eye on so many things."

That was precisely what she once thought. He was impressed by her, and she by him. "You don't really think that, Professor, do you?"

He smiled. "I do."

"But not as simpatico as you and Maria."

"Au contraire, Corinna."

"I don't think so."

"Attraction is a mystery," said the Professor. "It wasn't Virgil or Homer that drew me to Maria."

"That's for sure," she sneered.

The Professor looked at Corinna sideways. "I thought you were friends."

Clearly, he had no idea. How could a man of such intelligence be so thick?

"The night of the book party at the Brooklyn Historical Society, you introduced us. Maria was wearing a green dress that went magnificently with her red hair. They had a swing band and we danced. She was an excellent dancer, elegant yet in a most unassuming and modest way. A very attractive combination. I couldn't get her out of my mind afterward. That's why I was excited when you invited me to speak at the Senior Center."

Corinna felt her insides twisting. She thought it was because of her that he had come, not Maria.

"You saw right through me." He smiled.

His words sliced right through her. Like Dido, her heart was *desueta*: unpracticed and unaccustomed. She saw nothing, just as he saw nothing. Corinna was invisible to the Professor.

"What a marvelous picture," he exclaimed, examining Joe Flannery's portrait hanging on the wall above her desk. "It's you, Corinna, the spitting image. Your quickness. *Podos Okos*, as Homer describes Achilles in *The Iliad*. Fleet of foot."

Corinna frowned as he waxed on about the painting. The fire in her body had now been thoroughly doused a second time. There wasn't a shred of desire left among the ashes. It had been replaced by anger. How had she ever fallen for such a man? *You're right, Joe, he isn't worth it.*

"A quickness that is both physical and intellectual," he continued, "powering along on your Vespa and mastering Virgil's hexameters—"

"What are you doing here, Professor?" she stopped him. She had just about enough of him and his empty words.

"I'm here for two reasons," he said, turning away from the picture. "First, considering your new literary interests, I wanted to invite you to join Vincent and me for our Greek sessions."

He couldn't be serious.

"I'm certain you'd enjoy Homer, just as you've enjoyed Virgil. Will you at least consider it?"

"And second?" she asked impatiently.

"The second item is a bit more sensitive," he said. "I wanted to talk to you about history, Corinna. Your history."

She turned red.

"I realize we don't know each other well and . . ."

Was it possible that the Professor had been researching her past too? That her personal life might be part of his study sessions with Vinnie? She wanted to scream.

". . . and that this is none of my business—"

"You're damn right," she finally blurted out. "Did Maria send you here?"

"Of course not. She has no idea. I came because I wanted to, because this is yet another instance of our simpatico, Corinna. We may be even more closely aligned than I had imagined."

There was no end to the man's insolence. Her heart might be screwed up, but he was without heart altogether. "What are you talking about?"

"May I sit?" he asked, and without waiting for an answer, he pulled a chair over to the side of Corinna's desk and sat down. "Indulge me for a minute, Corinna, I want to tell you a story."

"I'm really not in the mood."

"Then I must insist." He stared at her intently, his hazel eyes sparkling. "It's important. You will see that soon enough, I promise."

"You better make it fast, Professor. I don't have all day."

"The story begins in the city of Munich in the 1930s," he told her. "That's where I was born and spent the first six years of my life. Our family lived at Lindenstrasse 48, two blocks from the Marienplatz. Our apartment was on the third floor of the building, reached by one of those grand, old circular stairways. My room was small and unimposing, but I imagined it to be the lookout tower of a grand castle. It was also the only room in the apartment with a window facing the street. One morning, peering out of my medieval turret in search of marauders, I witnessed a much more real and horrific scene. A squadron of brownshirts dragged my father out of his butcher shop on the ground floor and beat him with clubs."

"I don't understand," she said. "Why are you telling me . . . ?"

"Because it relates to you. I know this sounds convoluted, but please bear with me."

Corinna tapped her index finger against the desk.

"It was 1936. Hitler had been in power for three years and had already enacted the race laws. In a way, the vandalism and beating were positive things. Because of this incident, my father woke up to what was happening in Germany much sooner than most other Jewish families. He decided the only option was to leave the country as quickly as possible, and although we didn't have much money, he somehow managed to obtain the required permits. Four weeks later, we boarded a train to

Hamburg, and soon after, we were passengers on a ship bound for New York. I was six years old at the time, and despite what I'd witnessed, I cried every step of the way. I didn't want to leave my castle, my friend and fellow Teutonic knight, Peter, who lived upstairs, and, most of all, the bicycle my parents had bought for me for my birthday. It was a Fichtel and Sachs, the best kind in those days, bright red with wheels that went forward and backward. How I loved that bicycle and hated my parents for making me part with it." The Professor laughed. "Can you imagine?"

Corinna tapped faster. "I still don't see what this has to do with me."

"Because I know you to be a person interested in history, Corinna, and the smallest details of history, like the Tuscan stones that found their way into the tower of the Verrazzano Bridge. As it happens, my history may not be much different from yours."

"What's that supposed to mean?"

The Professor leaned in closer to the desk and put his hand on her arm. "You were on a ship too, Corinna. Only your ship, the *Bodegraven*, left from Holland four years later, in 1940. You were just under two years old at the time and traveling without your family."

Corinna swallowed hard as if something were stuck at the back of her throat.

"You don't remember?" he asked.

No, she didn't remember.

"Unfortunately, I don't have all the facts at the moment, but if you'll allow me, I'll do whatever I can to fill in the details. We are *Landsmann*, Corinna Hoffman." He pronounced her surname with a German accent—*Hawf-mahn*—and laid his hand on top of hers.

She wanted to pull away, but he tightened his grip.

"Not just because we are both German," continued the Professor, "but because we are both German Jews."

"Jews?" said Corinna, jerking backward. "I'm sorry, but your story is sounding more ridiculous by the minute."

"Maybe, but I'm almost certain it is true. The *Bodegraven* was used by the Kindertransport to help Jewish children escape from Nazi Germany. You were on that ship, Corinna."

No, it wasn't possible. It didn't seem right to her. None of it. When she looked backward in time, returning to her earliest memories, she saw only the house in Parkside, a two-story white colonial, the rocking horse and swing set in the backyard behind the dogwood tree, the Congregationalist church next door. The church where her father had preached the gospel and she had attended Sunday school. *Jewish?*

"I realize this is a lot of information to process, but there's no other way to interpret the facts."

Corinna didn't believe him. "Then what about my parents? Where were they in 1940? And why would they send me away by myself?"

"To save you from the Nazis. But you're right to ask these questions, Corinna, and I only wish I had all the answers." The Professor explained that, for the most part, the Kindertransport records were highly accurate and detailed, matching children's names to their parents and the towns they came from. Only not in her case. "Your name is on the passenger manifest, but there is no accompanying documentation about your family or place of origin. Vincent tried to search for any Hoffmans in the German-speaking countries—Hoffmans who were also Jewish and had a daughter named Corinna—but, so far, he's come up empty."

"Maybe there's nothing to find, Professor. Maybe it's all a big mistake."

"It's not," said the Professor. "There was a passenger on the *Bodegraven* named Corinna Hoffman who landed in Harwich on May 16, 1940. She spent several months at a facility in London until a placement was arranged with the Hale family in Parkside, Massachusetts. That much we know for certain."

"But I have no recollection of this. None whatsoever."

The Professor nodded sympathetically. "From what I read, Corinna, that's not surprising. You were a baby, and being separated from your mother at that age is traumatic. The majority of those who never saw their birth parents again don't retain any memories of their former lives. It's a natural defense mechanism."

Corinna was having trouble swallowing again.

"What I don't understand is how you got on that boat without the proper documentation. Keeping accurate records was the only way parents had a chance of finding their children at the end of the war."

She shook her head.

"That doesn't mean we can't sort it all out, Corinna. Just give me the word and I will help you. Vincent too. The truth is, he's the one who obtained most of this information. He's very skilled on the internet, which is not merely an infinite source of knowledge, as I've come to learn, but also a powerful means to connect with other people. If there's any hope of tracking down your family, we're going to need him. You do want to learn about your history, don't you?"

Corinna didn't know how to respond. She was confused by this barrage of information, overwhelmed, and wasn't sure what to believe. On the other hand, something about it—something she felt deep inside but couldn't quite put her finger on—made her unwilling to dismiss it outright. She recalled Maria's words: "Isn't this a good thing?" Corinna had spent most of her adult life erasing her history. If there was a possibility of an alternative, a completely different history, wouldn't she want to know about it?

"Yes," she finally answered.

"Excellent," said the Professor. "Then we won't stop until we learn everything." He reached for the manila envelope he'd brought with him, only it wasn't in his jacket pocket or on the floor next to him. Confused for a moment, he rose and returned to the classics section of the library, where he retrieved the envelope he'd left on one of the shelves. "This is what we've collected so far. Look it over and let me know if anything stands out."

The envelope was heavy, crammed with so much paper that it didn't close properly. She felt its weight pressing against her palms. Inside, supposedly, lay the proof that she wasn't who she thought she was, that a major part of her life had been concealed from her. Inside this ordinary-appearing manila envelope. Just thinking about it made her queasy.

"Why?" she suddenly asked him.

"Excuse me?"

"Why are you doing this, Professor?"

He tilted his head to the side. "Because you are my friend."

The word stung for a second. So that was what he considered her, despite all his talk of their being simpatico? A friend.

"I hope you feel the same about me," said the Professor.

She looked up and studied his face. There was no trace of meanness or sarcasm. He seemed sincere, not the heartless man she saw a moment ago. But could she ever think of him as a friend? Would she even want to? Especially if he and Maria . . .

"I'm excited about where this will lead, Corinna. I'm excited for you."

There was nothing in his expression to suggest he didn't mean it. And wasn't the stuffed envelope she held in her hands proof? In a way, it was a kind of swap. With one hand he had taketh, and with the other he had giveth.

"You put a lot of work into this," she said, trying to focus on the promise that resided inside the envelope.

The Professor smiled.

"I guess I should thank you."

"The person you should thank is Maria. I know you were upset that she started this without your approval, but I can assure you, she recognizes her mistake and truly regrets it. And remember, if she hadn't acted on her instincts, you would still be in the dark."

Corinna was gradually beginning to appreciate that, even though she was still angry with Maria.

"She has a good heart, Maria."

Corinna laughed. "Santa Maria."

"What's that?"

"Nothing."

"Excellent. Then I'll be in touch, Corinna," he said, bowing before he turned to go.

Just as he was leaving the library, she called to him. "You know, Professor, you're right about Maria. Somehow she manages to be both elegant and modest at the same time. Though maybe 'simple' is a better word. A big-hearted person with simple taste."

He nodded.

Corinna took a deep breath. She found it difficult to continue, but holding the envelope in her hand, she felt compelled. "Remember that about her and try not to go too heavy on the Latin poetry. The *Aeneid* bores her to tears. What she really likes is the cannoli at the Norwegian bakery on Third Avenue and watching the ships in the Narrows pass beneath the Verrazzano Bridge. And whatever you do, take it slow. Maria is very traditional. She talks about her dead husband as if they were still dating."

He smiled. "Thank you, Corinna. I'll keep that in mind."

24

The Temple

Gertie had given her friends an ultimatum last week, threatening to swear off the Temple for good if they didn't comply with her wishes, which they sure as hell hadn't, and yet that's exactly where she intended to go this Tuesday morning, two weeks before her trip to Europe. How could she not, after everything that had happened in the past few days: Maria spilling the beans on Vinnie's drug operation; Corinna's discovery that she was once a Jewish refugee from Germany; and she herself speaking to her daughter again after all these years? These were her best friends, regardless of their scheming behind her back. There was no way she could leave Bay Ridge without their blessing.

Gertie looked over at Elsa's letter on the kitchen table. Should she bring the picture of Kari with her? It was true what Elsa had said on the phone, she thought as she removed the picture from the envelope—Kari did have Gertie's blue eyes and the same dimple on her chin. *How will you turn out, little Kari? Like your grouchy old grandmother? Or your momma, who forgot she ever had a momma? Before you lies a vast, open plain that stretches on forever and ever. Only it doesn't, and it's not always easy. For your sake, I hope it's filled with everything you wish for, love most of all. It would be a shame if you had to do it all alone, like your grandma.*

Grandma. It had a nice ring to it.

But Gertie wasn't as delusional as Maria in this regard. *They take a lot more than they give, these kids. You may not see it, Maria, but I do. I've watched you over the years, slaving away for your daughter and grandson, only to see it blow up in your face. Vinnie isn't speaking to you, am I right? And Livy threw you out of her house. What was it she said? "Turn around and leave, Ma. Just go home."*

Naturally, I tried to reassure you, that Livy lost her temper and didn't really mean it. Who wouldn't be mad after finding out that her golden child had a nasty secret? But that was only part of it, Maria. The old dog becomes a burden after a while. Can't you see that?

Poor Maria, too good for her own good. Gertie had promised to walk with her to the Temple, hoping to cheer her up before leaving for Europe. She dropped the picture of Kari into her bag. It would put a smile on Maria's face, probably bigger than her own when she first saw it. Plus, she'd wear the hat Tom bought her for the upcoming trip. It was made with a special protective coating, he assured her, so that she wouldn't get another skin cancer. That might be true, but the straw hat with the oversized brim and chin strap was ugly as sin. It made her look like a clown, and the only reason to wear it, she decided as she placed it on her head, was to get a good laugh out of the girls.

She had better take one of the nerve pills before she left. The attacks had been getting worse lately, a fluttering in her chest that made her feel light-headed. She experienced them several times a day. The cardiologist said it wasn't her heart though. "Most likely stress, Mrs. Sundersen, and maybe even a component of depression. It happens to people at your age," he told her, handing her a sample container of the latest antidepressant from his medicine cabinet. "Depressed," she snapped back, "are you kidding? I never felt better." But now she started to wonder, since the nerve pills seemed to help, even if her cardiologist was a ninny.

Maria was waiting in the lobby when she arrived. If anyone looked depressed, it was Maria. Maybe *she* ought to take some of the doctor's sample pills. But it might not be necessary, since the hat appeared to be doing the trick. The minute she saw it, Maria's face brightened.

"Nice, huh?" asked Gertie. "If you play your cards right, I'll get you one. It protects you from ultraviolet radiation. Incoming Scud missiles too."

Maria smiled.

"How you holding up?" Gertie asked as they started down Shore Road.

"Okay, I guess," answered Maria. "Livy called to apologize. You were right, she didn't mean what she said about not wanting me around. But it's hard to know if that's true."

"You could still come to Europe," offered Gertie.

"No," Maria said, "I can't. Vinnie's problems will only complicate Livy's life further, and who will be here if she needs a hand? I have to stay in Bay Ridge, now more than ever. Besides, I wouldn't want to spoil the fun for you and Tom."

"Then we can make it a double date," said Gertie coyly. "You can bring along the Professor. Corinna tells me he has a thing for you. Personally, I thought she'd be better suited for the old geezer, but she claims she's not interested, not interested at all."

"Neither am I," said Maria.

"That's not what I heard. According to Corinna, you've been spending a lot of time with him lately."

"Who else am I supposed to spend time with?" asked Maria. "In case you've forgotten, the two of you deserted me—my best friends—just like that. Well, the Professor happened to be there when you weren't."

"Happened to be there?" Gertie snorted in disbelief.

"I was a mess when I left the Temple. He helped me get through that day. Believe me, I was surprised too. He turned out to be a lot nicer than I imagined."

"Oh, I bet!" said Gertie.

"Then I found the drugs in Vinnie's room and Livy went berserk. I felt like I was drowning. I needed someone to talk to."

Gertie looked surprised. "You didn't tell the Professor about the drugs, did you?"

"No, of course not. God forbid the Professor backs out of his promise to help Vinnie with Harvard. Besides, I don't know exactly what's happening with Vinnie myself. Livy says she's taking care of it, and I'm afraid to press her."

"I'm sure Livy will explain everything in time," said Gertie.

As they approached the end of Shore Road, just before the footpath, the glare from the sun became so bright that Maria had to shield her eyes. "Maybe I'll need one of those hats after all."

"I don't know how I've managed all these years without one," said Gertie. "Not only is it stylish—according to my very own knight in shining armor—but also a real lifesaver." She took off the monstrosity and began to dance, the two-step Maria had been practicing in her dance class at the Greek church.

"You're too much, Gertie," said Maria. "But you look great. The bruising around your eye is almost gone, and I can barely see the scab anymore. I think you look better now than before all this started."

Gertie grabbed the sides of her face and lifted her sagging cheeks. "I didn't want to tell you"—she winked at Maria—"but I had some work done in lieu of the cancer surgery. A little nip and tuck. Nice, huh?"

"More than nice. *Bellissima!* I only wish I could be with you to celebrate your birthday."

Gertie waved her off. "You'll just have to wait until I get back. We can go to your favorite place in Atlantic City. The Taj, right? Why don't you book a room for us, one with a view of the ocean?"

"Yes," agreed Maria. "That's just what I'll do."

Maria linked arms with Gertie and together they made their way down the footpath. They crossed the grassy area where two little soccer players were kicking a ball, the same ones from the other day, then climbed the small hill leading to the enclosure. When they arrived at the Temple, they were surprised to find it empty. No mat, no incense, no decoration. Just a few discarded beer cans. That was odd, thought Maria, checking her watch; they had agreed to meet today at the regular time.

"I hope Corinna's okay," said Maria, "with all this being thrown at her."

"Do you think she knows more than she's letting on?" asked Gertie.

Maria shook her head. "You weren't there when I told her about the adoption. She looked like she might go into one of her fits. No, she had no idea. I also worry about what the Professor told me, that very few of the Kindertransport children have any remaining relatives left in Europe. Most were killed in the concentration camps. I hope that's not the case with Corinna."

"So horrible," said Gertie.

"Everything about it is horrible. Almost seventy years of thinking she was one person, only to find out she's someone else. I can't begin to imagine what that might feel like. I just hope that once she gets used to the idea, there will be some comfort in it. Those people in Massachusetts weren't very nice to her."

"I hope so too," said Gertie, taking Maria's hand and leading her to the old stone bench. "Come, let's have a look while we wait. In two weeks, I'll be out there on the water, strolling along the promenade of the *Queen Mary* as it moves down the Narrows. Aren't you a little jealous?"

Maria smiled.

"Aren't you curious what it's like on the other side, on the water looking at the land? What it's like to see the bridge from below, to almost touch it with your hands? And the open sea, Maria, the open sea—all these years we've been marveling and imagining. Don't you want to be there in its midst, to feel it on your skin?" Gertie closed her eyes and took a deep breath. "You can smell it, Maria. The smell of the beginning and the end." She opened her eyes. "That's what Corinna once said, remember? I think it was a quote from one of her books."

The only thing Maria smelled was the faint odor of discarded beer cans, and it made her sad. Ever since their chance encounter years ago, she and Gertie had been best friends, attuned in a way she'd never been with another person. They loved spending time together, walking side by side along the shore, eating together at Sancho's on Third Avenue, laughing at the way the waiter pronounced paella as if it had a *j* in the middle rather than two *l*'s. They could almost always tell what the other was thinking before she thought it. Suddenly, all that had changed. Somehow Gertie got infected with the restlessness bug while Maria remained immune. Maria had no desire to leave Bay Ridge and was perfectly content to continue marveling and imagining from the shoreline.

"Come away with me, Maria."

"I can't," she said, her voice faltering. Would they ever be that close again?

Just then Corinna bounded into the enclosure with her helmet strapped to her head. "You're not going to believe this," she said, glancing from Gertie to Maria and back. "I have a sister in Germany. She lives in Eisenach. The same town where Johann Sebastian Bach was born." She bobbed up and down, barely pausing between sentences. "The Professor just called. Vinnie found her on Facebook. *My* sister. Can you believe it?"

As the news sank in, Maria could hardly contain herself. It was exactly what she had been hoping for.

"That's incredible," said Gertie. "Have a seat on the bench and tell us everything."

But as soon as she sat down, Corinna was on her feet again. She had forgotten her bag of goodies in the Vespa. The wine and cakes and incense. How could they celebrate without them? She'd be back in a second, she told them.

Maria was delighted by the smile on Corinna's face as she sped off. There was no trace of the anger that had consumed her the last time they were together at the Temple. Now that things appeared to be working out, maybe she'd be able to forgive Maria for her meddling.

As she climbed the footpath, Corinna felt the hammering in her chest that had started with the phone call from the Professor and hadn't let up since. Before the call, she had been in a trancelike state, reviewing the papers in the manila envelope over and over again. None of it seemed real: Hoffman. Germany. Kindertransport. Nazis. *Bodegraven.* England. Jewish. She wandered around the Center in a haze, trying to make sense of the bizarre details. She struck up a conversation with Alice Rosenberg, an émigré from Budapest and the only member of her family to survive Auschwitz, to see if anything clicked. But nothing clicked, neither Alice's thick Hungarian accent nor the black-and-white photographs of the old country hanging in her room. This morning, she accompanied Saul Cohen to the Bay Ridge Jewish Center and watched a handful of people in caps and shawls chant the morning prayers. There, too, everything seemed completely foreign.

Then came the call.

"Corinna, are you sitting down?" asked the Professor. "It looks like Vincent's efforts have been rewarded. He has made contact with a Joanna Neuman in Eisenach, Germany, whose mother's maiden name was Hoffman. The mother was born in Berlin in 1941 and had a sister three years older than her, named Corinna. Corinna Hoffman."

Is it possible?

"I'm almost certain Joanna's mother is your sister."

Almost?

"There are still a few inconsistencies we're trying to sort out. I mentioned the incomplete ship documentation for one. But the names, places, and timelines match up perfectly."

Is it possible?

"And she's most eager to speak to you."

She is?

"Once we're absolutely sure, Vincent will arrange a call with your sister."

My sister. My *sister.*

When she reached Shore Road, Corinna found her Vespa parked in the street with the engine still running. In her excitement, she had left the keys in the ignition. Thank God no one had taken off with it. She removed the keys, grabbed her tote from the basket, and placed the helmet inside.

There was so much more she wanted to know, so many questions she hadn't asked the Professor: what her sister's name was, whether her parents were still alive, if she had any other relatives—cousins, nieces, nephews—and so much more, if she could only think straight.

No matter. The haze was lifting on this strange, new chapter of her life. It was gradually becoming more and more real, something she might soon be able to see and touch. The Hales were not her parents, Henry not her brother. It made sense now why she never felt like she belonged, why there was always a distance between them. They were not related, not her blood.

Just like she never truly belonged in this country. She was German, not American. Her sister lived in the same town as her favorite composer. Bach's music had animated and fed her soul as far back as she could remember. And hadn't she always felt a special affinity for ships and the sea, the place where everything began and ended? As it turned out, in fact, her earliest adventure was crossing the Atlantic on a ship. It made sense all right. Maybe not the Jewish part so much, but hopefully, that would, too, in time. Her heart, she was certain, wouldn't stop hammering until she spoke to her sister and found out every single detail about herself and her family.

Corinna sprinted down the footpath for the second time that afternoon, her tote swinging by her side, the bottle of wine banging against her hip.

Reaching the enclosure, she immediately started clearing away empty cans, laying out the mat, lighting incense candles. "Now we're ready to celebrate," she said, holding up a bottle of white wine. "It's a riesling from the Rhine region in Germany, not far from where my sister lives." She poured them each a glass. "What shall we toast today?" she asked, looking over at Maria. "I know. We'll toast family." Corinna thrust her right hand in the air, fingers pinched together. *"La famiglia."*

Gertie repeated the gesture with even more gusto. "You said it, Corinna," she cheered, taking the picture from her purse, "and in that same spirit, let me introduce you to Kari, my new granddaughter."

"She's adorable," said Maria. "With a lot of you in her, I see. The eyes and—"

"I know, I know. The chin."

"She has the same little dimple. I can't wait to meet her, Gertie." Maria smiled deliriously. "What about your sister, Corinna? Does she have any children?"

"She has a daughter."

"Then that would make you an aunt," said Maria. "So now we have Grandma Gertie and Aunt Corinna!"

"Whatever you say, Maria. Here, have another glass of wine. It's not too sweet, is it?"

"No, it's perfect."

Corinna sat down on the mat and poured another glass for Gertie and then herself. "I don't know what to say, Maria. Last week, I wanted to kill you. The thought of Vinnie digging up old memories, my parents and brother. The thought of Henry knowing where I lived and worked, that he might show up on my doorstep at any moment and ruin everything." Corinna pumped her fists in the air.

"I'm sorry."

"Don't be," said Corinna in a calmer voice. "Actually, it's I who should be apologizing, Maria. I'm sorry for losing my temper and being so mean. I know you were only trying to help. Just do me a favor—from now on, will you please consult with me before you do anything crazy like that again?"

"I promise," said Maria.

"*Grazie.* Then as the Bard once said, 'All's well that ends well.' Better than well in fact. You see, Maria, you've been right all along. The smartest one in our group. Family *is* the most important thing."

Gertie glanced at the picture of her granddaughter. "I have to admit, I'm coming around to the idea myself."

"You're not mad, Maria?" asked Corinna.

"Of course not."

Corinna leapt up and, uncharacteristically, planted a kiss on Maria's cheek. "I have something for you." She took a cannoli out of the tote and placed it in her hand. "I'm going to make it up to you, Maria, I promise. We'll pick up where we left off in the *Aeneid*."

"Oh please, not that again."

"Don't worry, this time I'll make it more fun. I also want to introduce you to some of the Latin love poets."

"Why in the world—"

"To put you in the mood, Maria," she winked at her.

"The mood?"

Gertie croaked like a frog. "Another great idea, Corinna." She rose from the bench and took a formal bow in imitation of the Professor. Even Maria laughed.

"And don't think I forgot you, Grandma Gertie," said Corinna, plunging her hand into the tote and withdrawing a piece of sponge cake topped with whipped cream and blueberries. "Bluekaka," she said while sticking in eight candles, one for each decade. "We're celebrating a little early. Happy birthday, Gertie."

"It's called *blotkake*," Gertie corrected her. "My father's favorite. My mother used to make it every year for his birthday. You can serve it with any kind of fruit. He liked apricots. *Gratulerer med dagen, Pappa.*"

Gertie took a bite of the cake. It was delicious. Her father's birthday came in April, and when the weather was nice, they would eat in the backyard. Early in the morning, they would stop by the fish market in Sheepshead Bay and pick out the biggest lobsters they could find. Her father would grill them on the barbecue, and afterward, they would have *blotkake*. Except the one time that Archie, their golden retriever, climbed onto the kitchen counter and devoured the birthday cake while they were eating their lobsters. Poor Archie was up all night vomiting.

"Gertie, are you okay?" asked Maria.

Gertie didn't answer.

"You look pale," observed Corinna.

"The cake," cried Maria. "Maybe it got stuck and she's choking."

"Oh my God, not again."

Maria moved behind Gertie and wrapped her arms around her. Corinna inserted her fingers into Gertie's mouth. Maria began to squeeze. She squeezed harder.

All this time, Gertie was shaking her head. She wanted to tell them that it wasn't the cake, but she couldn't talk, she couldn't make a sound. The giant hand was clamping down on her shoulder again, as it did that night at the Center during bingo. She wanted to tell them, but she couldn't talk, and the hand kept tightening around her chest like a vise. It was getting harder to breathe. She *couldn't* breathe.

Corinna suddenly realized what was happening. "Gertie isn't choking, Maria, she's having a heart attack. Stop squeezing and run for help."

Corinna positioned Gertie on the bench with her chin up, just as she'd learned at the many CPR sessions she'd attended over the years at the Center. She blew into her mouth, five quick breaths. Then two chest compressions. She continued to alternate between blowing and compressions for what seemed like hours until she heard the sirens. A minute later, a team of EMTs rushed into the Temple with their rescue equipment and pushed her aside.

PART III

25

Gertie

She was swimming fast, faster than she ever swam. She could feel the muscles snapping as her arms spun in the air and her legs seesawed in a strong, steady rhythm, so that she was no longer fighting the water, it seemed, but skimming above it. One fluid movement, her father would say, like a fish. But when she glanced to her left, she saw Lily Waters ahead by a few strokes. Even her best might not be good enough today. She'd need a big turn and thrust on the final lap, then to swim with everything she had. *No, with more,* she heard Coach Sully roaring on the sidelines. *More.* She closed her eyes and willed herself forward. Flipping over at the turn, she slammed down on the wall and pushed off hard. Her arms spun around faster and faster, her legs kicked harder and harder, and when she was two arm lengths from the finish line, she shot both hands out and lunged ahead, straining and stretching all the way down to the tips of her fingers, as she reached for the wall . . .

—

"When was the last time you checked on her?" the head nurse asked her colleague. "She looks agitated and her pulse is up. Run the blood pressure monitor again."

The younger nurse walked to the panel at the head of the bed and pressed one of the buttons. A second later the cuff on Gertie's left arm began to inflate. "It's high, 160 over 100."

"I figured. Better page the doctor. They may need to raise her meds."

The head nurse watched Gertie's eyes flutter. "Are you in pain, dear?" she asked her silent patient. She adjusted Gertie's head on the pillow, straightened her breathing tube, and checked the flow on the IV line. She noted the crusted patch under her left eye, recorded in the chart as a skin cancer. "The least of your problems at the moment, I suspect." The nurse dipped her finger into the Vaseline jar on the bedside table and dabbed some on the patch. The rest she spread over Gertie's cracked lips. "I wish I knew what was going on inside that head of yours, Mrs. Sundersen." But her patient was unable to provide any help in this regard. "You don't look very good, Mrs. Sundersen. I'm worried you're not going to make it."

Gertie was stopped now, trying to catch her breath, the race over. The water felt good around her body, propping her up, the water she could rest in rather than fight against, the water caressing her exhausted limbs. A teammate came over to congratulate her. Lily Waters extended a hand but couldn't quite meet her gaze. Gertie looked up into the stands for her parents, but the seats were all empty. They must be on their way down to the pool. Coach Sully grabbed her hand and helped her out of the water. He was smiling, his face brimming with pride . . .

The first-year resident looked exhausted. It was his second straight night on call, and just as he was about to sneak in a few hours of sleep before morning rounds, his pager went off: *Room 2601, 79-year-old female, status post MI, agitated with rising blood pressure.* "Residency sucks," he grumbled, crawling out of bed and plodding to the ICU.

The light in the room was blinding. Shielding his eyes with his hand, he glanced down at the old lady. She was resting quite peacefully and didn't appear agitated in the least. "Any chance we could switch places for a while?" the resident chuckled while he scanned the numbers on the monitors. All were normal for a woman who just had a massive heart attack. He took up the chart and scribbled a quick note.

"Not sure why I was paged," he said peevishly to no one in particular at the nursing station. "The patient looks the same as she did a few hours ago. From now on, please don't call unless there's an emergency."

Gertie heard sounds, beeping and buzzing, footsteps, a periodic clanking, but they seemed far away. She tried to open her ears and eyes but couldn't, or maybe she preferred not to. Everything so dark and quiet. Was she dead? Funny, at the moment, the thought didn't alarm her. If this was what death was like, it wasn't so bad. The knots in her calves were gone. She didn't have to strain her eyes to see. The giant hand wasn't clamping down on her shoulder and making it hard to breathe. No, none of the bad stuff that had been plaguing her lately. Only a peaceful calm as she floated on her back, propped up by the water, cradling her, embracing . . .

Where was she now? In a pool? The ocean? She thought she'd smelled chlorine before, but now it smelled more like sea water. Coney Island maybe, after a plunge into the icy Atlantic with the Polar Bear Club. Or maybe many years earlier, after her father put her through a big workout, swimming without her arms, without her legs, without both, until she was exhausted and could barely move. Then they'd rest, side by side, floating on their backs, looking up at the sky that was always blue, clouds or no clouds, and he would talk about the future and the great things he predicted for her, his little *rokesild* . . .

At five o'clock in the morning, an orderly entered the room where Gertie and her father were floating peacefully on their sea bed. He swept the floor, emptied the garbage, and was about to refill the water pitcher on the bedside table when he took another look at the patient lying in bed. "You're pretty out of it, huh, Mr. Sundersen? Or is it Mrs. Sundersen? Hard to tell with all that stuff going in and out of you." The orderly shrugged. "In any case, I doubt you'll be needing any more water." He returned the pitcher to his cart and headed to the next room.

26

Corinna

The sun was an orange ball resting on the surface of the ocean; it hadn't yet thrown off any color to the dark-gray sky above. A gentle breeze from New York Harbor plied the Narrows. The streets were empty and traffic on the Verrazzano light—almost no movement on the upper deck at all. Bay Ridge was still asleep as the spring morning emerged full of promise.

The wine bottle next to her sleeping bag lay unopened. She must have been so tired, she conked out without a nip. That didn't happen very often on the roof deck. But neither did anything else that happened yesterday. One minute they were celebrating over cannoli and *blotkake*, the next Gertie was in an ambulance racing off to Lutheran Medical Center, a breathing tube shoved down her throat.

"Are you the one who did CPR?" asked the ER doctor after Gertie had been stabilized.

Corinna nodded.

"You saved your friend's life," the doctor said, glancing over at the bed where Gertie lay motionless, her eyes closed, a tangled web of lines and tubes running between her body and the machines encircling it.

She didn't look very alive to Corinna.

"I can't say whether Mrs. Sundersen is going to make it, but if it hadn't been for you, she wouldn't have stood a chance." He patted her on the shoulder. "Nice work."

If it hadn't been for Maria too, Corinna wanted to inform the doctor, but he had already left the room. "And it's not the first time either, right?" She was trying to cheer Maria up, remind her of their long-ago heroics under the Verrazzano, but Maria, sitting in the chair next to Gertie's bed, seemed as lifeless as their friend.

"Gertie the Bull. You remember that, Maria. She'll pull through."

Corinna still believed what she'd told Maria yesterday in the hospital, especially in the promising light of what the day held for her. The Professor had given her the good news after Gertie was transferred to a bed in the ICU. They were walking to the vending machines down the hall from the ICU to get something to eat. "I realize this isn't the best time," he said, "but Vincent made contact with Theresa."

It was the first time she heard the name, yet somehow it sounded familiar. She smiled. "My sister?"

"Yes."

"And you're sure now? Absolutely sure?"

"I am."

She took in a deep breath. Theresa. A beautiful name, it evoked the great female ruler of the Habsburg empire, Maria Theresa. She pictured her sister in a fancy lace dress, ruddy cheeked and bejeweled.

"Do you have her phone number? I want so much to speak to her."

The Professor smiled. "Your sister is just as eager. Joanna and Vincent thought the best idea would be a face-to-face meeting over the internet, on Skype. They will set everything up. When you're ready, of course," he said, looking grimly in the direction of Gertie's room.

"I'm ready now."

She felt guilty the second the words tumbled from her mouth. How could she be so selfish when her best friend was fighting for her life? Poor Gertie.

She felt the same this morning on the roof deck. Still, she couldn't hold back the excitement surging from the depths of her being. She'd almost bitten off the Professor's head when he told her they couldn't arrange the meeting until the following day because of the time zone difference between Germany and the United States. For Corinna, nothing was so important as speaking with her sister and filling in the blank parts of her past.

She felt especially guilty when she thought of Maria, glued to the chair next to Gertie's bed. Maria would have slept there all night if they hadn't kicked her out when visiting hours ended. If the tables were turned, and it was Maria about to meet her long-lost sister for the first time, she would postpone it until she knew Gertie was all right.

It was true what they said about a crisis, Corinna was beginning to realize. It illuminated things you might not have otherwise seen, that you might not want to see. They had been best friends for twenty years—Gertie, Maria, Corinna. The Three Musketeers, one for all and all for one. But maybe that wasn't the way it really was. Corinna winced as if the orange ball on the horizon was shining directly into her eyes.

Gazing down at the Verrazzano, she imagined another bridge, never far from her thoughts. *The Bridge of San Luis Rey* was one of the first books she'd read to the girls at the Temple. She wanted to see how they'd react to its author's deeply troubling insight that, even in the most perfect love, one person loves less than the other.

"It doesn't have to be like that," Maria had insisted when they discussed the book afterward. Although Gertie agreed with Maria, Corinna could tell they weren't as sure as they let on, and the more she pressed, the more uncertain they became. "Husbands and wives maybe," conceded Gertie, "but a father and daughter would always love each other equally."

"How about a mother and daughter?" asked Corinna. The question made Gertie uncomfortable. Maria began to fidget and squeeze the sides of her handbag. Before long, she was wiping down the stone bench with a Kleenex.

"You're right, Maria," Corinna told her. "It *doesn't* always have to be like that. And the best way to disprove Thornton Wilder is to look at us, our special friendship."

That was something the three of them—spinster, widow, and divorcée—could agree on. They broke open a second bottle of wine that day, a year or so after they'd first met, to toast their budding friendship and pledge their support and loyalty to each other. And so it seemed to continue for almost twenty years.

The orange ball lifted off the ocean surface and slowly rose through the sky.

She was beginning to see more clearly now, a series of snapshots from the ICU spread out before her: Maria sitting next to Gertie's bed, Corinna leaning against the door; Maria holding Gertie's hand, Corinna standing apart.

Maybe that was how it had always been—the day they stuck up for her at Dunkin' Donuts and all the times they helped her out at the Center. It was never one plus one plus one equals three, but more two parts plus one adding up to three.

Their love was stronger.

Corinna remained on the outside.

Now there was a chance to change that. Not in their circle but in another one. A chance for Corinna to finally be on the inside. Wouldn't that be easier if the parties were the same, the same blood, the same genes? Her real parents might no longer be around, but she had a sister, a sister who would accept and love her without condition.

Gertie had been right about one thing. It *was* their last chance. For Corinna, though, it was her last chance to finally belong, not to travel to some far-off destination.

"There is a land of the living and a land of the dead," Wilder had written, "and the bridge is love, the only survival, the only meaning."

Corinna spotted a cruise ship by the Sixty-Ninth Street Pier. Soon it would pass under the Verrazzano. She noticed the upper deck of the bridge was still empty.

Things happened so fast it had been hard for her to process, ever since Maria told Corinna that she was adopted and the Professor began to fill in the details. Yet strange as those details were, they seemed right. Hadn't she always been drawn to German culture, its literature and music? Her temperament—serious, bookish, willful, regimented—had a German cast too. She pictured herself marching a group of seniors through the Brooklyn Museum like a Prussian general, Clausewitz or von Mecklenburg. "Do we have to see the entire museum in one day," complained Joe Flannery, as they swept through the Egyptian wing and advanced to the Greeks. Yes, she felt it in her bones, a connection always intimated but never fully known.

There were still a few things to do before the big meeting with her sister. Corinna had to find someone to take the residents to the park, make sure Zadie Sandusky got to the doctor, and pick up a new batch of supplies for art class. The rest of the morning she'd spend at the hospital with Gertie and Maria. She hoped the promise of the day would extend to them too—that Gertie's condition would soon improve and that that, in turn, would lift Maria's spirits. She hoped this with all her heart.

Corinna took one last look at the orange ball, now suspended directly above the twin towers of the Verrazzano. There was some commotion on the upper deck. She reached for her binoculars and saw the fire engines and ambulance. Now she understood: a jumper.

It always made her jittery. She'd thought about it once or twice herself.

Flying through the air and falling into the sea like Icarus. So much more poetic than any of the other ways to escape.

But today, the bridge didn't smell of death.

Not to her at least.

27

Maria

Maria was exhausted, her lids heavy as stones, but she couldn't sleep. There was a fly buzzing inside her head, driving her from one thought to the other without a moment's peace. Who was with Gertie at the hospital now? What if something happened in the middle of the night? Who would comfort her if she woke up? The clock on her night table showed it wasn't yet midnight. There were still hours to go before the night ended. Maria tried to remember everything the doctors had told her, but it was hard to follow and often contradictory. One minute they seemed reassured that Gertie's blood pressure had normalized, the next they worried about her low oxygen levels.

The buzzing grew louder when she thought of what the cardiologist had said. "I don't understand," he told Maria after reviewing the chart. "I put Mrs. Sundersen on a new medicine for her heart, but the levels in her blood were negligible. Do you know if she stopped taking it?"

Maria turned over on her right side, then her left, but she couldn't get comfortable. Had Gertie stopped taking her medicine? Had she run out and not renewed her prescription? No, of course not. She might be strong willed, but she wasn't reckless. Yet something Gertie said after they left the travel agency that day made her wonder: "With the special they're running, it works out to two hundred dollars a night for the *Queen*. That's not bad, Maria. Just about what I pay for my heart pills every month."

Gertie had never been one to discuss her finances, and Maria simply assumed it wasn't an issue. Although it did take her almost a year to replace the refrigerator, which barely kept the milk cold by the end. Maria figured that sort of thing didn't bother Gertie as much as it would her, but maybe that wasn't the case. Maybe Gertie didn't have much of a cushion.

Could she have stopped her medicine to pay for the trip?

Maria bolted up. *Mannaggia. I would have given you the money, Gertie. If something happened because . . . I'll never forgive you.*

She had tried everything to change Gertie's mind. When she showed her the article from the *Daily News* detailing the prohibitive costs of travel to Europe, Gertie had laughed. But maybe she wasn't laughing inside, just scrambling for a way to come up with the money. How could Maria have been so thick? If only she'd guessed what was going through her friend's mind, she would have offered to help. Of course she would have. She would have given Gertie everything she had, everything, and then maybe this could have been averted.

If only the buzzing in her head would stop.

She wished there was someone to talk to. The phone sat on the night table next to the clock. She grabbed it and dialed her daughter's number.

"Yeah, Ma, I know, it's awful," said Livy. "Just awful."

"They're not sure if she's going to—"

"For God's sake, Vinnie, turn down that music. I'm on the phone with your grandmother."

"Do you hear what I'm telling you?"

"Yeah, of course, Ma, but I can't say I'm shocked. Gertie has a lousy heart. It was only a matter of—"

"Livy, how could you?"

"Sorry, Ma, but I can hardly think straight with everything going on in this screwed up household. Vinnie, will you turn down the damn . . ."

Livy was yelling so loudly Maria had to take the phone away from her ear.

"Let me call you back tomorrow, Ma. It's late anyway and you could use some rest."

"Sure."

Everyone, it seemed, had their share of problems: Livy, Vinnie, and certainly she herself. Yet you couldn't always comfort—or take comfort from—the people closest to you.

She called Lutheran hospital next. It took forever to be transferred from the operator to the ICU. Maria tapped on the floor with her bad foot while she waited. It was close to 1:00 a.m. when a nurse informed her that Gertie's condition hadn't changed and she should check back again during regular visiting hours.

"Gertie the Bull. You remember that, Maria. She'll pull through."

Thank God for Corinna. She would have been a wreck without her. Corinna knew exactly what to do when Gertie stopped breathing at the Temple, the chest compressions and mouth-to-mouth resuscitation, just as she knew what to do when Gertie choked on the pit twenty years ago. Nor was she intimidated by the nurses and doctors at the hospital and would do all the talking whenever they were in the room.

Maria still had the phone in her hand and dialed Corinna's number, but there was no answer.

She threw off the covers. No point trying to sleep with the buzzing in her head. She slipped on her robe, lumbered to the kitchen, and filled a glass with water. She gazed out the window. The street was dark and deserted. She walked over to the living room and plopped down on the recliner. A week ago, the Professor had been sitting across from her on the couch and they were having tea. She was upset then too, but looking back, that was nothing compared to this.

"You had a fight with your friends. It happens. But they are your friends for good reason. They will be back."

"You were right, Professor," she said to the place on the sofa where he had sat.

She was glad when he showed up at the hospital. She practically expected him—the minute a crisis arose, there he was.

"I came as soon as I heard. I'm so sorry," he said, taking her hands in his.

Livy had said she was sorry too, but it wasn't the same. The Professor really meant it. Maria could tell by the way his face went slack.

"Can I get you anything?" he asked.

No, she didn't want anything.

"I just spoke to one of the doctors. He says Gertie's doing a little better."

Yes, she nodded, hopeful.

She was nodding now too. The Professor always seemed so calm and confident and caring. She imagined him taking the teapot off the tray and pouring her another cup, adding a teaspoon and a half of sugar. How did he know that was just the way she liked it?

"I made contact with Elsa," he told her shortly after arriving at the hospital. "She'll be here as soon as she can."

That should have been the first thing she did when they stabilized Gertie and transferred her to the ICU. But Maria was so distraught, she completely forgot about Elsa. Thank God the Professor hadn't.

What if Corinna was wrong? What if Gertie didn't pull through?

The fly was buzzing louder than ever. Maria rose from the recliner and started pacing. Outside the window, the street was still dark and deserted.

What if Gertie never woke up?

The dull ache in her hip suddenly erupted into a shower of searing pain that rained down her leg and into her foot. Life without Gertie. She couldn't imagine what that would be like.

Corinna would still be around, of course. Livy, too, and Vinnie.

Somehow that didn't feel like enough.

Life without Gertie.

It would be as if large parts of herself had suddenly been erased, like the bridge on the day of the fight, when the rain had stopped: one tower standing and the rest—the second tower, deck, and anchors—all obliterated by the fog.

Maria already felt smaller.

Had Gertie been right about friendship, that it could be just as important as family?

The buzzing in her head had become unbearable. If only the night were over.

She tried Corinna again, but there was no answer.

Should she call the Professor, even though she'd never called him before? She searched for his name in the phone book. He wasn't listed. *Mannaggia mia.*

She turned to the clock on the wall and sighed—still hours to go before daylight.

28

The Temple

Two days after Gertie's heart attack, the Temple remained empty. As the Fort Hamilton High School bell rang, Vinnie Donofrio prepared for his first day of rehab at Phoenix House in downtown Brooklyn. He was angry at his grandmother, angry at his mother, and angry most of all at himself for being so stupid. Regardless, he wouldn't forget to set up the Skype session for Corinna at the internet café. His grandmother and the Professor were determined to bring the sisters together, and he had to admit, it was turning out to be one heck of a story. Maybe things wouldn't be as bad as he imagined.

Livy hadn't slept all night. She felt as though she had failed her son: having spent more time at work than at home when he was younger; not disciplining him as much as she should have; and not providing him with a male role model after his father died. No wonder he was screwed up. If only she could make things right so he wouldn't ruin his life for good.

She felt guilty, too, about how thoughtless she'd been with her mother, who was beside herself over her best friend's condition. Her mother had been so supportive over the years, always putting her daughter's and grandson's needs before her own. After she took Vinnie to Phoenix House, she'd drive over to the hospital to be with her.

The Professor had just signed in at the front desk and was on his way to the ICU with bagels and spreads from Bagel Boy. These sudden, tragic twists of fate had never failed to rattle him. No one was immune, as he learned years ago when his wife discovered the lump in her breast and, six months later, was gone. Yet he couldn't help feeling hopeful at the moment. Gertie's misfortune had given him an opportunity to spend more time with Maria.

Tom Jurgen stood in his bedroom, as of yet unaware of what had happened at the Temple. He'd spent so much time preparing for his upcoming trip that he hadn't checked his answering machine. Staring at the pile of clothes set out on top of his dresser, he suddenly decided they wouldn't do, that Gertie would want him to be more stylish on their trip abroad, more like the dapper Professor. He'd ask Gertie to take him shopping later for a new wardrobe.

Joe and Rose Flannery sat in Dr. Sandler's waiting room, watching CNN breaking news: a new round of powerful tornados was expected to hit the Southeastern United States in the coming days; there was dramatic new video of the killing of Osama bin Laden in Abbottabad; and Prince William and Kate Middleton were sighted on their honeymoon on a private island in the Seychelles.

Outside, the sun was shining, the sky blue. The water on the Narrows lay flat and still, glittering in the morning light. A freighter glided along effortlessly, about to pass under the great wingspan of the Verrazzano.

29

Gertie

She moved without hurry now, gliding along the surface one moment, plunging below it the next, winding and rolling, shooting up into the air and arcing back down into the sea. Salmon, bluefish, dolphin. No starting guns, no confining lanes or other swimmers to contend with. She was on her own now, swimming at her own pace. Only in the water could Gertie move so easily, even gracefully. On land she was a clunker, a lumbering bull. The water was her home, thanks to her father. Now it was time to pass on the tradition.

We better start soon, she advised Elsa, *before the year is up. Kari definitely has the right constitution. Like you said after the meningitis scare, she's a fighter, and she'll need to be if she wants to be good. I'll teach her the way your grandfather taught me. I'll show her how to move in one fluid motion, like a fish. Rokesild. That's the name he . . .*

I remember, Momma.

Did she just call her Momma?

I never told you, but I loved watching you swim.

You did?

I wasn't very good in the water, but I'd give anything if Kari could swim like you.

Do you mean it, Elsa?

Elsa?

Elsa, can you hear me?

But the voice that answered wasn't Elsa's.

"It's me, Gertie—Maria."

She opened her eyes and gazed at the familiar face above her.

"Elsa is on her way," said Maria. "She'll be here soon."

That was good. She'd wanted to see Elsa and tell her about her plans for Kari.

"Her plane was supposed to land—"

"It's okay, Maria. You're the one I want here right now." Her voice was hoarse and weak.

Maria brushed Gertie's hair to the side. "I'm so glad they took the breathing tube out. How do you feel?"

"Like a champ." She grinned. "Only a little out of shape."

"You'll get it back," she said, squeezing her hand. "Just in time for the next race at the Y."

She had to smile, watching Maria try, as she always did, to put things in the rosiest light.

"But you better listen to what the doctors say."

If her mouth weren't so sore, she'd laugh. How the hell could Gertie *not* listen to what the doctors said? They had her pinned to the bed and chained to a gazillion lines and machines.

"Gertie, please tell me you didn't stop taking your medicine. I've been thinking about it all night. If there was a problem, I could have . . ."

"Relax, Maria, it's not your fault. That was my decision, and I'd do it again."

Maria shook her head. "I don't understand."

"I can see that and it worries me."

"It worries *you*? You're not making sense, Gertie."

"Time was ticking, Maria. It's ticking now," she said, tapping her on the hand. "Not just for me, but for you too."

"I would have given—"

"Now, you listen to me, Maria, before it's too late." Gertie held her hand with all the strength she had left. "Stop worrying about everyone else for a change and think of yourself."

"How can I do that when you're—"

"I need you to promise me a few things."

"Of course. Whatever you want."

"Promise me, you and Corinna will board the *Queen* at Red Hook and ride with it down the Narrows. Promise me, the two of you will be on the promenade deck as it passes the Temple and the Verrazzano, that you'll get the hell out of Bay Ridge for a while and see some of the world."

"I promise, Gertie. The minute you're back on your feet. We'll all go together."

"No," she sighed. "You're not listening. The tickets are in a folder on my kitchen table. Take them and go with Corinna. Maybe you can fit Germany into the itinerary and visit Corinna's sister. I'm sure my pal at the travel agency can arrange it."

"But—"

"No buts, Maria. I'm asking you to promise."

Maria hesitated.

"Please."

She nodded reluctantly.

Gertie wasn't finished. "Promise me you'll also spend more time with the Professor. I know he's not your type with all his hoity-toity. But no one's perfect, and the man genuinely cares about you—I've seen it with my own two eyes."

Maria looked away, unable to respond.

"You're going to need someone to talk to when—"

Maria winced. "What are you saying?"

"You could take him dancing with you at the Greek church. Corinna says he likes to dance. That's what I hear attracted him to you in the first place. Point is, you need to live a little more. You hear me?"

She nodded yes and no at the same time.

"One last thing. Promise me you'll look after Tom."

Maria had had enough. "*Basta*, Gertie. The doctors just took out the breathing tube and said you were doing better. Why are you asking . . . ?"

"Maybe Corinna could get him a place at the Center. That's where he belongs, with other people around to prop him up. Hannah was right about her husband—that man won't last a minute by himself."

Maria's eyes began to tear.

"Don't get upset, Maria. I'll be fine, as long as I know you'll keep your promises. Now let me rest awhile. I'm awfully tired."

As Gertie's head fell back on the pillow, Maria started to cry. "Why aren't you fighting?" she asked. "You're the Bull, Gertie, you can't give up now. We'll all go on the *Queen* together—that's the promise I want to make."

But Gertie didn't hear her. She was already fast asleep.

30

Corinna

Her senses tracked and magnified everything around her as she rounded the corner: the pungent, peppery smell of the kabob truck, the sounds of honking horns and footstep clatter, the shadows cast by sunlight on the sides of cars and buildings. The hospital was already a million miles away.

The capricious winds of the Narrows had shifted again, thrusting the three women in different directions: Gertie had been unresponsive since the morning; Maria remained inconsolable despite the Professor's attempts to calm her; and Corinna was rushing off to meet her sister.

Yet the day was also full of promise—a present lying under the tree on Christmas morning, wrapped and bowed, waiting for her to open.

She was greeted at the internet café by none other than Mr. Tongue Ring. "I didn't know you worked here."

"Yup. My official job." Zach grinned.

She noticed he'd changed his hair color from purple to yellow.

"I got everything thet up for you in the back. Vinnie thaid you'd want some privacy."

"Some privacy would be nice."

"You got time. Want a cup of coffee?"

"Just the bathroom."

The tiny cubicle had no mirror, but Corinna brought one with her, along with a brush and makeup. She didn't want to paint her face before her visit to the hospital. It was bad enough how she felt inside without parading it before Maria and the Professor. There was no doubt where his affection lay now, yet she didn't feel a shred of anger or jealousy. It no longer mattered.

She fixed the collar on her blouse and straightened her hair. She applied some blush to her cheeks, then wondered if it might be too much; she could hardly remember the last time she wore makeup. She did the same with the lipstick, a glossy cherry red, which the lady at Century 21 said was their number one seller. Better to apply more than less, she told her, since cameras tend to make things darker.

When Corinna finished, she was ushered into the privacy room, every nerve in her body tingling.

"Nothing to it, ma'am. All you got to do ith talk. I'll be up front if you need me."

The room was only slightly bigger than the bathroom. A small table with a desktop computer and folding chair. The walls bare, a dulled, dirty white with areas of chipping paint. It was depressing, like an interrogation room or jail cell.

She glanced at her reflection on the screen. Thankfully, you couldn't see much of the room behind her. She wished there were music, but wasn't in the mood to confer with Mr. Tongue Ring. Instead, she played a Bach violin concerto in her head while she waited.

Suddenly, the view on the screen changed. A stately table in dark wood was framed by a window hung with plush burgundy drapes. She heard people speaking German in the background. A large woman appeared and lowered herself onto an embroidered chair with great difficulty. The resemblance to the picture in her head of the Habsburg empress was striking. The woman was white and fleshy with a small, sharp nose, blue eyes, and gray hair pinned in a bun. The lace collar of her dress fit snugly around her neck.

"Theresa?"

"Corinna?"

Despite the formal appearance, her sister's voice was soft and soothing.

"I wish we were meeting in person. It is strange talking to a computer screen."

Corinna watched her sister closely as she spoke. Her teeth were white and straight, none of them crooked or missing. In fact, as far as she could tell, there was nothing physically wrong with Theresa.

"Look at you, Corinna, your hair is still blonde and not a wrinkle on your face, while I, three years younger, am so old and ugly."

Corinna blushed, gripping the sides of the folding chair so that her hands didn't wander into the picture frame.

"That's not true. You are as beautiful and elegant as I imagined," said Corinna. "And you speak English so well." She had a million questions for her sister and didn't know where to begin. "Can you tell me about our parents? Are they still living?"

"I'm afraid not. They passed on many years ago," answered Theresa.

"Were they killed in the camps?"

Theresa's eyes narrowed. "The camps?"

"The concentration camps."

"The concentration camps?"

Corinna wondered why Theresa kept repeating her words, as if she didn't understand. Maybe her sister's English wasn't as good as it appeared. "Our parents must have realized we were in grave danger. Why else would they put me on the ship with the other Jewish children? Did they try to smuggle you out of the country too? I hope to God you weren't in a camp. How awful for someone so young."

Theresa, who previously seemed confused, now became genuinely agitated. She turned around and began speaking excitedly in German to someone behind her. The back and forth with her invisible interlocutor continued for several minutes. When she finally returned to face the camera again, she was calmer. "I'm sorry, Corinna, I thought you knew. My daughter and your friend's grandson have been in communication."

"Yes, Vinnie Donofrio—I call him Mr. Smarty-pants. He was the first to find out about my great escape from Germany on the Kindertransport. I guess I was one of the lucky ones too."

"That is true—for the most part."

"For the most part?"

"It is complicated, Corinna, and I prefer to tell you the rest in person."

Corinna wanted to know the rest right now. "Please, tell me what happened back then to you and to our parents. Why didn't we try to escape together, as a family?"

Theresa didn't answer immediately. "Our parents died soon after the war ended. I was a young child at the time and don't remember much. The one thing I do remember, however, is that our mother loved you deeply. She took great risks getting you on that ship. But my dear Corinna, this is not a day to talk of sad things. Today is a happy day when I meet my sister for the first time. This is what we must focus on. Please, tell me more about yourself. I want to know everything about you."

Corinna didn't mind talking about sad things, eager as she was to learn her history, the entire unedited version—what her parents looked like, their tastes in music and books, where they lived and worked. But she could see that Theresa was uncomfortable with this line of questioning and didn't want to push. She would comply with her sister's request.

Corinna decided to skip over the early chapters of her life with her adopted family, leapfrogging to the much happier years she'd spent at the Senior Center, the place where she found her calling. "Even when I was young, I understood older people and knew I could help them. Now I realize they might have helped me more."

"How interesting, Corinna, because I see things very similarly. I, too, am drawn to the more vulnerable and needy. Did you know I was a doctor?"

"No," she answered, suddenly embarrassed. How many doctors she had seen over the years, especially as a child, groping, gawking, judging her. "You know about my condition?"

She nodded.

"Do you have any imperfections?"

Theresa laughed. "I suspect that I have a lot more than you, including this mountain of weight that I drag along with me wherever I go."

Corinna held up her hand for Theresa to see. "A lobster claw deformity is what they call it. Very attractive, don't you think? And I'm not much bigger than—"

"Sister, all that may be true, but what I see before me is a seventy-two-year-old woman who looks more like a young girl, and most likely with the health of a young girl."

She blushed.

"When you have practiced medicine as long as I have—or taken care of the elderly as long as you have—you come to see not only the weaknesses of a person, but their strengths. In fact, what inspires me most is how those strengths are used to compensate for the weaknesses. How my patient with arthritis, for example, manages to walk a mile to the clinic for her appointment despite the difficulty and pain, and more often than not with a smile on her face. It makes me smile too."

Such a lovely way of seeing things, thought Corinna. The same way she had come to see things over the years, in herself and others. "My other passion is books," she told her sister. "I trained as a librarian and over the years built a well-stocked library at the Senior Center. I see books as living, breathing things and love them for their different personalities and energy. Like people, but even better."

"Then we will have much to talk about, for I also love books."

Corinna told Theresa about her friends, Gertie and Maria, and their special place beneath the Verrazzano Bridge that they call the Temple. "We meet there every Tuesday to chat, drink wine, and watch the boats go by. I read my favorite poems and novels to them. Right now, we're in the middle of Virgil's *Aeneid*."

"That sounds wonderful. A magnificent bridge, the Verrazzano, with its long and sinuous wingspan. More so than the Brooklyn Bridge in my opinion."

Corinna agreed.

"I can't wait to see it when I come to New York and visit your temple. I arrive in two weeks' time."

"Oh no, Theresa, I wanted to visit Germany first. It's all I could think about." She tried to make her sister understand. "Ever since I was a child, I knew I didn't belong here, and not just because of my problems," she said, gesturing toward her hand. "When I found out I was born in Germany, it suddenly made sense. I'm from the same country as Johann Sebastian. Not a day goes by that I don't listen to his music."

"We are sisters, Corinna."

"Beethoven and Brahms too. And German literature—Goethe, Heine, and Mann—right up to the present. Günter Grass's *The Tin Drum* is one of my favorites, with little Oskar, the boy that never grows up. Just like me," she laughed. "You see, Theresa, the German spirit has always been inside of me, waiting to spring out. It wants to go home. I want to go home."

"I know you do, but first I come to New York and we talk. There is much to talk about."

"Why can't we talk now?"

"You must trust me, Corinna. It is better this way. And if, after our talk, you still desire to see Germany, we can return to Eisenach together. I promise."

Corinna didn't understand why Theresa was being so evasive. She was absolutely certain that nothing her sister said would ever change her mind about returning to her homeland.

"You know, Corinna, I, too, have always felt there was something missing in my life. When our parents died, I went to live with our mother's sister in Switzerland and so spent most of my childhood and adolescence in a foreign country. But even after I returned to Germany, got married, and had a family of my own, there was an empty space inside that I could never seem to fill."

Corinna had always considered herself an expert on empty spaces.

"I didn't even know you were alive until a week ago, when the boy began speaking to Joanna. But like you said, it made sense. Somehow I always knew there was someone out there, someone looking for me just as I looked for her. Someone who might fill the empty space inside me. My sister! How happy I am to have found you."

Theresa's eyes narrowed and she began to cry. Until then, she had been so composed. Now her entire body shuddered. A younger woman with the same sharp nose and blue eyes crouched down beside her and put her arm around her. "*Es ist alles in Ordnung, Mutter,*" she comforted Theresa, then turned to the screen and said in a thick German accent: "She is crying from happiness, Aunt Corinna. I am Joanna, and I, too, cry from happiness."

The happy tears continued for a good while, followed by more talk about Theresa's upcoming visit and how it would be when the sisters were finally reunited, until the time came to say their goodbyes. As the screen went dark, Corinna jumped from her seat and let out a yelp. The tiny room with peeling paint suddenly seemed palatial and full of light. She almost hugged Mr. Tongue Ring on the way out. In a few days, Theresa would be in New York.

31

Gertie

She leapt off the block and dove into the water, the biggest race of her life, the 200-meter butterfly final at the nationals. A win would enable her to compete for a spot on the US Olympic team. She felt strong and quickly attained a good rhythm—no hint of the cramp that bothered her the day before. She'd keep this pace until midway through the third lap, then make her move. In the stands, her mother cheered loudly while her father willed her on in silence. As Gertie approached the target point, she took a deep breath, accelerated the snap of her kick, grabbed the water with both hands, pushed back as hard as she could, then swung her arms around again, the words of Coach Sully reverberating in her head: *No one but you is going to push you across the finish line.* She kicked, grabbed, pushed, swung with everything she had, breathing harder and harder until she realized it was no longer necessary. She could move effortlessly now . . . without the need for air and oxygen anymore . . . like a fish moving through the water.

—

At 2:30 p.m., as he passed the handpiece over Gertie Sundersen's chest, the technician at the echo lab noticed that his patient's heart rate had slowed precipitously. He ran to get the doctor who was supervising a case next door. When they returned, the patient was no longer breathing. The monitor showed her heart had stopped. "Should I call a code?" asked the technician. The doctor shook his head. There was a "Do Not Resuscitate" order on the chart. He pronounced Gertie dead at 2:41 p.m. and called the ICU so they could notify next of kin.

The head nurse noted that Mrs. Sundersen's daughter had still not arrived from California. She would have to inform one of the deceased's friends—either the distraught redhead who sat by the bed and cried most of the day, or the well-dressed man with his bow ties who brought in food for them to eat. Afraid the news might send another old lady into cardiac arrest, the nurse decided to direct her words to the more even-keeled man.

32

The Temple

Tuesday morning, the twenty-fourth day of May 2011. A dense fog swept in from the Atlantic, partially blanketing the Narrows and much of the Verrazzano Bridge. The horns of invisible ships sounded every now and then. There was no one walking or jogging along the water, no tourists snapping pictures of the famous Brooklyn landmark.

The fog didn't seem to bother two little boys playing soccer on the grass or their mothers sipping coffee and chatting about preschool and play dates. A surprisingly strong kick sent the ball just over the portable net and up the hill, disappearing in the trees below Shore Road. The boys ran to retrieve it. Some time passed before their mothers realized the boys were missing, and when they finally did, they panicked. One looked around frantically while the other kept yelling their names until they finally heard a child's voice.

Racing up the hill after it, they entered the tree line and followed the narrow, winding pathway. It led to a small enclosure where the children were running around in circles.

"Look, Mommy, a secret hiding place," said one boy.

His mother picked him up and squeezed him hard. "I was so worried about you. Promise me you'll never run off like that again."

"Can we play here awhile?" asked the other boy, smothered in the arms of his own mother.

Now that the danger had passed and the women could breathe easier, they began to notice their surroundings: the stone bench and columns, the circle of trees.

"Sure," answered the mother. "It's nice here. Except for that smell."

"Someone left candles," said her son.

She remembered the old lady walking up the hill a while back. At the time, the woman thought it odd, since she never suspected there was anything in this remote part of the park. Her friend remembered too: the old lady with red hair.

"What's this, Mommy?" asked her son.

On the ground at the edge of the enclosure was a plastic face mask used to deliver oxygen. Next to it lay a pair of gloves and a roll of medical tape.

"It's to help you breathe." She wondered who might have needed such help. She hoped it wasn't the lady with the red hair.

"Check this out," said her friend, pointing to a small opening in the trees. "You can see the bridge from here. It's like looking through a telescope."

"Wow! There's the Staten Island Ferry going by."

The mothers lifted their sons onto their shoulders. The boys couldn't see the ferry through the fog, but they did see a helicopter heading straight for the bridge. "Watch where you're going, Mr. Helicopter Pilot!" the boys shouted. They wished they could fly a helicopter one day. "Do you think it's hard, Mommy?" "How does the bridge stay up with all those heavy cars on it?" "Why doesn't it just fall down into the water?"

"What a great spot," remarked one mother. "We should come back tomorrow when the weather is better. We can have a picnic."

"Yeah, let's come back!" shouted the boys.

"We can make it a regular thing," agreed the other mother.

Tom Jurgen sat on the grass at the bottom of the hill and barely turned his head when he heard the boys' shouts. They seemed to come from somewhere up in the trees behind him. That must be where the Temple was, he thought despondently. If he had any strength left in his legs, he would have gone and had a look.

Instead, he remained rooted to the spot, still in a daze after the phone call he'd received four days ago. "I'm sorry, Tom," Maria had said. "Gertie's gone." If there had been anything else said in the conversation, he couldn't remember. It was all a jumble in his head.

He gazed up at the great bridge, the water flowing beneath it, cold and silent, on and on and on. He was alone now. Gertie was gone. There would be no trip to Europe. No one to play gin rummy with or to protect from the elements. No one to kiss. And there was so much more he wanted but would never have.

He probably deserved it. After all, he wasn't so nice to Gertie when they were younger, always needling her about her butch qualities, that she was more man than half the firemen in his firehouse. But he never meant any harm. If anything, he was jealous. Not only that she could outrun and outswim him, but that she never cared what anyone else said or thought. She was a tough son of a bitch, just like she said.

And just like the Verrazzano, with all its steel and concrete, two of the most fire-resistant construction materials known to man. Even in a massive conflagration, the steel would absorb the heat of the flames, allowing the heat to diffuse along its length, and no matter how fiery the steel's conduction, the concrete at the bridge's base would hold.

Gertie had been his steel and concrete. He felt stronger, more a man, whenever he stood next to her. Now he felt like a rag doll, all wobbly and weak. He would never stand next to her again. Nor carry her bags home from the market or hold an umbrella over her head. He'd never imagined these small moments, where nothing much happened, would make him so happy. Yet there it was, an unexpected windfall after Hannah died. And now there'd be no more of them.

33

Corinna

Corinna had left the internet café on that fateful day in the best of moods, but it quickly changed when she returned to the hospital and found Maria in tears and the bed where Gertie once lay empty. At the very time Corinna was talking to her sister, Gertie had died. The Professor sat next to Maria, trying to console her. Gertie's daughter, Elsa, due to arrive in just a few hours, would never see her mother again. "It's not fair," Maria kept repeating.

Corinna tossed and turned in her bed that night and for nights afterward. She worried how Maria, the most sensitive in their group, would get through this. She fretted over the fact that Gertie had stopped taking her medicine and that neither she nor Maria had ever questioned whether Gertie could afford the trip. She felt guilty about not spending more time in the hospital and wondered if it would have made a difference. She brooded over Maria's promise to Gertie that she and Corinna would go to Italy in her place. But how could Corinna leave Brooklyn now that Theresa was coming? And how would she tell Maria this without upsetting her even more and dishonoring the memory of their friend?

Then there were the nagging thoughts that followed her conversation with Theresa. Why had her sister been so evasive? Why did she react so strangely whenever Corinna mentioned the Jews and the concentration camps? And why didn't Theresa want to talk about their parents? As the questions piled up and gnawed at her, Corinna decided she couldn't wait another day for answers. She would find the Professor first thing in the morning and get Theresa's number.

The phone rang shortly after 6:00 a.m. Corinna had given up sleep by then and was halfway through *Austerlitz*, a novel by the German writer W. G. Sebald. The protagonist's story was practically identical to her own—a man who learned late in life that he had been adopted and was one of the Kindertransport children.

"Corinna, is it too early to be calling?"

"Theresa?"

"Yes, it's me."

"No, of course not. I'm glad you called. I was just about to call you."

"Good. I feel terrible about not being as forthcoming as I should have when we last spoke. And I would hate if you heard anything more from the boy or his teacher. I should be the one to tell you."

So it wasn't just in her mind; Corinna's sister had kept things from her.

"It's because I didn't want to hurt you," said Theresa.

"How could you possibly hurt me? I just want to know about our family."

"I know you do, so bear with me and let me try to explain."

Corinna listened while her sister took several deep breaths before continuing.

"First of all, Corinna, you are not Jewish. None of us are. That's not the reason you were put on the boat."

She didn't understand. "The whole point of the Kindertransport was to rescue Jewish children."

"That is true, but not in your case. I don't know how to say this. In fact, it makes me sick just to think about it."

Corinna could hear the quivering in Theresa's voice.

"You were placed on that ship because of your congenital anomalies," explained Theresa. "The Nazis decided you weren't a pure enough German for them. They considered you unfit to live and were going to . . . This is very hard to talk about, Corinna. They were going to euthanize you."

Corinna began to feel light-headed.

"It makes me so angry. Disgusted. For this, too, is our people, Corinna, a part of the great German heritage. Not just Bach and Brahms, but Hitler and Himmler and Mengele. Our mother refused to go along with the order. Somehow she was able to arrange a place for you on the Kindertransport. Maybe she knew someone, maybe she paid off an official, or maybe she just begged and begged until someone took pity on her—it's not entirely clear. But it couldn't have been easy since, as you just said, the transports were meant to save Jewish children and you weren't Jewish. On top of all that, she was somehow able to keep this from our father; the day you left Berlin she supposedly told him that she was taking you to the assigned hospital as planned."

"Our father? He agreed?"

"Yes, I'm ashamed to say."

A tightening at the back of her throat made it difficult for her to breathe.

"You mustn't think of him, Corinna. Only our mother. She loved you and mourned for you. I don't remember much—I was only six years old when she died. She wore a locket around her neck with your baby hair and picture inside. I remember her weeping at night and clutching the locket. I have that locket and will bring it to you when I visit."

"Do you have pictures of her?"

Theresa did have some and promised to bring them. "Our mother never told me her secret, Corinna. She told me you died of scarlet fever.

I only learned about the Kindertransport when your friend's grandson made contact with Joanna. At first I didn't believe it. I begged Joanna to call the Jewish agencies herself to verify the story. She was able to find a woman living in Berlin who remembered our mother, the Christian lady pleading for her child—the lady, pregnant with her second child at the time, who took a big risk in defying state orders to save her daughter's life. People were shot for lesser crimes in those days. The woman from the Jewish agency told Joanna how awful it was to watch parents having to part with their children as they boarded the trains that would take them to the port in Holland. She remembered hearing that it was particularly painful for the pregnant Christian lady. They had to pry you from her arms."

Corinna's head spun from the dizzying rush of new information, as she tried and tried to make sense of it all.

"Corinna?"

"Yes."

"Our mother loved you. That is what you must remember. And now that we have each other, I will always love you."

Corinna could barely utter the word goodbye before hanging up the phone, could barely utter any words for that matter, for when the storm in her head eased up, she was left with an aching emptiness, as if every particle of matter in her body had been sucked out.

Her father had agreed to have her killed.

Put down like an animal.

How would she be able to live with that?

34

Maria

"Come in," said Elsa, opening the door to Gertie's apartment.

Maria forced a smile, determined to be stronger today. She'd been a wreck the last twenty-four hours and probably had no tears left by now. The Professor had allayed some of her guilt about not realizing her friend was strapped for cash, not appreciating how much the trip meant to Gertie, and not getting Elsa to New York faster when things began to unravel.

"You can't blame yourself, Maria," he told her. "There's a famous Latin expression, *carpe diem*. Gertie seized the day, she made her choice. So did you, Maria, and I believe Gertie has benefited from both those choices—she was able to plan her trip and talk to her daughter again. Thanks to you, she got more than she hoped for."

It hardly seemed that way to Maria, with Gertie's unused travel tickets and passport in her pocketbook and Gertie not being able to see her daughter before she died. But what Maria couldn't deny, as the Professor had pointed out, was the peace and calm in her friend's voice the last time they talked. "Don't get upset, Maria. I'll be fine, as long as I know you'll keep your promises."

"I've been going through her things," said Elsa regretfully. "She kept a lot more than I would have expected."

Maria wasn't surprised. Gertie may have been gruff on the outside, but deep down she was a softie, a side most people never saw, including her own daughter. Maria tried not to be angry with Elsa for that. How could she, when it was obvious how badly Elsa felt?

"This thing must be a hundred years old," said Elsa, gesturing to the green couch. "It was in our living room at Howell Street. No one was allowed to sit on it except when guests came. I remember the couch always smelled like moth balls."

Maria watched Elsa speak, looking for resemblances to her mother, but there weren't many. Elsa was tall and thin, her face long, her nose angular. Even her blue eyes were different, squinty and skittish compared to Gertie's larger, more resolute ones.

"And the same tapestry still hangs above it. The White Bear King, Valemon, an old Norwegian folktale. My grandparents brought it with them when they came to this country." Elsa laughed. "It's like Gertie took her entire living room and set it down here."

"What's wrong with that?" asked Maria. She had done the same when she moved to Bay Ridge.

"It was the '80s," Elsa explained. "The 1980s, not the 1880s."

Maria nodded. "You look like your father."

"That's what everybody used to say. I'm not sure it was a compliment, looking like a man. But he was a handsome man."

Maria had seen pictures of Thorvald, and he was indeed handsome, at least on the outside. That wasn't the case on the inside. The very opposite of Gertie.

"You probably think he was a monster. That he was to blame for everything that happened."

"He walked out on your mother," said Maria.

"You didn't know Gertie back then. She had her priorities, and neither me nor my dad were high on the list."

"I don't believe that."

"You weren't there," snapped Elsa. "My mother was always away, and I was always making excuses—why she couldn't make my birthday party or come to a softball game, even the big ones, like the Little League World Series when I was thirteen. My father, on the other hand, never missed a game."

That couldn't be true, could it?

Elsa collapsed on the couch and frowned. "The White Bear King in the tapestry had a curse put on him by a troll. I used to think it was the same for me—my parents hating each other, my difficulties getting pregnant." She tapped her finger on the old wooden chest Gertie used as a coffee table, another relic from Howell Street. "Who knows, maybe I was wrong all this time. I'm not sure of anything anymore. Except how I felt back then—my mother loved swimming more than me, and I could never forgive her for that."

Maria took a deep breath. "It wasn't just a hobby, Elsa. Gertie almost made it to the Olympics. That's a huge accomplishment."

A large cardboard box filled with papers and other objects lay at their feet. Elsa bent down and opened the top flap. "I've been going through everything. I can't believe she still has my old jewelry box." She took out the white wooden box with the unicorn on top and rattled off its contents: "Baby teeth. Old pictures. Report cards. Birthday cards." She reached back down and grabbed a tattered baby blanket. "My blanky too," she laughed, wrapping the blanket around her arm. "And my trophy from the Little League World Series."

Maria smiled.

"She kept everything." The words caught at the back of her throat, and Elsa began to cry.

"It's okay, dear."

Elsa flinched. "No, it's not. I screwed up. I believed everything he said. Never anything she said."

Maria wanted to comfort Elsa, even though what she said was true.

"I should have made more of an effort. Called more. Visited."

Yes, Maria thought, *you should have.*

"I screwed up, and now it's too late."

Maria put her hand on Elsa's shoulder. "You can't only blame yourself, dear. I loved your mother, but she had her faults too. I didn't know her when you were a child and she was focused on her swimming career. It couldn't have been easy. But one thing I'm sure of: she loved you, Elsa. I know because I saw how much it hurt her not speaking to you. Gertie was a proud woman and would never let on how she felt. That's why I kept calling."

Elsa looked down and ran her hand over the frayed, green upholstery of the couch she had always hated. "I don't know what to say. We'd been mad at each other for as long as I can remember."

"I'm sure you were hurting too."

"That's just the thing. I wasn't." Elsa shook her head. "At some point, I figured out my father wasn't the angel he claimed to be. That he played a part in their breakup. And yet I didn't do anything about it."

Maria watched Elsa pick a hole in the couch fabric.

"I had my own life three thousand miles away. A job, good friends, a man I loved. Plenty to keep me busy. Why should I care about someone who didn't care about me?"

Maria could think of more than a few reasons.

"It's only now that I feel bad and realize how selfish I've been," admitted Elsa. "Now, when there's nothing I can do about it. Serves me right."

"Don't say that."

"You don't understand. How could you? From what you told me, you get along perfectly with your daughter. A gift was what you called it."

Maria blushed, remembering their last conversation. She had tried to convince Elsa how much there would be to look forward to if she started speaking to her mother again. But maybe things weren't as black and white as she imagined.

"I'm going to do everything I can so that Kari never feels like I did. No matter what happens in my life, I'll make sure she knows how much I love her."

That's important, thought Maria. It was the way she'd always been with Livy, the way it should be with every mother. But it should also go in the other direction—a child has to show her love too. Where was Elsa all these years? Maria recalled what Gertie once said: "They take more than they give, these kids." That wasn't the case with Livy though. She gave back plenty.

She did, didn't she?

Elsa held a photograph in her hand, the one of Kari she'd mailed to Gertie. "What a joke!" she said. "I finally want to see my mother again. I want my daughter to see her grandmother, and now that I decide it's time, now that I'm ready . . ."

"The old dog becomes a burden," Gertie used to say. Did Livy appreciate how much her mother had done for her, how much she still did for her? Or was Gertie right, that Livy saw her mother more as a burden? Maybe, like Elsa, she'd rather be three thousand miles away.

". . . it's too late."

The words pricked at Maria. She'd heard them before: "Listen to me, Maria, before it's too late. Stop worrying about everyone else for a change and think of yourself."

Elsa covered her face with her hands and cried.

Maria felt like crying too. "Gertie loved you, Elsa. I promise you that. Yesterday morning at the hospital, she spoke to you as if you were in the room with her. I wish you could have seen how happy she was when you called her Momma."

"You're just saying that to make me feel better."

"I swear," said Maria. "She talked about teaching Kari how to swim. She wanted to start early, just like her father did with her."

Elsa looked up at Maria. "That's so weird. I was thinking the same thing."

"Then you should do it. What a nice way to remember your mother and honor her wishes."

"Yeah," nodded Elsa, brushing away her tears. "You're right."

Later, as she walked home, Maria realized that she, too, must find a way to honor Gertie's wishes. *Wake up*, she heard her friend telling her. *Stop worrying about everyone else.* How could she do that, she wondered, when she had lived her whole life worrying about everyone else?

Think about yourself for a change. She wasn't even sure what that would mean, what she might want for herself.

Time is running out. This, unfortunately, Maria did understand, understood only too well now. Oh, if she could only talk to Gertie; she'd help her figure it out.

As Maria passed Ida Levitsky standing guard in front of her apartment building, she glanced over to the sitting area where the Professor had been waiting for her the day of the big fight at the Temple. Although he wasn't there now, she saw him, rising from the couch: *Carpe diem, Maria,* he said. *Seize the day.*

35

The Temple

Corinna was surprised to find two little boys running out of the Temple, chasing a soccer ball. Their mothers, each balancing a coffee cup in one hand and donuts in the other, trailed closely behind them. She'd never seen anyone inside their secret place before and was upset by the intrusion. Then again, maybe she shouldn't think of it as their place anymore. One of the boys fell on the way down the hill, and his mother rushed over to help him. She took the crying boy in her arms and gently patted the bruised side of his face.

Corinna reimagined the scene: now, she was the child who had fallen; now, it was *her* mother, her real mother, who swept Corinna into her arms. Ever since her phone call with Theresa, Corinna had been tortured by what she'd heard—yet another evil man in her life, another father, this one of her own flesh and blood, willing not just to cast her aside but to have her killed. She had used every ounce of willpower to force herself not to think of him, to follow her sister's advice and block him out. The only part of her history that mattered was her mother: the mother who loved Corinna unconditionally; the pregnant woman on the station platform who couldn't bear to part with her child; the grieving woman who wept at night clutching her locket. From now on she would find this woman wherever she looked. The image of her mother sweeping a bruised Corinna into her arms soothed Corinna, fortified her, as she entered the Temple to prepare for her friend's send-off.

Gertie had been clever with her timing. The *Queen* departed Red Hook at 11:00 a.m. on Tuesday, May 31, her birthday, and would enter the Narrows just around the time of their weekly gathering. Only this Tuesday, everything would be different. Corinna would be in the enclosure with her binoculars, gazing out through the opening in the great oak trees, while Maria and Gertie were out on the water—no longer viewers like her but objects to be viewed. How strange and sad. Corinna felt compelled to mark the occasion, an ending that was also a beginning.

When he heard of the *Queen*'s departure from the Red Hook Terminal, Joe Flannery had volunteered his artistic services. Corinna immediately accepted the offer, grateful that he would be standing beside her, anchoring her, as she said goodbye to her friends. Joe was already at Red Hook when Corinna had arrived that morning, sitting at his easel and painting the scene. He'd brought along a brooding Tom Jurgen, soon to be his new neighbor at the Senior Center, as well as a bottle of Jameson single malt whiskey. "In the open air, like the Impressionists," Flannery said with a smile. "And no computer to mess up, right, Boss? I'm in heaven."

"I know an even better spot," Corinna replied. She invited the hapless pair to watch the *Queen Mary* pass beneath the Verrazzano with her at the Temple, promising them that the view would be unforgettable. While Joe had given her the thumbs up, Tom made no response; he continued to stare glumly at the ground before him. "You won't be needing that today," she had told him, gently prying the umbrella from his hands. "I know you're sad, Tom. I am too, but that's not what Gertie would want from us right now. Today we're going to send off our friend in style."

Now at the Temple, Corinna spread her mat over the ground and laid out incense candles. She climbed onto the stone bench and peered through the opening to the Narrows below. The earlier cloud cover had given way to brilliant sunshine. The water was lake calm, a giant mirror reflecting trees and sails, beams and cables. For a moment, she wished she were out there with Maria and Gertie on the *Queen Mary*. Maybe she could convince her sister to return to Europe by ship.

Poor Gertie. This was all her idea, and she didn't even get to enjoy it. Then again, who knew what in this crazy world Gertie might or might not be able to enjoy at the moment. Gertie should have seen Maria this morning. In the span of a few days, she had transformed herself, trading in her granny frock and clunky orthopedic shoes for an outfit straight out of *Vogue*: a light-green summer dress, white espadrilles, and a chic leather handbag. She'd put on makeup and colored her hair, restoring it to the magnificent auburn of her youth. "You look positively radiant, Maria," Corinna told her at the terminal in Red Hook, and she meant it. She didn't begrudge her friend one iota, not today, after all she'd been through and done for her. If anyone deserved to be happy, surely it was Maria.

Finally, the bow of the *Queen Mary* jutted past the Sixty-Ninth Street Pier—white on top, black in the middle, a thin strip of red at the bottom. Soon the massive floating city would pass the Temple. Corinna felt her stomach flutter. Where were Flannery and Jurgen? She hoped they didn't get lost on the way from the terminal; she could use a little nip of Jameson at the moment. She wondered if Theresa liked to indulge as much as she did, some schnapps now and then to revive mind and body. There was so much she had planned for her sister's visit: the Statue of Liberty, the Metropolitan Museum of Art, opera and theater tickets, and of course plenty of time by the Verrazzano. She couldn't wait to hear more about her mother, her sister, and her niece. She couldn't wait to hear more about her family.

Maria stood on the top deck of the ship facing the Brooklyn side of the Narrows. As a light breeze brushed across her face, she tightened her grip on the railing and listened for Gertie's voice: "Aren't you curious what it's like on the other side? And the open sea, Maria, the open sea . . ."

The words barely registered back then. It was different today. *Yes,* she answered, *I am curious.* She took a deep breath, inhaling as much sea air as she could. *I smell it now. The smell of the beginning and the end, just like Corinna said.* She licked her lips. It had the taste of tears. *Did you know it would taste like tears, Gertie?*

Maria opened her bag. In it lay the metal urn with her friend's ashes. She ran her fingers over the top.

I didn't understand, but I understand now.

The breeze rustled her hair as the ship passed Owl's Head Park, the Sixty-Ninth Street Pier, the grand two- and three-story houses along Shore Road. Soon Fort Hamilton High School and the Temple and the Verrazzano Bridge. *You're right, Gertie, it does look different from this side. Everything on land stands still while the ship moves on.* She felt a tingling in her fingers and toes. It wasn't just the ship. *She* was moving on.

She laughed. Santa Maria, the Homebody. The one who loved familiarity and routine. It made her feel safe and secure, how she kept things just so in her apartment, her toothbrush in its holder, her medicine laid out in the pill organizer, the microwave needing an extra tap to start. Living a few blocks away from Livy and Vinnie, being able to call when there was a problem. Knowing all her neighbors in the building, Ida Levitsky, Manny the Super, the entire staff at Key Food. Everything had its place, and there was nothing to worry about, no surprises. She could sleep easy.

But that was just what you were trying to tell me, Gertie, that I was asleep all this time. I understand you now. Time is precious, and we have no say in how it's allotted. The other day we were together, and now I'm out here and you're in there. After all these years, Elsa wanted to see you again, but she arrived too late. My daughter also has good intentions—look how nice she dressed me up for my big trip—but I know her life is elsewhere.

Vinnie's too, now that he's spending more time at rehab than at school. I asked him on the phone the other day if he was still mad at me. "A little," he said, "but I'll get over it. Hey Granny, I never told you this, but your friends are pretty cool—Corinna with her Vespa and Gertie with her big travel plans. I'm glad you decided to listen to them and go away. You never know what tomorrow will bring."

He's right, Gertie. On the news, they keep showing pictures of Joplin, Missouri. Those poor people. In just a few hours, the twister took away everything: their homes, their possessions, and, for many, their lives. Gone. Without the slightest warning.

I was afraid, Gertie. Afraid of losing the people and things I loved and depended on. I was afraid of change. Of being alone. That's a lot of fear to accumulate. And for what? We lose something every day. That's just the way life is. And we're always alone, even though we have parents and children and friends.

"I ga-beeesh," she declared to the sea air with her fingers pinched together, in the exaggerated way her friend would have said it. *I'm not afraid anymore, Gertie. It feels good being on the water, being on the move, leaving Bay Ridge. My cabin isn't quite as nice as you might have imagined, this being the* Queen *and all. Not much bigger than a closet, with just one small, round window and a bed hard as nails. But I don't mind. I can survive without my apartment for a while, without my mattress and pillows and sheets. Without Livy and Vinnie. What was I so afraid of?*

How strange, Gertie. Not long ago we were sitting next to each other at the Temple, and I had never felt so far away from you. And today, when the distance can't be greater, I feel close again.

She tightened her grip on the urn, holding back the tears.

We're almost at the Temple, Gertie. It's just behind those trees. I can't see Corinna, but I'm sure she's there, standing on tiptoe on the stone bench, watching us through her binoculars. I'm going to wave now, Gertie. I'm going to say goodbye.

"Maria," the Professor called out, jauntily striding toward her. "You look smashing in that dress. There is no question that green is your color. To whom are you waving?"

She pointed to the dense tree line just below the end of Shore Road. "Corinna. She's at the Temple now."

"I should have known. *Salve*, Corinna." He waved to the shore. "One of these days you'll have to bring me to the famous Temple. Today, however, we have an invitation to join the captain on his private deck. A friend of mine arranged it, and I'd like to be there when we pass beneath the bridge. Come," he said, taking her hand.

The upper deck was crammed with people, already nostalgic about leaving New York. Young and old, single and grouped, members of just about every color and race. They were dressed for the occasion and jostling for a good view. Normally, Maria avoided crowds, but today it didn't bother her, especially with the Professor leading the way, his cane rapping against the wooden planks.

"Did you hurt yourself?" she asked.

At first he didn't understand. "Oh no," he laughed. "This is my travel stick. I never leave home without it. Naturally, it was made in Rome. The handle carved from the horn of a stag. Nice touch, eh? And it can also be used as a weapon if necessary." He smiled, thrusting the stick in the air.

Toward the front of the ship, there was a stairway guarded by a man in uniform. The Professor gave his name, and they were allowed up. They arrived at a rounded deck encircling the ship's cockpit. Directly ahead, no more than one hundred feet away, rose the Verrazzano Bridge.

"I've been waiting for this moment, Maria. Just look at that magnificent structure. They can talk all they want about the Brooklyn Bridge or the Golden Gate, but the Verrazzano is the most noble of all."

Maria was speechless. She had seen the bridge a million times, but always from the side and always from a distance. Now she could practically reach out and touch it. It was so much bigger than she'd ever imagined.

"The main span is over forty-two hundred feet across." The Professor gestured with his stick. "That's about ten football fields. And almost three times the size of the Brooklyn Bridge, might I add."

"Three times?"

"The towers are just about seven hundred feet high," he continued without a beat. "And look at those massive cables—each one three feet in diameter."

She shook her head in wonder; the Professor seemed to know everything.

He winked at her. "Don't tell anyone, Maria, but I have it all written down here," he whispered, producing his cheat sheet. "I wanted to impress you, so I reviewed Corinna's chapter in *The Bay Ridge Chronicle* last night and took notes. You have to admit, the numbers boggle the mind. Especially the cables, so massive and yet possessing such delicacy, the way they drape from one tower to the other."

Maria felt the same way. Her friends did too. "It reminds me of a necklace," she told him. "Gertie thought the cables looked like the strings of a harp. And Corinna imagined a giant bird. I wish they were here with us now."

"They *are* here, Maria. Isn't that the magic of a bridge? It's built to connect things, to bring people and places together. The way it once brought the three of you together."

Yes, she thought, opening her handbag; she wanted to make sure Gertie could hear what the Professor was saying.

"The way it will always bring the three of you together in your thoughts."

Suddenly, the bridge was directly before them; it seemed as if they were going to crash right into it. Maria shielded her face with her hand and ducked.

"Don't be afraid," he reassured her. "The *Queen* has a clearance of thirteen or so feet."

The space around them darkened as the ship passed beneath the Verrazzano. The Professor might have been right about the clearance, but they sure cut it close, thought Maria, gradually recovering her composure. She could see the rivets and bolts in the beams, patches where the steel had rusted. She heard the rumble and roar of the cars and trucks above, watched the roadway shudder under the strain. All that weight held up by the delicate string work of her necklace, Gertie's harp, Corinna's bird.

She was glad when they reached the far side and daylight returned.

"Say goodbye to Bay Ridge, Maria."

She looked inside her bag. "Say goodbye," she whispered to her friend.

"Of course, it's only goodbye for now," he added. "A bridge may take you somewhere, Maria, but it also provides a way back."

Maria liked how that sounded. It reminded her of something that had stuck in her mind for many years. "There is a land of the living and a land of the dead," she recited the memorable lines, "and the bridge is love, the only meaning, the only survival."

"That's beautiful, Maria."

"It's from a book Corinna once read to us about a bridge that collapsed in Peru, killing five innocent people. A priest spent years trying to figure out why God would have allowed such a terrible thing to happen."

"I don't imagine he was very successful."

"No," she replied, "he wasn't." They stood quiet for a moment until Maria turned to the Professor. "I want to thank you for helping Corinna. She also spent a good deal of time searching for answers. Thanks to you and Vinnie, she's finally found some."

"Your grandson is an exceptional boy," said the Professor. "A bit of a rebel, as I'm sure you know, but that often happens with the smart ones. It was a lot worse in the '60s and '70s, believe me. I'm not worried about Vincent, Maria. He has a good head on his shoulders. He's going to be very successful at Harvard and at whatever he decides to do with his life. I'm sure of it."

Maria hoped so with all her heart, as did Livy. They hoped that Vinnie would be able to straighten himself out over the summer and start off fresh in the fall.

"The truth is, you deserve most of the credit for helping Corinna," he added, smiling. "Naturally, it will take some time for her to adjust. Her story didn't turn out exactly the way I envisioned. There are a few details I withheld," admitted the Professor. "I thought her sister should be the one to tell Corinna."

There was more? From the expression on the Professor's face, Maria could tell that the latest information wasn't positive.

"Corinna escaped from the Nazis as we suspected, Maria, only not as a Jewish refugee."

"Didn't you say she was on that boat with the other Jewish children?"

"Yes, but her case was exceptional. Corinna was one of the *lebensunwertes Leben*—life unworthy of life."

Maria didn't understand.

The Professor sighed deeply. "The Nazis were the most racist people that ever inhabited this earth. They believed in the supremacy of a German master race, that all inferior elements had to be purged—the mentally ill and disabled along with the Jews. First there were forced sterilizations, and then, under the cover of war, they brazenly exterminated people they deemed subhuman, people like Corinna."

"My God," gasped Maria.

"Thousands of innocent Germans were killed, children as well as adults. The most despicable part is that physicians went along. Physicians sworn to the Hippocratic oath: first do no harm."

She had no idea.

"It turns out that Corinna's father was one of those physicians. After the war, he was put on trial and convicted. He hanged himself in prison. Her mother, pregnant at the time with Theresa, was the one responsible for smuggling Corinna out of the country. She died shortly after her husband, supposedly of natural causes."

Maria grabbed the side rail. Poor Corinna. How could so many bad things happen to one person? If the priest couldn't figure out why God had chosen that time for those unlucky souls in Peru, how would anyone ever make sense of Corinna's lot?

"There's so much ugliness in this world."

"True, Maria, but there is also plenty of beauty," he said, gesturing to the brilliant blue sky and the seagull soaring overhead, the shimmering of the water and the lush green Brooklyn shoreline. "The cards might have been stacked against Corinna from the outset, but she's made a good life for herself. She has her library and Vespa, her work at the Center, friends who love her. And now she has a sister and a niece and whatever else may follow. A new family. Isn't that what you wanted for her?"

Yes, but not all that other stuff.

"Come, Maria, let's meet the captain of this behemoth."

"Do you mind—I need a few minutes alone first."

"I understand. I'll be waiting for you."

Maria watched the dapper Professor stroll toward the bow of the ship, tapping the ground with his stick.

Suddenly, she was confused.

She put her hand on the urn. *Did you hear what the Professor said, Gertie? Corinna's father was a doctor who killed children like her, who might have killed his own daughter if her mother hadn't intervened. How is that possible?*

And Livy—she bought me all these nice clothes and took me to the terminal this morning. "Have fun, Ma," she said, and I'm sure she meant it. But I could tell she was happy to see me off. She has her own life to live, and maybe I get in the way.

And here I am leaving Bay Ridge on a ship with a stranger. On an ocean that tastes like tears. Headed for who knows what.

Mannaggia mia!

I know I promised to scatter your ashes under the Verrazzano, but I can't right now. I need you here with me. Besides, you wanted to go on a trip. Not like this, of course, but still. I'll do it on the way back, I promise.

It's a comfort, knowing we'll return, isn't it? The bridge brings people together. It takes you places, then shows you the way back home.

And the bridge is love.

There are many different kinds of love, Gertie. My love for Jim. My love for Livy and Vinnie. My love for Corinna. For you.

I don't know if I could ever love the Professor.

Looking back, I guess my Jim had his faults, yet I loved him dearly.

The Professor isn't so bad really. He's with the captain now, most likely reeling off statistics about the Verrazzano from his little cheat sheet. Oh my, is he vain! You should see him with that walking stick. But he's also kind, Gertie. He listens, and that's important. And he makes me laugh—like you.

Maria opened her bag. *I'll try to have fun, as long as I know you're with me.* She patted the urn, took it out of the bag, and gave it a little hug, then held it firmly on the railing in front of her, facing the horizon. *Happy birthday, Gertie!*

We're passing Coney Island now, the Ferris wheel and the boardwalk, the hot dog stands and the cotton candy, the beach where your father taught you to swim. We're leaving Bay Ridge, just like you wanted, moving past the noise and the fog, past the confusion and anger and sadness at what we once thought was the end.

Soon we'll be on the open sea.

ACKNOWLEDGMENTS

Thank you to my friends and most loyal supporters: David Rothenberg, Steven Fisch, Allison Schneirov, Howie Lipson, Neal Merker, Kenny Brachfeld, Eric Silver, Shannon Russell, Giulia Melucci, Eric Hofmann, Howard Altmann, Monica Cohen, Rhonda Pomerantz, Alan Rosenbach, Mert Erogul, Charles Messina, and Nellie Hermann.

Thank you to those who have read and reread my manuscript too many times to count: Beth Rothenberg, Matthew Kneale, Jillian Kearney, Donna Maddalena, Jeanne Morris, Sandy Gruenwald, and most of all, Ellen Tien.

Thank you to my agent, Jennifer Lyons, for sticking with me and being so supportive during the drought years.

Thank you to my editor, Jodi Warshaw, and everyone else at Lake Union, for loving this book as much as I do and helping me make it better.

And thank you to my family, Daniella, Daniel, and Luca, for putting up with me during a writing process that never seemed to end.

ABOUT THE AUTHOR

Photo © 2019 Donna Maddalena

David Biro is a physician and a writer. He is the author of the novel *This Magnificent Dappled Sea* and two works of nonfiction, *One Hundred Days: My Unexpected Journey from Doctor to Patient* and *The Language of Pain: Finding Words, Compassion, and Relief*. He lives in New York City with his wife and two sons. For more information visit www.davidbirobooks.com.

Made in United States
North Haven, CT
19 October 2021

10429927R00148